KILL BY NUMBERS

KILL BY NUMBERS

IN THE WAKE OF THE TEMPLARS   BOOK TWO

LOREN RHOADS

NIGHT SHADE BOOKS
NEW YORK

Night Shade Books may be purchased in bulk at special discounts for sales promotion, corporate gifts, fund-raising, or educational purposes. Special editions can also be created to specifications. For details, contact the Special Sales Department, Night Shade Books, 307 West 36th Street, 11th Floor, New York, NY 10018 or info@ skyhorsepublishing.com.

Night Shade Books™ is a trademark of Skyhorse Publishing, Inc.®, a Delaware corporation.

Visit our website at www.nightshadebooks.com.

10 9 8 7 6 5 4 3 2 1

Library of Congress Cataloging-in-Publication Data is available on file.

Cover illustration and design by Cody Tilson

Print ISBN: 978-1-59780-831-6
Ebook ISBN 978-1-59780-848-4

Printed in the United States of America

This book is dedicated to Brian Thomas,
partner in crime and shining light.

CHAPTER 1

Something caught Raena Zacari's attention. She glanced over at Ariel and Gavin, but they were engrossed in feeding each other pieces of some bright yellow alien fruit. Nothing strange there, except that they were being nice to each other.

Shoppers filled the souk today. Even though they ranged from humanoid to feathered to she didn't know what, they were all acting like privileged rich people at a mall, haggling unnecessarily with the shopkeepers. Nothing seemed out of place, but adrenaline poured into Raena's blood. She clenched her fists, ready for the fight to begin.

Something stung her thigh. Raena glanced down at her leg, bare in the slit of her parrot-blue dress. A tiny dart, fletched with silver foil, pierced her skin.

The drug hit her so fast she couldn't call for help. Gavin saw her going down and lunged forward to catch her. She saw her terror reflected in his expression. Then his head came apart. She couldn't even reach up to wipe his blood away.

Screaming people fled into the maze of the old Templar city. Kai was supposed to be a weapons-free world. Everyone paid enough to guarantee their safety here.

Ariel knelt beside Raena, staring at Gavin's corpse, trying to figure out what had happened.

A second Gavin fought his way through the panicked crowd. He knocked Ariel aside and pulled Raena up over his shoulder. Then he dodged away through the souk.

This Gavin turned a corner to charge down a narrow street. He didn't see the teenaged boy hiding there. Jain Thallian stepped out from a doorway to fling a shock net over Gavin and Raena both. Its initial jolt knocked Gavin from his feet. Raena fell to the dirt with him. With the drug in her system, she couldn't raise her hands to break her fall.

Raena fought her way awake from the dream before the Thallians could take her prisoner. Then she lay on her back in her bunk, trying to slow her hammering heart. She breathed deeply, concentrating on the sounds of the *Veracity* around her. Its engines hummed with a steady, reassuring sound. She could hear the hiss of its air exchangers and the gurgle of water in its pipes. All appeared to be right in the galaxy.

Except for this dream. It felt wrong. Its weight—if that was the word she wanted for it—was too great for a soap bubble created from her subconscious. Rather than a mere nightmare, it felt more solid, almost like a memory: a memory of something that hadn't really happened to her.

She scrubbed the tears from her eyes with her fists. There hadn't been two Gavins. There had been only one. And on that day on Kai, he'd gotten knocked out as soon as Thallian's soldiers attacked. Raena had killed as many of the attack team as she could, disabled the rest, and kidnapped Jain. Then she'd left Gavin and Ariel behind, stolen the *Veracity*, and assassinated the rest of the Thallian family. She was free now.

Suddenly Raena needed to get out of her cabin, into the company of people. It had been a month since she'd felt that way—and Jonan Thallian, the man who had been hunting her then, was dead. She'd watched his body burn.

Still jittery, Raena climbed off her bunk. She pulled a clean catsuit from the locker and shimmied into it. This one was poisonous magenta. She hoped the color would lift her mood.

She rubbed some static into her short black hair to make it ray out from her head. Then she strapped on her high-heeled boots like she was putting on her armor.

Ariel Shaad woke up herself by reaching for the gun that should have been holstered on her thigh—except that Ariel herself was worlds away from the events on Kai, safe in bed in her villa on Callixtos.

Shivering, Ariel examined the vestiges of the nightmare still fogging her head. There had been two Gavins. The new one murdered the Gavin she had been traveling with and ran off with Raena flung over his shoulder. One of Thallian's sons had thrown a shock net over Gavin and her sister. Raena, paralyzed, was weeping in fear.

Ariel rolled over in bed, seeking coolness in sheets that were soft as water, but her thoughts were still entangled in the dream. That hadn't been how things really happened. True, Thallian's soldiers had attacked the three of them in the souk, but Gavin hadn't died there. He'd merely gone down after his hard head met someone else's even harder fist. One of Thallian's men had grabbed Ariel's arm. She'd lost precious time reaching after her nonexistent gun on the weapons-free pleasure planet. Raena stepped up, going on the attack, barehanded and in heels, taking down the kidnappers with a fluid poetry of motion that neutralized the threat until only one teenaged boy and his uncle were left. Then remorseless as an angel, Raena killed the uncle, squashing him like a bug. The boy fled, the only sensible course of action left to him. And Raena ran after him, legs flashing in the parrot-blue sheath dress. She'd been laughing.

That was real. It was over. Raena was safe and all the Thallians were dead.

A shudder crawled over Ariel's flesh and impelled her to get up. She would get no more sleep today.

She switched on the screen by her bed and checked messages, but saw nothing from Raena. Ariel told herself that the silence signified nothing. It had been only a nightmare.

Two Gavins, Ariel's thoughts repeated, circling back to the weirdest part of the dream. The second Gavin had seemed—what? Older? More focused? He reminded Ariel of the era when Gavin had been using the Dart, a Templar drug that focused his personality into something so hateful that Ariel had broken off with him and hidden. In those days, she'd slept with a Stinger under her pillow, just in case.

Somehow, in the dream, Ariel felt that the second Gavin had been the one to drug Raena, just so he could steal her away. It didn't make sense. In real life, in those final days on Kai, Ariel and Gavin had tried to hide Raena, to keep her safe from the Thallians. Luckily, the outcome had been the best anyone could hope for. Anyone who wasn't a Thallian, of course.

Or, Ariel supposed with a wry twist of her mouth, anyone who wasn't Gavin Sloane.

She sighed, glad to be rid of her ex at last. She scrolled through her messages again, but saw no more word from him. It had been a couple of weeks since Gavin left his last haranguing message. Did that mean he'd found a new obsession? Not bloody likely. Maybe he had checked himself in somewhere, gotten the help he so desperately needed. Taken some time out to rebuild his life without Ariel or her sister in it.

Probably he had been arrested again. Ariel tried to decide if she cared enough to check the news. In the end, she signed off the computer and went in search of breakfast. Business wasn't going to do itself today.

Raena came out of her cabin into the *Veracity*'s passageway. She paused, as always, listening to establish the locations of the rest of the crew.

Something smelled good. Mykah, the human captain, must be busy in the galley. Raena had never eaten as well as she did in Mykah Chen's crew. Before her imprisonment, when she'd served in the diplomatic service of humanity's Empire, military rations had always been provided by the lowest bidder. Mykah, who'd worked in food service on Kai before Raena tempted him to become a pirate, insisted on fresh ingredients when he could get them—and knew how to combine them to best effect to please the spectrum of palates on the *Veracity*. Raena counted herself lucky to be serving with him.

She'd asked Mykah once why the others let him become the *Veracity*'s captain. At the time, Mykah laughed. "I'm an excellent cook and an apprentice journalist. Everyone else has useful skills." Besides, captaining the *Veracity* wasn't time-consuming. Mostly, Mykah's job was a matter of entertaining himself with minor media hacks.

At this moment, Haoun, the pilot, and Coni, the resident hacker, were on duty in the cockpit, chatting about a solar wind race, critiquing the media coverage. Neither of them seemed to have placed any bets.

A faint tang of solder burned Raena's nose. Somewhere toward the back end of the *Veracity*, Vezali must be tinkering. Upgrading the antique diplomatic transport ship—registered as the *Raptor*, before Raena stole it—seemed to fascinate Vezali endlessly. Raena supposed that had to do with the sheer amount of cobbling together Vezali was called on to do.

Galley first, Raena decided. She started in that direction, moving down the passageway silently, just to keep in practice.

When Mykah saw her reflection in the coffee pot he was filling, he smiled. He'd reshaped his beard again. Today he'd twisted it into two coils under his chin.

"Morning," he wished amicably, even though it wasn't morning any longer. Mykah didn't seem to mind whatever hours

Raena kept. He grasped that sleep was elusive for her, that she only captured it after hours of stalking it. He always wished her good morning the first time he saw her for the day, no matter the Galactic Standard hour.

"Is it almost lunchtime, Captain? That smells wonderful."

"I was just about to call the crew. You want to eat first?"

Raena appreciated that he tried to accommodate her, but really, she had to start trying to fit in or else she needed to move on. The longer she held herself apart, the harder it was going to be to settle in—and nowhere else was likely to be a whole lot better than the cushy gig she had now. This crew was small and the work wasn't demanding. And she had the largest cabin, since she'd been the one to provide the ship.

"No," she said quietly, picking an apple out of the crisper. "I'll join you, if you think it won't put Coni off her food."

"Nah, czyk is her favorite," he teased. "Nothing will stop her from eating it." He pressed the intercom chime.

Raena chose the corner of the table where she could get her back against the wall. Once the crew settled in around the table, she'd be penned in, but they posed no real physical threat to her. Well, maybe Haoun did. The big lizard was strong and could move faster than one might expect, if only for short bursts. He had a calm temperament and quick reflexes, which made him a stellar pilot, but he also calculated for safety rather than excitement. He wouldn't stir anything up.

Raena watched them all come in, note her presence in the galley, then pick their seats at the table. Coni sat diagonally from her, holding a spot at her side for Mykah. Haoun settled on Raena's left, easing himself onto a stool designed for a smaller, more humanoid, creature. Vezali slipped into the banquette at Raena's right, arranging her tentacles under the table. Raena meant to watch to see if the same tentacles always served Vezali as hands, but it was hard to keep track. The tentacles seemed to be in constant flux, changing from feet to hands as Vezali required.

"There's been a new request to interview you," Coni said. The blue-furred girl didn't raise her gaze from the plate Mykah set in front of her. Nothing was stopping her from eating the czyk, Raena was amused to note.

"How was the interview request addressed?" Raena asked.

"They didn't know your name."

One of the earliest requests had called her by name. Others had addressed her as Fiana, her mother's name, which she'd used on Kai while hiding out with Gavin and Ariel. Ariel wouldn't contact her so obliquely, wouldn't ever do anything more than leave a message on the Shaad family's private channel for Raena to retrieve at her leisure. Anyone who called her by name or the Fiana alias knew or was working for Gavin Sloane. Raena didn't respond to those calls.

"I don't do interviews," Raena repeated, same as she always did. She thought Coni must hate acting as her secretary, but she also expected that was the least of her behavior that freaked the blue girl out.

"Is it from a legitimate news outlet?" Mykah asked. Since everyone had been served lunch now, he joined them at the table.

Raena looked down at the plate he'd placed in front of her. Today they were having a slab of some kind of meat glistening in a rich yellow sauce. Ever since she'd come back into the galaxy after her long imprisonment, it amazed her that people still ate meat. With creatures whose heritage looked saurian, octopoid, and some weird pastel-shaded vaguely feline mammal, Raena wondered how the *Veracity*'s crew found any flesh safe or appropriate to eat, unless it was some form of avian creature. Wasn't everything else someone's distant relative? Was there a galactic measure of sentience that edible creatures had to fail before they were fit for the table? Raena might be able to ask Mykah, who was continually entertained by her naiveté, but she wouldn't risk offending any of the others.

On her plate, beside the meat, sat a cluster of roasted grain, garnished with some kind of fancy leaf, and a blue vegetable they'd eaten before. Apparently that was czyk, Coni's favorite. To Raena, it tasted like tree sap. Not unpleasant, really, just not what she expected when she put a blue stalk of vegetation into her mouth.

She ate her apple first. It was probably the most expensive thing on the table, but since the *Veracity* had collected the Thallian bounty, the crew could afford a few luxuries. Anyway, Raena always tried to ease her stomach into eating with something that passed for human food.

The others tucked into their meals with gusto.

"The interview request seems legitimate," Coni said between dainty bites. "They asked to talk to the human responsible for hunting down the terrorists who spread the Templar plague. No names were mentioned, other than the Thallians'."

Mykah was watching Raena when she glanced up.

"You're the press agent," Raena told him. "Talk to them only if you want to. Feel free to tell them the same thing you told the others. Keep me out of it."

"Do you think that smuggler is still looking for you?" Vezali asked.

"Maybe," Raena said in such a way that it sounded like yes. Gavin Sloane was just as obsessed with her as Jonan Thallian had ever been, without the added fun of psychosis. "Maybe Gavin's gotten himself a new girlfriend," she added, but, really, she didn't think that was likely.

"We need some other work," Haoun said. The translator around his neck made him sound very urbane, while the actual sound of his sibilant voice still raised the hairs on the back of Raena's neck. It was some kind of uncomfortable vestigial reaction, completely unconnected with the affable lizard's presence. Raena refrained from reaching up to rub her neck. "We can't just hang around," the big lizard continued. "We can't just keep living off the last big score."

Raena had headed up the *Veracity*'s last two big jobs: assassinating the Thallians and revealing the looting of the Templar cemetery world, but she had run out of wrongs she felt morally responsible for righting in the galaxy. Her old scores were, for the most part, settled. The only one that remained she was content to let slide.

"Since the last two jobs were human malfeasance," Mykah said, "I'd like to uncover someone else's responsibility for a change."

"Even humans have rights," Haoun said. Everyone laughed, save for Raena. The phrase was the punch line to an almost twenty-year-old joke that had circulated the galaxy after the Templar plague and the consequent destruction of the human Empire. Mykah had tried to explain the joke to Raena, had even played her several recordings of it, but as far as Raena could tell, everyone laughed at the punch line because they found it so improbable. Humanity had really screwed things up in the galaxy; many felt that, after the Templar plague was revealed, it was quite likely that the purges hadn't gone far enough. Human rights were a polite fiction, granted by the rest of the galaxy, but continually subject to reconsideration.

Still, whether she understood the humor or not, she'd chosen the seat with her back to the wall, so Raena knew she had to ride the laughter out. It wasn't directed at her personally—and Mykah joined in, anyway. Raena inclined her head over her plate and ate in silence.

Then a thought occurred to her. "I don't suppose there's anything we can do about the Viridian slave trade," she asked casually.

"That's bigger than we are, unfortunately," Mykah said apologetically. "Slavery has been outlawed on a system by system basis, but even the Council of Worlds hasn't had any luck wiping it out galaxy-wide."

"For the future, then," Raena said. "For now, the four of you will have to decide what work to take. I don't even know which wrongs can be righted. Just let me know if you find anything that requires some security."

Ariel walked from her bedroom to the office, where Eilif was already at work for the day. From the back, the woman looked alarmingly like Raena: same shape to her head, same sharp alignment of her shoulders, same ramrod-straight spine. Although she was much younger than Ariel, Eilif had gone gray prematurely, her formerly black hair now pure white. She wore her hair long and loose, flowing down her back as Raena once did. These days, Raena wore her black hair short. She'd whacked it off with a knife last time Ariel had seen her.

"Morning," Ariel wished.

Eilif jumped, even though she must have heard Ariel come into the room. Poor thing. The widow's life had been a hell that Ariel struggled not to imagine.

"Good morning," Eilif answered cheerfully. She got up from her screen to fix Ariel a cup of coffee, something she did every morning without being asked. Even though Ariel told her often how unnecessary the gesture was, Eilif did it anyway. It seemed to make her happy. She'd had so little happiness in her life that Ariel indulged her in this.

"How are things today?" Ariel asked.

"I found a home for the twins," Eilif said. "Can I give them the news at lunchtime?"

"Tell me about it first," Ariel said, but she was sure the placement would be secure for the boys. Eilif treated each child as if he or she was one of her own. She wouldn't send the kids anywhere that might endanger them. Once Ariel had showed her how to search, Eilif was more determined and vigilant than Ariel had ever been when looking into the backgrounds of potential parents.

Ariel wondered if any of Eilif's own sons had survived Raena's attack on their father. She knew she would never, ever ask.

Since they'd made the *Veracity* their home, the crew had set about customizing it. It had started life as a troop transport carried aboard the *Arbiter*, an Imperial warship that had masqueraded as a diplomatic courier. After Jonan Thallian and his family followed the Emperor's command and spread the Templar plague, Thallian had taken the *Arbiter* and its crew into hiding with his family. All through the dissolution of the Empire and the hunt for the plague's disseminator, the warship and its complement of transports rested beneath the ocean on Thallian's homeworld. One of Thallian's brothers commanded the *Veracity* in its middle age, when it served to carry private soldiers on the family's errands—mostly supply runs, Raena understood, until they'd been ordered to come after her.

The ship's larger hold had served as a barracks for Thallian's soldiers. Once the *Veracity*'s crew had settled into their stolen ship, they had dismantled the bunks, added walls, and converted the hold into several nice-sized cabins: one for Haoun—too tall to fit into a human-scale room—and another for Vezali, who preferred to sleep in a tank of water. The others they used as storerooms.

Raena had taken over the smaller secondary hold for her gymnasium, which Vezali helped her to construct and stock. Mostly Raena did resistance training, working against the increased gravity in that room, practicing cartwheels and flips, climbing the walls or hanging from the ceiling, anything to strain her muscles and help her sleep.

And sleep never came easily any more. Raena suspected that was because she'd slept away so much of her imprisonment. During the years of lying in total blackness, she hadn't noticed much difference between sleeping and waking anyway. Perhaps her body felt it had stored up all the rest she would ever need. Or perhaps some part of her feared to drift away and release its grip on wakefulness, lest she find herself imprisoned again.

Still, she needed rest to recharge. She knew her reflexes got dangerously hair-trigger if she didn't sleep. Raena had spent enough time drugged against her will that she had a horror of doping herself. The odds of anything creeping up on her while she was vulnerable were slim now—she'd killed most of the creeps herself—but the years of vigilance made relaxing difficult.

To Raena's way of thinking, a spaceship was all too similar to a prison, whether the lights were on or not. Sometimes, if the *Veracity* wasn't going anywhere, she'd suit up and go explore the outer hull, just to get *out*. Space might not have air or gravity, but it didn't make her feel penned in, either.

The only problem with that kind of escape—other than the inability to use it when the ship was traveling—was that she'd inherited her spacesuit from Jain Thallian. No matter what she did to sanitize it, the spacesuit continued to smell like teenaged boy inside.

Today Raena retreated to her gymnasium, to hang from her hands and see just how many times she could raise her feet over her head. The exercise was tedious, but she hoped it would also prove exhausting.

Someone rapped on the hold's door, metal against metal. Raena looked up to see Mykah peering through the hatch. He grinned.

"Come in," she called.

"Want some company?"

"I'd be glad for it." She let go of the chin-up bar and flexed her fingers.

"Wanna spar?"

"Sure."

He toed out of his deck shoes and stepped barefoot into the room. "Wow," he grunted. "How high have you got the gravity dialed up today?"

Raena turned a handspring. "Just trying to keep things interesting," she explained. One of the things she liked about the old Earther ship was its location-specific gravity system. "You want me to set it back to Earth Normal?"

"It's kind of hard to breathe in here."

He let her walk past him, her back to him as she adjusted the gravity, before he attacked. She heard him coming, big bare feet slapping the deck, but she didn't turn. He almost had her before she dodged right, using a grip on his forearm as a pivot point.

He'd gotten too close to the wall to swing his left hand to grab her. Raena continued on around and released him, dancing back.

"Heard me coming?" Mykah asked.

"Like a loader."

"You'll have to teach me how to move quieter."

She stuck out one booted foot. "The higher the heels, the stealthier the step."

"I doubt that." He struck out with one leg, trying to catch her off balance. Raena kicked up higher and used the momentum to pull herself over into a walkover. She followed that with a handspring, twisting in midair so that she landed on both feet somewhere to his left, far from where he expected to find her when she came up.

He spun to face her, found her in a crouch. "I'd be dead, wouldn't I?"

"Depends on what I was armed with," Raena said.

"Gun? Knife? Bad language?"

Raena laughed. "I've never killed anyone with bad language yet. You'll have to teach me the words first."

"Nah. It may be my only advantage."

She launched herself forward as Mykah charged again. This time she aimed for his waist. If she'd gone high and caught his head, even on accident, she could have snapped his neck when she changed trajectory.

He managed to close one hand on the neckline of her catsuit. She heard it tear as she twisted her body. Still, she got behind him, used his moment of surprise and embarrassment and the corner of the wall and got her shoulder against his back. It was a matter of leverage. He'd leaned too far forward and couldn't get his long legs under him to correct.

She rode him to the ground, then rolled away before he could turn over and grab her.

Mykah flopped over to look at her, breathing hard, winded by the fall. He'd remembered not to put his arms out to break the drop, which risked a broken bone, but he hadn't curled up or relaxed into the fall as she'd tried to teach him.

"Are you okay?" Raena asked. "If I broke you, Coni will kill me."

"Okay," Mykah wheezed. "Good lesson."

Raena looked at him on the floor. She had plenty of time to move in, pin him, feel his body warm and lithe beneath hers. She wanted to do it. Wanted it bad enough that her mouth watered. So she didn't. Instead, she folded her legs in the middle of the room and joined him on the floor, more than one of his arm's lengths away.

Mykah was Coni's. Until the blue girl said he wasn't, Raena wasn't going to step in, no matter what her body might think it wanted. Shipboard life was complex enough for Raena without getting into the middle of someone else's relationship, especially when she actually liked one of the members. She wanted to do him the favor of not complicating things. Besides, whether Coni liked Raena or not, Coni was a very good hacker, equally adept at teasing things out of the *Veracity*'s elderly computers or from the galactic news grid. Raena respected her. She wouldn't want Coni for an enemy.

It made Raena a little melancholy, though, to think that this might be her last sparring round with Mykah for a while. Maybe she could redirect him into kendo or something where they could wear armor and not actually touch—or even meet each other's eyes.

Mykah pushed himself into sitting up, his back against the wall. He was rubbing his ribs, which was a good sign. It meant that nothing was broken. Otherwise, he wouldn't be able to stand touching them. "I almost got you this time," he panted, nodding at her.

Raena glanced down to assess the damage to her clothes. Good thing she'd slept in the exercise band. He'd ripped her neckline down past her shoulder, revealing the starburst scar from her assassination of Thallian. She lifted the flap of her torn neckline and wondered if the catsuit could be repaired. Maybe Vezali could sew, in addition to everything else she could do.

"You may have killed my catsuit," Raena conceded. "One of these days, you're gonna catch me."

"Then you'll be in trouble," Mykah teased.

No doubt, she thought. Raena glanced down at the deck and let the silence be awkward all on its own. She didn't trust her voice to come out as anything other than flirty.

He belongs to someone else, she reminded herself firmly, but loneliness was clearly not doing her any favors.

Raena unwound herself from the floor. "Will you excuse me, Captain?" she asked, holding the torn catsuit in place. "I think we've done enough damage for today."

Coni sat back from the screen, flexing and retracting her claws. It still shocked her how extensive the surveillance system was aboard the *Veracity*. Despite the work Vezali had done putting up new cabin walls, there seemed to be no corner of the former diplomatic transport that couldn't be spied upon. The ship's previous owners had eyes *everywhere*.

Coni had just unlocked the cameras in Raena's makeshift gym. It was fascinating to watch her boyfriend working out with the little assassin. Mykah was practically half again the little woman's height. His skin was a deep brown, still warmed in color from working on Kai, while Raena's skin hadn't lost its dusty grayish tone from her imprisonment. Coni would have called Raena stone-colored. That was one of the subtle things that had attracted her to humans in the first place: the variety and changeability of their hues.

Coni had grown up feeling sorry for the fragile underdogs of the galaxy. She studied humans at school, with a life plan to become a social worker and make certain that humans had safe places to live, safer jobs to work, and healthcare that took their delicacy physiology into consideration. Her job on Kai had been meant to be a stepping-stone. There hadn't been many humans on Kai—most couldn't afford the pleasure planet, so it didn't require much in the way of human staff to serve them—but the job led her to Mykah. He changed her life.

After Mykah's mother's died during the War, his father had shipped out on any freighter that would have him. In consequence, Mykah had grown up in a group home. He hadn't spent a lot of time around his own kind.

Coni wasn't jealous of Raena, because she saw Mykah's curiosity as just that. But she didn't trust the human woman not to take advantage of it, all the same.

Coni told herself that she wasn't really spying. She trusted Mykah. She only wanted to make certain he wouldn't get hurt. She wanted to be able to step in before Raena did anything they would all regret.

The Thallians probably had a master password to control all the cameras, but Coni was having to unlock them one at a time. Some, like the one in her cabin, she disconnected at the source. She left Haoun and Vezali their privacy as well. But Raena's cabin had the most extensive set-up. Jonan Thallian apparently had not trusted his older brother and had monitored him whenever Revan was sent off on a mission. That made Coni's fur ruffle uncomfortably, but she didn't disconnect the cameras to Raena's cabin. Just in case.

CHAPTER 2

Tarik Kavanaugh swallowed his smirk. The kid wasn't nearly as smart as he thought he was. That description might have applied to Kavanaugh himself for so much of his life that he was amused to be on the other side of it. Now Kavanaugh was older, experienced, and he'd seen what came of trusting your friends to watch your back.

He set his cards down carefully on the tabletop and listened to the happy chime as the computer declared him the winner. Still blank-faced, he leaned forward to collect the heap of credit chits from the center of the table.

"Dammit, Zhon!" The kid directly across the table flung his own worthless cards down. "I thought you had it figured."

Kavanaugh swept the pile of chits into his pouch, cinched it tightly, and tucked it inside his jacket. These kids just couldn't count as fast as he could, especially after all the xyshin they'd sucked down. Tolerance—and grown-up liquor—would come in time.

If they didn't get themselves killed first. Zhon reached for his gun, some kind of shiny model that Daddy probably bought him when he went away to some expensive business academy.

Kavanaugh smoothly drew his own pistol—a Stinger, hot off the factory floor, courtesy of Ariel Shaad—and leveled it at the feather-boy's shoulder. Kavanaugh's hand didn't waver. The kid froze.

"Drop it back in your holster," Kavanaugh advised. "You don't want to get into it with me, kid."

Defeated before he began, the bird boy let his gun drop home again.

Kavanaugh eased the bottle of xyshin from the tabletop with his free hand. Really, the liquor was so sweet it made his teeth hurt. It was a lot like something college kids would drink, but the boys certainly didn't need any more of it, if they were going to make it back to school alive. Kavanaugh thought he probably still had some of Ariel's bourbon to cut it with. This bottle would make the good stuff she'd left him stretch a little further.

He nodded to the boys and left the bar. Once outside, he melted into the crowd and ambled back to the *Sundog*. He kept one eye on the shopping displays as he passed. He had no interest in this year's frocks, but it never hurt to keep an eye peeled in case someone with a few more years under his belt tried to follow Kavanaugh to his ship and help himself to some of Kavanaugh's winnings—or less likely, if the college boys managed to grow a pair between the set of them and decided to try to get their money back.

Time to be moving on, Kavanaugh thought. Winning a card game here and there kept food on the table, but it didn't net enough to keep his ship in the air. He'd need to find some paying work soon.

Raena was headed back to her cabin for a nap when she heard Mykah's voice coming loudly from the cockpit. "No, we had no contact with any of them before we reached the solar system," he lied.

There was a pause, during which Raena couldn't hear the question. She stopped to listen to Mykah's answer: "That's right. The crew of the *Arbiter* was on the planet's surface when we found them. They had very little in the way of supplies, not even shelter from the elements, so we dropped everything we could spare for them and amplified their distress call. As you remember, the planet's surface was destroyed after Jonan Thallian was found guilty of the spreading the Templar plague."

Raena stayed carefully out of range of the cockpit recorders, eavesdropping as Mykah did yet another interview about finding the Thallian hideout. He'd told the story so many times now that it sounded completely honest. And he was a good enough actor that it sounded unrehearsed.

Too bad that it wasn't what really happened. She'd taken one of Thallian's clones hostage on Kai, stolen the shuttle he'd hunted her in, and turned them both into weapons against her former commander. The adventure hadn't worked out entirely the way she'd intended, but Mykah and his crew had, in fact, been responsible for the rescue of the *Arbiter*'s survivors, whom they'd really found unprotected in the nuclear winter on the planet's surface. In that sense, the crew of the *Veracity* were honestly heroes.

Not that it mattered. Raena had no desire to set the record straight. It was enough that the galaxy knew there had been a saboteur amongst the Thallians, someone who cracked their sea domes and let the ocean swallow them. Some of the interviewers suspected the saboteur had been part of the *Veracity*'s crew—why else had the ship been in a position in the backwater corner of the galaxy to hear the distress call when it came? Even though Raena hadn't been the one to drown the city, she planned to protect Eilif as long as they both lived.

Anyway, Mykah had made himself an expert on the Thallians, capable of reeling off every possible statistic, every death for which Jonan Thallian bore responsibility, every step of his journey to disseminate the Templar plague. Mykah sounded just like the truth-and-justice-obsessed kid that he was. His enthusiasm and outrage made it easy to believe that he had just happened to be headed to explore the Thallians' supposedly abandoned homeworld when the destruction took place.

Mykah seemed to adore the attention. Raena counted herself lucky to have met the one man on Kai who would love every minute of pranking the media.

It didn't hurt that he always arranged to have Coni, Haoun, or Vezali in the cockpit with him when he recorded an interview, so that the nonhuman majority of the galaxy could be vicariously represented by the nonhuman majority of the crew. The three other crewmembers drew lots so that everyone got their turn on camera.

Unlike the rest of the crew, however, Raena had no desire for fame. She was content that the universe should continue to take no notice of her. Having her likeness immortalized on a twenty-year-old Imperial wanted poster had been notoriety enough.

She hadn't reckoned with the fascination the Thallians and their evil would continue to hold over the galaxy. After she'd killed the man and his clones, she'd allowed Mykah to break the news to the rest of the galaxy, thinking that would expedite the rescue of the *Arbiter*'s hundreds of survivors. They could tell the tale of the madman's exile under the sea, the ancient mystery could be solved, and everyone would be ready to let the past be past and move on into the future. Instead, different news organizations kept picking over the story like they were sifting the bones.

Raena was certain that at least some of the media figureheads had worked for Gavin Sloane. That was why she'd released the footage of the avalanche on the Templar tombworld: as a warning for Gavin to back off. She'd left the clear implication that the Thallians were responsible for the looting of the Templar tombs—and who but a handful of people could say that they were not? Any of the others, especially Gavin, would incriminate himself if he spoke up.

She knew Gavin would understand the threat: leave me alone, or I'll pull the final curtain back.

After she'd released the recordings, the interview requests hadn't slackened, but their tenor changed. Raena felt like she was safe for the moment. She didn't trust Gavin not to look for another way to reach her, but she'd checked him for now.

The current interview moved on to the looting of the Templar tombworld. "What did the Thallians want with the things they stole from the Templar tombs?" the interviewer asked.

Mykah deflected it deftly. "That's a better question for the survivors of the *Arbiter*."

"How did you know that the Thallians had been there?"

"Old Imperial footage showed Marchan had visited the Templar tombs before the Plague began. We were curious to know what had interested him there."

"Did you visit the tombs yourself?"

"All of them were sealed except for the one you see in the avalanche footage."

"And what did the Thallians find there?"

"It's impossible to guess," Mykah said.

Raena grinned to herself. That was the tomb in which she'd been imprisoned. Thanks to Kavanaugh and Sloane, she'd been out for nearly a week before the Thallians came to look for her.

Coni rounded the corner out of the galley and stopped short at the sight of Raena just standing in the passage outside the cockpit. "What are you doing?" she blurted, surprised.

Raena waved Coni to follow her back into the galley. "I was eavesdropping on the interview," she said. "I guess I've never listened to one before."

"They all tend to ask the same questions," Coni admitted. The sight of the little assassin standing so still in the hallway had really startled her, although she wasn't sure why. Maybe it was the sense of seeing Raena *working*.

Before Coni could puzzle it out, the little woman surprised her by asking, "Coni, could you help me with something?"

Coni knew Mykah was openhearted enough to say "Sure" to anything anyone asked. She was more cautious by nature. "What do you need?"

"If we take work on any civilized world, I'm going to need a new identity record. I don't even know what all I'll need. Could you help me figure it out?"

"Yes." Coni found she was relieved by the request, but couldn't name what it was she had feared to be asked.

"I'd like to keep my own name," Raena said. "Since I'm genetically identical to the person in the old Imperial databases, does it make sense to claim to be my own daughter?"

"I think we could do that."

"Good." Raena sighed as if honestly relieved. "Any idea where I could have been born that there wouldn't be a record of a hospital birth? Even my mother, crazy as she was, recorded my real birthday."

"I'll see what I can turn up as a likely possibility." Coni's thoughts were already ticking ahead on the problem. It sounded like an intriguing puzzle. "Who would you like to claim as your father?"

Raena poured herself a glass of water and had a long swallow. "Thallian would be the obvious candidate, except that I don't want to be linked to him. If I claimed Gavin Sloane—another reasonable possibility—maybe I could get a court to award me some support." She grinned as if the idea amused her, but then shook her head. "I don't really want or need Gavin's help, though. I guess it's better if I'm just orphaned."

Then she grinned again. "How about this? What if the old Raena—the Raena of the Imperial era, the one on the run from Thallian—had a child while she tried to hide from the Empire? Maybe she got pregnant on the *Arbiter*, some torrid affair with one of her shipmates under Thallian's nose, and ran away in order to protect her unborn child?"

"All right," Coni agreed. Clearly, Raena enjoyed the idea of the fictional romance. "If that was the case, where could you have been left behind on your mother's flight?"

"I don't know. I'm not sure I even remember all the places I ran through. I really only remember the places I was captured—and I don't see how that can help us now."

Coni slipped the handheld from her jacket pocket and made some notes.

"Whatever else we do," Raena said thoughtfully, "I hate to think that this imaginary self grew up a slave, so let's make sure that doesn't happen to her. I spent three years legally enslaved myself. They were probably the safest, most secure years of my childhood, but I always understood that my purpose was to do whatever was necessary, even die if I had to, in order to allow Ariel time to escape. I wouldn't wish that pressure on even a made-up person."

"I understand." Coni's attention was already absorbed with the problem. The trick was to fill in the intervening years—the years when Raena had been imprisoned—with plausible occurrences.

She turned the question of Raena's past around a different way. Where could she have been educated? It had to have been somewhere that would explain why no one had ever heard of her, why no schoolmates would argue with her schooling: some dumping ground for human orphans that the Empire would have ignored in its death throes and no do-gooders like the Human Safety Commission would have disrupted.

Really, though, since Raena wasn't likely to ever apply for any sort of legitimate work, Coni didn't feel the need to force any accreditation. She just didn't want it to look like the woman had sprung, fully formed, from a hole in the ground—even if that was exactly what had happened.

"Thanks, Coni," Raena said softly.

Coni glanced up, saw that Raena was already withdrawing. "My pleasure," she said, using one of Mykah's favorite phrases, but her attention didn't stray far from the puzzle at hand.

Kavanaugh wove through the docking area on Tacauqe, which was mostly deserted at this hour of night. Everyone must either be off in town, enjoying being on the ground, or locked in their ships already, headed for bed. He checked the time. In another hour or so, the commonways would be hopping as everyone stumbled home from the bars.

He checked over his shoulder one last time. No one trailed him as he ducked into his own docking slip.

The *Sundog* was a little human-made hauler, perfect for a man alone to handle. He'd fallen in love with her retro-futurist style as a young man, purchased her with a loan from Doc when he was ready to start out on his own. The hold was a nice size, easy enough to fill without big equipment to shift things and simple to reconfigure for passengers if he decided to take them on. Generally Kavanaugh preferred to haul freight and to travel alone. Fewer complications that way.

He stepped inside and turned by reflex to lock the door. Then he didn't bother to turn on the lights as he moved through the little ship. The running lights were enough to guide him, although really he could have moved through the familiar ship in complete darkness. The *Sundog* was the only home he had known in his adult life.

Kavanaugh entered his cabin and locked that door after himself, too, as he did every night. Even though the Thallians were gone and Kavanaugh didn't have anything to fear from them any longer, he still didn't want to discount force of habit. He remembered what they'd done to Lim, Kavanaugh's engineer from the grave robbing team on the Templar tombworld. A locked door wouldn't have stopped them, but it might have given Lim enough time to arm himself before they came in to cut him apart.

Kavanaugh turned on the news in order to have some voices for company as he brushed his teeth and tried to amp down from the day. He told the computer to scan programs in Galactic Standard, switching every minute or so. In this media-saturated galaxy, millions of channels broadcast constantly, but at this hour, celebrity gossip dominated the news. Kavanaugh never paid enough attention to know whom they were gossiping about.

Just as he was going to shut the screen off, footage of sheer black cliffs scoured by gritty winds caught his eye. He sank down onto his bunk, captured. He didn't feel homesickness so much—who could feel homesick for *that*?—but he had spent a couple of months in that nightmare of wind and obsidian sand. Why, he wondered, would anyone be interested in the Templar tomb-world now?

The cameras panned over the bunkers he and his crew had left behind when Sloane broke down the "archaeological dig" and paid the grave robbers off. Kavanaugh had been only too glad to get off that rock.

The next video showed a grainy surveillance recording of some human men, dressed in black livery that harkened back to the Imperial days, exploring the bunkers. Kavanaugh had never seen Thallian in person, for which he thanked the stars. The commentator identified the soldiers' commander as Revan Thallian, older brother of the infamous Jonan, the Imperial diplomat who'd been convicted in absentia of disseminating the Templar plague. Apparently no one knew for certain if Revan had also been involved in the creation or spread of the plague, but he seemed implicated in the genocide as he ordered his men to explore the Templar graves. It was assumed he had also overseen the looting of them.

Kavanaugh knew the truth of that.

More grainy surveillance footage followed. Directed by a boy who was obviously yet another Thallian, two soldiers attempted to open one of the tombs. The avalanche that followed was almost too quick to comprehend: first there was a mountain. The men were placing charges to shift the slab that sealed its entryway. Then the men, the slab, and the mountain's face were gone, buried in a rubbish pile of broken stone.

Kavanaugh fumbled the bottle of xyshin out of his coat pocket and knocked back a hefty swallow. His hands shook. Then he set the footage to play again.

While working for Sloane, Kavanaugh and his team had opened more than a dozen Templar tombs. Nothing had ever been booby-trapped. Kavanaugh shuddered at the sight of the death that might have been his.

The third time he watched the avalanche footage—slowed down as much as he could make it—he recognized the dimly colored Templar characters painted above the tomb's doorway. The voiceover said it labeled this as the Templar Master's tomb, the grave of the leader of the Templars at the time of their genocide.

The tomb was empty, the narrator said. More recent—less grainy—footage showed the plundered tomb as it stood now. The fallen stone had been cleared away, piled neatly on either side of the entryway. The camera moved past the silent heaps of rock and entered the tomb itself, empty save for the lone catafalque in its center.

The video crew had set fire to a collection of pots around the edges of the room, highlighting the massive tomb's interior dimensions. The cave was much larger than Kavanaugh had suspected. Its ceiling soared upward inside the mountain, easily twice as high as its diameter.

"What was here?" the narrator wanted to know. He raised an antique hand torch. Kavanaugh recognized it as the Imperial-issue torch he'd tripped over the day his men had opened the tomb. Revan's men hadn't left it behind; the Emperor's had, when they imprisoned Raena Zacari there.

The documentary's narrator was a spindly creature with a pinched mouth and oversized black eyes, as much a bug as the Templars had been. Kavanaugh could see that the barely restrained anger evident in his voice wasn't feigned. "Did the Thallians steal or destroy the Templar Master's body?" the narrator asked. "Wasn't the genocide of the entire Templar people enough for them? Did they have to desecrate the lost people's graves as well?"

Kavanaugh had another drink. He knew who had been in that tomb, because he had been the one to let her out.

He watched the documentary to its end, then watched it again from its very beginning. All throughout, it remained solely focused on the Thallians, blaming them and no one else for the desecration of the tombs. Kavanaugh, Sloane, and Raena Zacari were never mentioned.

Kavanaugh was tempted to call Sloane, to tell him to watch his back. If the Thallians had been able to trace the archaeological dig back to members of Kavanaugh's crew—and thereby identify Sloane and find Raena—then others might be able to do so, also.

Except that Kavanaugh and Sloane weren't on speaking terms any longer. Kavanaugh certainly owed the older man no more loyalty. Anyway, even if he did, he told himself he didn't know how to go about reaching Sloane easily. He'd have to do his own searching around. It wasn't as if Sloane wanted to be found by anyone other than Raena.

Kavanaugh skipped back in the documentary and watched the collapse of the Templar Master's tomb again. Raena had rigged that, he was certain of it. It must have been in the interval between the time Kavanaugh's men roused her and let her out of her prison cell and later that night, when she'd showed up outside their bunker and asked for Kavanaugh's help to get off the tombworld. He hadn't known where she'd gone in the meantime, but he'd assumed she had been attempting to steal their hopper. Sloane had trashed it to keep them planet-bound. Once she'd seen the damage, she would have known she couldn't escape without help from above.

Now Kavanaugh understood what Raena had done to occupy herself in the interim. She'd set the booby-trap, knowing that the Thallians would follow her to the Templar tomb planet. As soon as she'd escaped her imprisonment, she was already scheming not to be taken back in again. The level of justified paranoia she'd perfected was inspiring.

Where, he wondered, had the video of the Thallians come from? While his men worked in the Templar tombs, Kavanaugh had known about the old Imperial surveillance cameras, but most of them were damaged by the constant gritty winds. At least, the few he'd bothered to test hadn't worked. He wouldn't have put it past Sloane to repair some of the cameras in order to spy on the looters in his employ, but why would Sloane release the footage of the Thallians on-world to the news? Why would he want to draw any attention to the looting at all? As a matter of character, Sloane was wily enough to keep himself beneath the radar.

Kavanaugh sped ahead to the credits of the documentary. Among the experts thanked were the crew of the *Veracity*.

That rang a bell. Kavanaugh keyed in a quick search and found the connection. The *Veracity* had been the first ship to pick up the distress call from Thallian's homeworld. The *Veracity* had saved hundreds of lives, all the soldiers who had survived hidden for decades after Jonan Thallian took his Imperial warship into the depths of his home ocean and enslaved its crew. After all the Thallians were dead, the *Veracity* had been the ship to break the news of the collapse of the domes of Thallian's underwater city.

Kavanaugh reached into the octagonal metal box on his desk. Inside the Templar box lay coiled a length of black hair, easily more than a meter long. He knew who had killed the Thallians, who had destroyed their city and set their slaves free.

He'd bet good money she was on the *Veracity* even now.

So why would Raena release the recordings she'd made of the booby-trap she'd set on her Templar tomb? She wasn't condemning Sloane for funding the grave robbing. Was she trying to misdirect the media: to protect Sloane—or Kavanaugh himself?

He was too tired to figure out Raena's motives tonight—and after finishing the too-sweet bottle of xyshin, he was too drunk. He powered the screen down and kicked off his boots, stretching out on his bunk in his clothes.

He fell immediately into a dream, as if it had been waiting for him.

CHAPTER 3

Kavanaugh had serious qualms about robbing Templar graves. It was bad enough that the rest of the galaxy blamed humans for exterminating the Templars. If the galaxy discovered that a human team was now looting their graves, he didn't like to think where that would lead.

Still, as Sloane said, it wasn't as if the bugs inside the tombs were using the weapons and armor buried with them. And it wasn't as if Sloane hadn't paid off every official in the quadrant who might be intrigued by what the "archaeological" team was doing.

That Sloane could loot the Templar tombs without a second thought saddened Kavanaugh. And yet here Kavanaugh found himself, leading the team, wondering how in the hell he'd volunteered for this.

At least the impossibly hard stone kept the caves' contents incorrupt: metal was as polished as the day it had been entombed, corpses as fresh. In the past couple of weeks, Kavanaugh had seen more than he wanted of dead bugs contorted by the Templar plague.

Nothing indicated that this particular cavern would be different than the others. If it had been up to Kavanaugh, he'd have let the men close down the machinery for the night, sent them back to the bunkers to get out of the knifing, granular wind. Unfortunately, Sloane had made it clear to him that not meeting the quota would cost Kavanaugh his job.

He was on the verge of saying, "Fine, I quit," but the boss, long ago, had been a friend.

When they opened this tomb, the huge explosion dropped the ground from beneath their feet. Then the blast wave knocked the team back against the loader, holding them in place a moment, air crushed from their lungs. When it released them, Kavanaugh commented, "Think you used too much."

"I used just enough," Taki huffed.

Kavanaugh always had a moment, as he slithered past the edge of a slab, when he feared it would rock back into place and crush him. Or worse, it would rock back after he'd passed it, trapping him inside the tomb. No telling how long it would take someone to die inside one of those graves, how long until the air ran out or dehydration made breathing cease to matter. It wasn't as if Sloane would feel he had enough invested in the team to rescue anyone.

Most of the tombs they'd entered had warehoused whole companies of bugs, the dead warriors of a single starship buried together. Kavanaugh played his light around the inside this cavern to find only a single cata-falque, an uncarved slab of obsidian roughly in the center of the room. Whoever lay atop it must be important, *he thought.* Shouldn't take too long to loot one body.

Kavanaugh peeled off his face shield and lifted his flask, sucking down the last half of its contents. His boot knocked something over. When he bent down to retrieve it, he found an Imperial-issue electric torch. Damn. Had someone beaten them to this one?

"What's a human girl doing in here?" Taki asked.

Kavanaugh stopped fiddling with the torch to see his team had con-verged around the catafalque. He couldn't make sense of what they were saying. Why would there be a human girl inside a Templar tomb?

"There's your dancing girl," Curcovic teased. "Maybe you can wake her with a kiss."

"'Cept for the dust," Lim commented.

"Well, yeah, 'cept for the dust, Lim. Damn, man, don't you have any imagination?"

"What did you have in mind?" Lim asked skeptically.

"Are you sure she's human?" Kavanaugh asked as he took another drink.

"I think she's just a kid," Curcovic added. "No armor. You think she was somebody important's kid?"

"She's the best thing I've seen on this rock so far," Taki pointed out.

Kavanaugh was crossing the uneven floor to join them when a low female voice said clearly, "No."

From that point on, she took down all of Kavanaugh's men. She could have killed them as if they'd been standing still, but she'd disabled them instead. He suspected that was because they posed no real threat to her.

Cold sweat ran into Kavanaugh's eyes. He held the flask in his gun hand. He'd have to drop it to draw his weapon.

"We didn't mean you any harm," he said gently as he let go of the flask.

She wheeled toward him. "I know you." Her voice was rusty. "Switch on your light. I want to see your face."

With his left hand, Kavanaugh pulled his torch out of his pocket. He held it to illuminate the left side of his face.

"No," she said, her voice desolate. "You only remind me of someone I used to know." She was moving toward the mouth of the tomb. Kavanaugh shivered at the thought that she might knock the chocks aside and seal them in.

"Where will you go?" he asked desperately. "It's a rock out there. Barren. You can't get off-world without our help."

Somewhere in the darkness, she laughed. The sound wasn't entirely sane. "You're grave robbers. You're going to help me?"

"We're archaeologists," Kavanaugh lied. "We work for Gavin Sloane."

Her response was completely unexpected. "Gavin? Still alive?"

"I'm here, Raena," Sloane said calmly. He switched on a torch, angled down at his feet. He stood just inside the mouth of the tomb.

"Is it really you?" Raena asked. She made Kavanaugh think of a child, desperate for comfort from the dark.

"It's really me." He crossed the room to her, engulfed her in his arms.

Kavanaugh jerked awake as he turned over. Too many years of living on shipboard, sleeping on this narrow mattress, saved him. He caught himself just before he rolled right off his bunk. With adrenaline coursing through his system, Kavanaugh found himself completely awake.

Why had he dreamed that Sloane had come down to the planet? Sloane hadn't ever seen the tomb, as far as Kavanaugh knew. Sloane hadn't been one to get his hands dirty, if he could bully someone else into it. He lurked in his base on one of the planet's tiny moons and let Kavanaugh and his men take the risks to find Raena.

Everything else happened in the dream just as he remembered in real life. In fact, it seemed less like the messy chaos of a real dream and more like he was living the memory again. Kavanaugh fumbled the blanket out from beneath himself and pulled it over his body, but still he shivered.

At the time, he hadn't known that Sloane's operation had a goal beyond stealing as many of the Templar artifacts as they could pack into crates. That had only been Sloane's cover story—and a way of funding the expedition. He never let on to the men doing the actual work, but all along he had been really only looking for Raena.

Once again Kavanaugh counted his blessings. He knew Raena had never done well with enclosed spaces. She might have come out of that tomb like a caged animal and killed them all.

In fact, once he'd realized how things might have gone, Kavanaugh had struggled to forgive Sloane for putting him into that kind of danger. Once upon a time, he had counted Sloane as a friend, almost like a big brother. Probably it had just been luck, but when Kavanaugh had been a kid, Sloane was always nearby when he needed help.

Then, after they'd finally rescued Raena—well, after Kavanaugh had rescued her—Sloane paid Kavanaugh a goodly sum to get lost. He might have been able to forgive that, if Sloane hadn't hurt Ariel so badly on their last ride together.

Kavanaugh punched his pillow into a better shape and flopped over into a new position. He might be more comfortable if he'd just get up long enough to take off his clothes, but he didn't want to get out from under the blanket.

The dream felt wrong in his head, more nightmarish than actual events—and actual events hadn't been a joy themselves.

Kavanaugh shrugged and tried to settle himself back to sleep. Obviously, the dream must have been brought on by studying the documentary before he passed out. It was nothing but his conscience taunting him. If he were like Sloane—or Raena, for that matter— events in his life wouldn't trouble his dreams. He'd be immune.

He curled tighter under the blanket and hoped the chill wouldn't keep him awake long.

Back then, as her imprisonment dragged on, Raena didn't really sleep any more. She didn't think of it as sleep, anyway, more like perpetual rest. She lay on her catafalque with her hands folded across her stomach, her legs crossed at her ankles. Maybe it was meditation or maybe she'd just been alone in the dark for so very long that it was the only way she had left to pass the time. Whatever it was, she lay there, still as stone, listening.

For some time, she had heard something she couldn't identify: a deep booming that echoed and sang through the mountain at whose heart she lay. At first she thought the sound was an explosion, maybe bombardment from space, but it only happened intermittently, with long silences in between. She had no way to measure the intervals, but eventually they stopped making her jump.

She decided that the sound was the precursor to an earthquake, something so massive that it might break the mountain open and allow her to walk away. Hoping for that day wouldn't bring it closer; she had hoped for release since the slab closed on her tomb. She had no way to measure how long ago that had been. So instead of hoping, she lay still on her catafalque and waited.

The next boom sounded closer, but distance was difficult to judge inside her cocoon of rock. Perhaps this time it was an earthquake, since the mountain around her actually shuddered. Fine grit drifted down, falling onto her face, but Raena didn't bother to reach up to brush it away. What difference did it make? It wasn't as if anyone was going to see her.

She heard a new sound: grinding, as if rock slid against rock. She was so calm that she lay still and waited for the ceiling to fall. If she were luckier than she had been so far, the falling rock would kill her. She thought about what it would be like to be dead. It was hard for her to imagine an afterlife. What she really wanted was to be blotted out. Her luck had been so bad for so long, though, she figured her fate was to be crushed, maybe pinned in place, but not killed. Pain would bring a new kind of waiting.

Then she heard something like men's voices. Her imagination had to be working overtime. She listened to them banter, silly things men would say to each other when they felt there was no one to overhear. They were clearly so comfortable amongst themselves that they had a patter, a rhythm, that spoke of camaraderie. Longing submerged her and she wished, more than anything, that she had someone to speak to once more.

"Are you sure she's human?" one of the men asked.

"I think she's just a kid," another suggested. "No armor. You think she was somebody important's kid?"

"She's the best thing I've seen on this rock so far," a third pointed out.

Just as she was trying to sort out how many of them there were, a hand brushed across her breast.

That got her attention. This was real, she realized belatedly. There was someone in her tomb . . . and they were touching her.

She said, "No," and sat up, straight-arming one of the men away from her. He hit his head on the stone floor and didn't move again.

Another man backed away, holding a wavering torch beam on her. That allowed her to see a third man fumbling his gun from its holster. She skipped sideways just as the gunslinger cleverly shot his companion. The fallen man's curses were amusingly creative.

She spun toward the one with the gun, turning a one-handed cartwheel that left her in range to kick the gun from his hand. As it flew from his grip, she twisted around and cracked her fist hard into his chest. The man dropped with satisfying speed.

"We didn't mean you any harm," someone else said. His voice seemed somehow familiar. Someone she knew a long time ago . . . someone from when she was running? A boy's face rose in her memory.

"I know you." She grimaced at the rusty sound of her own voice. "Switch on your light. I want to see your face."

He held the light awkwardly, pointed toward the side of his face with his off hand. Raena slipped sideways, so he couldn't flash the light her way and blind her.

He was no boy. Warm brown eyes nestled amidst crows-feet above a tousled red-gold beard.

"No," she said sadly. "You only remind me of someone I used to know." Raena turned toward the mouth of the tomb, eager to make good the escape for which she had waited so long.

"Where will you go?" the grave robber asked desperately, trying to slow her down. "It's a rock out there. Barren. You can't get off-world without our help."

She laughed—and recognized that the sound wasn't entirely sane. "You're grave robbers. You're going to help me?"

"We're archaeologists," the man lied. "We work for Gavin Sloane."

Her response startled her. As if the whole relationship she'd been imagining between them had been real, she asked, "Gavin? Still alive?"

"I'm here, Raena," Sloane said calmly. He switched on a torch, angled down at his feet.

"Is it really you?" Raena begged.

"It's really me." He crossed the room to her, engulfed her in his arms.

She clung to Sloane as if she were drowning. His beard was scratchy against her cheek. One of his hands cupped her butt and squeezed, which seemed at odds with the pair of kisses that had been all they'd shared in the brief time they'd actually known each other. Perhaps he'd been imagining a relationship with her as well, all the time she'd been imprisoned.

Still, she'd been a slave. She knew how to respond to the arousal of her masters. She owed her rescue to Gavin Sloane and his team of "archaeologists." She leaned against his body, pressing her hip against his groin with an excitement more calculated than his. She got just the reaction she intended to.

Sloane led her toward the door of the tomb. He handed her a helmet with a full-face screen. "The air is full of grit," he warned, "bits of Templar stone. It will slice through any exposed skin."

She slipped the helmet on, accepted the cloak that he gave her as well. She wondered if he would kick the chocks loose as they passed the tomb's slab, but he didn't seal his men inside. Nor did he spare time to help with the wounded, she noticed, not even to acknowledge them or say goodbye.

Instead, he escorted Raena to an opulently appointed yacht. Once he had her strapped safely into the copilot's chair, he lifted the ship from the rock. At the edge of the atmosphere, he turned the yacht back toward the planet. He released a barrage of missiles, destroying the tombs and the men left behind on the planet below.

"Thallian would have used the encampment to connect your rescue to me. He would torture Kavanaugh's men in an effort to find you. This is kinder," Sloane explained. "At least this is quick."

Raena knew the sort of agony the men would face, when Thallian tried to hunt her down. It probably was safer to kill them now. Still, she had liked Kavanaugh. She was sorry he was dead. She turned toward Sloane and shot him with the gun she'd taken from the fallen archaeologists. If Thallian could connect her to Sloane, she needed to get away from him as quickly as possible. She unhooked the crash restraints and dragged Sloane's body back to the airlock.

She'd always been happier running alone anyway.

Coni was taking a shift in the cockpit while the others slept. The puzzle of piecing together a new identity for Raena was more entertaining than she expected. For once, during her shift, she wasn't the least bit sleepy.

After they'd hijacked the *Veracity* from the Thallians, Coni had seen Raena's Imperial wanted poster and the recording of her trial in its log. It surprised Coni how much more information she could find about the little assassin in the Imperial archives. Following up on the crimes Raena had been accused of opened up all sorts of records. Fascinating reading, if one had the patience to wade through the human-centric propaganda.

The old files inspired the new biography Coni was writing for Raena. She wanted to tie in planets that Raena had actually visited, skills she honestly possessed.

The work felt like compiling an ironclad telenovel. Coni found wry amusement in using the search capabilities of the *Veracity's* computers to craft this elegant fiction.

Then again, Mykah had been the one who changed the ship's name from the *Raptor* to the *Veracity*—and he'd encouraged Coni to add another false record of sale atop the *Raptor's* already complicated series of falsified registrations. After the Thallians had illegally prevented the *Raptor* from being melted down as war surplus, they obscured their ownership for fifteen years. The ship's current crew was only continuing that tradition. Coni loved Mykah enough to make sure the final transaction moving the ship into his possession looked very, very legal. She'd even refinanced a fake loan on the ship, then paid it off in reality with part of the bounty they'd claimed on the Thallians.

All the same, Coni was aware of the difference between the literal truth and the apparent truth. She had never had any aspirations to becoming a journalist, as Mykah had. She hadn't even really planned to become a hacker. She had only wanted to protect the ship and its crew to the best of her abilities.

Some strange noise raised Coni's hackles. She reached out one finger to mute the Haru singer she had been listening to.

There it was again: a quiet voice, a note of protest, raised in the sleep of one of her crewmates.

Coni had forgotten she'd turned on the speaker for the monitor in Raena's cabin. Thank the stars one of her crewmates hadn't caught her spying. She reached over now and turned on the picture.

Raena was alone in her cabin, of course. Coni couldn't imagine anyone keeping her company, although she supposed Mykah might have, if asked. No, Raena lay in her bunk, sleeping face down, arms wrapped around her pillow.

The quiescent monitor screen in Raena's cabin cast bloody red light across her skin. She was bare from nape of neck to the ribs, but weird shadows striped her skin. Was it a tattoo? Coni tried to make out the image, but the video resolution was too grainy for clarification.

Raena whispered again. She stiffened, straightened her legs, and the shift of her body propelled her from the nightmare.

Coni toggled the monitors off. Her surveillance felt intrusive now, too intimate. It was one thing to watch Raena awake and moving about in her gym—and another entirely to spy on her as she awoke from a nightmare.

Why was she doing this, Coni asked herself. Of all the illegal things she did for her shipmates, spying on Raena was by far the one that felt the worst.

Raena opened her eyes on her darkened cabin. Only the power light of her screen glowed, a cheery red light in the shadows. She rolled over, chasing sleep. Of course, it wouldn't come back.

That wasn't how it went, she thought. Gavin hadn't come down to the tombworld to get her. He'd been waiting in his base on one of the planet's moons. When she'd shown up there with Kavanaugh and a couple of Gavin's bodyguards as an escort, Gavin hadn't recognized her. He accused her of working for Ariel.

With eyes closed, Raena could picture it all again: the ludicrous white fur carpet, the crystal glass from which she'd drunk her first sip of water in twenty years, the pretty girl with the big gun who stood guard for her boss. Gavin had a beard then, like he did in her dream, but he seemed younger in her true memory than he had in the dream just now, even though the drug he'd been addicted to at the time had whittled him down to little more than a skeleton.

Weird. Now that she pondered it, the man she'd identified as Gavin in her dream didn't really look much like him at all.

Anyway, why was Kavanaugh getting dragged into her dreams? She wondered if he understood how much danger Sloane had put him in. When Kavanaugh opened her tomb, Raena had been just as disoriented as she had been in the dream. She marveled now that she hadn't simply killed Kavanaugh and his men just for startling her. At the time, it hadn't seemed necessary.

Thinking about it now, Raena finally appreciated how much she had changed during her imprisonment.

Poor Kavanaugh, she thought. She'd always liked him. He seemed like an honestly good-hearted person, fair and reliable, maybe too kind to survive in the galaxy. At least she'd avenged his death in her dream.

Raena got out of bed to splash some water on her face.

Why was her subconscious bringing up Kavanaugh and her escape from the tomb now?

Yeah, she was sorry that she'd ended things with Kavanaugh with her fist to his head. Tarik didn't deserve to be left unconscious on the floor of Ariel's ship. When she was leaving them behind on Kai, Raena had been angry at being spied upon by her supposed friends. She'd been in a hurry to steal the *Raptor* and get off Kai before Planetary Security caught up to her. She was supposed to meet Mykah and the crew. The clock was ticking.

She ought to apologize to Kavanaugh, but she wasn't sure how to look him up. What would she say, anyway? Sorry you were in my way?

Poor Kavanaugh. He deserved better friends.

The dream circled around and around in her thoughts. Raena shook her head, trying to shake the dream images away. Her mind just wouldn't clear.

Disgusted with herself, she went to dress. She might as well get some use out of the day. Maybe she could get Vezali's help making some modifications to her gym to make working out more of a challenge.

The lights flickered on in welcome as Raena stepped into her gym. She stood in the doorway, wondering whether she knew the room well enough that she could work out in the dark.

She stepped back into the passageway and opened the panel by the door, hitting the switch to kill the lights.

That didn't make the room completely dark, she realized. Light still filtered through the windowpane on the door. She caught herself wondering how to turn out the passage lights. Right. She could blackout the whole ship and creep around in the dark. Her crewmates would be sure to understand that.

Were the disruptions to her sleep making her irrational? Not, she supposed, as long as she recognized the craziness before she acted on it.

What was she trying to do, anyway? Hurt herself? What did she have to prove? She was never, ever going to be anywhere that was completely dark again, if she could help it.

She flipped the gym's lights back on. Maybe she could heat the room up, find a way to make it humid. She wanted to exhaust her muscles with running and vaults. Movement. The illusion of flight. She wanted to tire herself out to the point of sleeping without dreams.

Coni waited until she was sure Raena was occupied before she switched off all her monitors and pinged Haoun to wake up for his shift. Then she backed up her notes and went to catch some sleep.

The sound of their door opening roused Mykah, who smiled sleepily at her. He inched over in their bunk, making room, as she hung up her jacket and stepped out of her skirt. Coni slipped under the coverlet and snuggled close to Mykah, breathing him in. The salty metallic smell of his body had turned her stomach when she met him on Kai, but she'd gotten used to it. Usually she found it erotic, but her brain was too tired to act on her impulses now.

Mykah stroked his fingers through the fur under her chin. "How'd you spend your evening?"

"Raena has me setting up a new identity for her," Coni said sleepily.

"Really?"

"Well, it's only sort of new. She wants to keep her name and masquerade as her own daughter. But she wants a birth certificate and school transcripts and some record of herself as a real person in the galaxy."

"That seems reasonable," Mykah said. "She can't really leave the ship on any sort of civilized world. If she gets picked up for anything, there are going to be questions about who she is and where she's been. If they run a DNA trace on her and find out who she was, they're going to connect her to Thallian—and she's going to stand trial for his crimes unless she can prove her imprisonment. And we didn't find any evidence of that. Did we?"

"No," Coni said. "We have her word that she was imprisoned all those years, along with the knowledge she had of the grave robbing and the recording she hacked of the avalanche that killed Thallian's men. But we don't have any evidence that she was actually imprisoned in that tomb."

"Except that she's physically twenty," Mykah pointed out. "She hasn't aged since the War, so some kind of Templar tech was involved."

"I'm still trying to figure that out," Coni said. "She says the Templar stone kept everything inside it from rotting or falling apart. Does that mean it's like a super-refrigerator, cold inside? Or does that mean that it warps time somehow?"

"Whoa," Mykah said. "Are you serious? You think the Templar stone warps time?"

"I don't know. There's no research on it, but that's not unusual. There's so little research on most Templar tech. Let's say that it does warp time somehow. That would explain her apparent age. Maybe if we all slept inside Templar caves, we could become immortal."

"That would be a story to unveil," Mykah said, yawning.

"Except that who would want to be immortal?" Coni argued. "I don't know what other use the time warping might be . . ."

She realized that Mykah had fallen back to sleep already. She curled up against him, her face buried in his shoulder, breathing his salty metallic smell. This was home to her now.

CHAPTER 4

Hours later, Raena was still working out. At her request, Vezali had routed the heat exchangers to vent into the gym, just for the day. Raena had kicked over a tub of water, leaving a slick on the floor to evaporate into the air, making the room sufficiently steamy. She was trying to replicate jungle conditions.

Sweat plastered her short black hair to her head in clumps. She'd stripped off her shirt, leaving a breast band on for modesty's sake. In general, the others left her alone while she was working out, but she was glad when Coni tapped on the door. She could use some distraction from worrying about her dreams.

"Wow," Coni gasped as she stepped into the room.

"I can come out," Raena said. "There's no reason you should come in and be uncomfortable."

"No, it feels wonderful," the blue-furred girl said. "Like home." She stretched, rolling her shoulders around, soaking in the heat. "What possessed you to warm it up in here like this?"

"I was bored of exercising at ship temperature," Raena said simply. "Do we keep it too cold for you normally?"

"I'm used to it," Coni answered. "It's why I always wear a jacket." She slipped the boxy black coat off now and hung it on the peg beside Raena's top.

When she turned back, Raena realized she'd never seen Coni without her jackets before. The top half of the girl's body looked genderless under its luxuriant blue fur. She looked upward into Coni's face, but as always, couldn't read her expression.

Coni said, "I think I have a good start on your identity. You've got a birth certificate now and transcripts through lower school. Did you want to continue on to trade school?"

"Would that make the most sense?" Raena asked. "Maybe I studied human computer systems or something? Don't make it too technical or complicated, though. I don't want anyone to challenge me on something I should know, since my knowledge is mostly out of date. Is there a way to have me be self-taught or home-schooled or something? Or a student of martial arts?"

Coni nodded. "What do you want to have done after school?"

"Bodyguard work? Something unconnected to legal security."

"Got it." Coni made a note on her handheld. Without looking up, she asked, "Do you want to take credit as the person who executed the Thallians? You could say you were avenging your mother or something."

"No," Raena said decisively. "Let the assassin remain anonymous. I don't want my new identity connected to the Thallians in any way. I want a new life, free and clear."

"All right, then. I can finish this up this in another day or two. I'll send it back to your cabin."

"That will be perfect, Coni. Thank you so much for your help."

"It's been fun." Her voice fell back into the toneless pitch that Raena couldn't interpret.

Raena tried to think if she'd ever heard Coni speak her own language, or speaking anything other than Imperial or Galactic Standard. Maybe she should do a little research on Coni's species, about the way they communicated amongst themselves. Probably, if she put a little work into it, she would understand the relationship developing between her and Coni much better.

Raena crossed the gym to sip from her water bottle. She heard Coni's deep, shocked intake of breath and spun back to see what was the matter. Coni's eyes were round and wide above her muzzle.

"Sorry," Raena said immediately. "I forget what my back looks like."

"If you keep your scars," Coni said cautiously, "we will have to write them into your biography, too."

"You're right. Thank you for understanding that. I do want to keep them. They're a talisman to protect me from ever belonging to anyone again."

"Are they from when you were a slave?"

"No," Raena said. Then she added, "Those are love marks from Thallian."

"May I?" Coni drew closer, one taloned hand upraised. Raena turned away and let the girl examine her.

"What did he hit you with?" Coni asked.

"They're burns. He poured accelerant on me and set it afire."

"It must have hurt like hell. He didn't send you to the infirmary afterward?"

"He didn't think the crew knew what went on in his cabin. Jonan thought that as long as I refused to scream, no one could hear a thing. No one would jump to conclusions. That alone should have made me realize how delusional he was."

"How did you stand it?"

This was a longer conversation than she'd ever had with the blue girl before, and much, much more personal. Something had shifted between them. Raena was glad for the change, even if she didn't completely understand the thaw.

"I stood it because he owned me," she said. "Legally, of course, I had enlisted in the Empire's diplomatic corps, but in reality I served as Thallian's aide only at his pleasure. If I'd refused him anything, given him any provocation, he would have had me thrown into the cells on the *Arbiter,* where he could have tortured me to death for any reason or no reason at all. None of the crew would have cared to stand up for me. As long as Jonan thought I liked what he did to me, liked it as much as he liked doing it, he kept me around. I was the mirror that reflected his perversion and made it beautiful."

The pads on Coni's fingers were rough, but her touch was extremely gentle as she explored the ridges and troughs of scar tissue.

Raena asked, "You understand now why I killed him?"

"Yes." Coni took her hands away and Raena turned to meet her gaze. "Yes," she said again. "I think the galaxy would understand, too, but I respect your privacy in this."

"Thank you." Raena went to the door and retrieved her shirt, sliding it back over her head. Having someone touch her scar tissue made her feel chilled, despite the sweltering heat in the room. Those memories, apparently, were still too close to the surface.

She didn't tell Coni not to say anything to Mykah. It would be interesting to see if the blue girl would want to get her boyfriend outraged over something that happened to another woman or if she really did respect Raena's privacy enough not to share her discovery.

After Coni left her, Raena realized her fever to exercise had passed. She re-routed the heat exchangers and started mopping up the floor with a towel.

Mykah came into the gym while Raena was crawling around on all fours. His hair was an explosion of ringlets today and he was letting his beard go dark at the roots. "Wanna spar?" he asked hopefully.

"No, I'm done," Raena said.

He looked disappointed.

"Go ahead and use the equipment," she added quickly, "if you just want a workout."

"Thanks." He moved into the room listlessly, trying to decide where to start.

Raena paused in the doorway. "Can I ask you a question?"

Mykah turned from the equipment as if glad of the interruption. "Anything," he promised.

"Do you remember your dreams?"

That was clearly not the direction he expected her to go. "Yeah," he said, "doesn't everyone?"

"I don't know. I never asked anyone before." She leaned against the doorframe, trying to steel herself to ask what she really wanted to know. "Mykah," she said slowly, "do you ever dream about your past? Like reliving your memories?"

He frowned, thinking about it, before he shook his head. "Not really. I mean, things from my past turn up, like the day we disrupted the jet pack race. I remember what it was like to fly. But I end up flying out over green fields or above forests or the ocean, stuff we never did on Kai. The memory is kind of a jumping-off point for the rest of the dream."

"Thanks," Raena said, letting the door open.

"Why do you want to know?" he asked, before she could get away.

"I've been having a lot of bad dreams lately," she said. "I wish they were as wonderful as flying over the ocean. Maybe, now that you've put the image in my head, I'll dream of that next."

Coni waited until Raena had gone into her cabin to shower, before she slipped back into the gym to talk to Mykah.

He also had stripped off his shirt to exercise. She came over to lick the sweat beading on his chest.

He laughed at her. "Did you come in just to get a taste of me?

"That, too," she said, savoring the lingering salty flavor on her tongue. "But . . . no. I wanted some reassurance."

He released the bar he had been hanging from and dropped back to his feet. "What's wrong?"

"I came in here earlier, when Raena was working out. I saw . . . I saw her back. I saw what that monster did to her."

Mykah rubbed a towel over his skin before he came to hug her.

"I know," he said, looking up into Coni's lavender eyes. "I've caught glimpses of them. We knew she'd been shot several times in his service . . ."

Coni interrupted him. "It's her back. She said they were love marks. She said he'd set her on fire."

Mykah squeezed Coni tighter. "You know he was crazy," he reminded.

"How could humans do that to each other?" she demanded. "I know he was evil. I know all the things he was charged with. But to hurt someone you love . . ." She shuddered, smoothing the pads of her hands down Mykah's muscled back as if to wipe the memory away.

"She said the crew she served with knew," Coni reported. "They knew and no one helped her. She said she had to take his abuse because otherwise Thallian would have tortured her to death."

Mykah reached up to take Coni's face in his hands. "I know," he said softly. "She's withstood terrible things. But she's avenged herself. He can't hurt anyone any more."

"It's not that," Coni argued, but maybe it was. "How does she get up every day, get dressed, face other people . . . How do you recover? How do you act normal? How do you . . . ?" She ran out of words, unable to articulate how deeply she was touched by all that Raena had endured.

"She's able to do it, because she was shut in that tomb for twenty years," Mykah reminded, "where she was safe from him. She couldn't die, so she had to heal."

Coni bent down to rub the top of her head under his chin.

"You're welcome." He scratched her gently behind the ear. "You know you can always come to me with your questions. I don't know all that Raena's survived—I don't think she's let anyone know it all—but I understand pretty well how she did it."

There were times when Raena missed her bubble bath. When Kavanaugh had delivered her to Gavin's moon base up above the Templar tombworld, the two men had adapted a rocket casing so she could have her first bath in decades. Even though the water had cooled faster than she would have preferred, it was still heavenly. Raena wondered if Vezali could rig some kind of bathtub out of the weapons the Thallians left behind.

In the meantime, she stepped into the shower in her cabin. She set the water to be practically scalding, but didn't allow herself to luxuriate in it for long. No telling how many times that water had been cycled already.

Her thoughts had finally quieted. After she toweled herself off, she couldn't think of anything she particularly wanted to do. So she crawled back into her bunk and let her eyes slide closed, hoping for the peaceful sleep that had eluded her earlier.

If not that, then some nice pastoral dreams about flying.

In her tomb, Raena experimented with turning the electric torch off for short periods of time. She knew the torch's batteries were not going to last forever. As far as she knew, her imprisonment was intended to be for life, so she was likely to outlive the light. Whenever she considered what life would be like once the light was gone, she wanted to weep—but her tears had apparently used themselves up. Her inability to cry didn't make the emotion any less intense.

She was trying to memorize the boundaries of the tomb. She started by walking to the cavern's entrance, where she put her hand on the slab and switched off the torch. Then she paced forward slowly, counting her steps.

She wondered if going crazy was a choice. Could she choose madness? If she went crazy, would the darkness fill with ghosts? Would they attack her, gang up, avenge themselves on her? Would it be better to have company, any company, than to have the fear of the dark so clear in her mind?

She halted abruptly. She realized she had forgotten her count. She turned around carefully, one hand always on the wall, and walked back toward the tomb's slab to begin again.

The fear began to spiral: how far had she gone? It seemed like she was walking back farther than she'd already come. Was she lost? Was it possible to get lost? Was the cave rearranging itself around her in the darkness?

Panting, unable to catch her breath, she snapped the torch on. The entrance of the tomb was a mere arm's length ahead of her.

Raena sank to the floor with her back against the wall. She took a deep breath, held it as long as she could, then blew it out slowly. Then she switched the torch off again.

Sometime later, a huge boom shook the cave. Raena scrambled to her feet, her body on fire with adrenaline. Was it an earthquake? She wanted to race around in the dark, find somewhere to hide, but the cave was big and open and bare to the walls except for the catafalque where she slept. There was nothing inside the mountain that would protect her. Her hands clenched and unclenched, desperate for anything to hang on to. All she had was the torch.

A grinding sound set her teeth on edge. Raena couldn't figure out what it was, why it wouldn't stop. Any avalanche would be quicker than this slow, steady scrape.

Then she noticed the blackness around her had lightened subtly. Someone was opening her tomb.

Of all the people who knew she was inside, only one would come after her.

If she could drop dead in an instant rather than face Thallian again, she would have counted herself the luckiest girl in the galaxy. Instead, she swiped her clammy hands against the legs of her jumpsuit, then crept as quietly as she could to the far side of the tomb's entrance. That was as much of a hiding place as any.

Not a moment too soon, either. A beam of light flashed around the inside of the cave. It did not find her.

"Raena?" a man called. "It's okay. I've come to rescue you. You're safe. I've come alone."

She recognized the voice, but couldn't picture its owner. It wasn't Thallian. Of course, he wouldn't come himself. She should have expected that. He'd sent a minion: someone from the Arbiter, she thought. The voice made her think of the ship.

She held her breath until the man slipped past the slab that had sealed the tomb's entrance.

Then she leapt on him, yanking the helmet from his head. She flung it out of arm's reach into the darkness. She followed up with her other hand before he had a chance to react. She hit him with the Imperial torch, beating it down into his skull over and over and over until the bone gave way with a satisfying crunch and hot blood slicked her fingers.

When at last she'd expended her fury, the man's face was unrecognizable. Raena stood back and wiped her long hair from her face. She tasted blood on her lips and shivered. How long had it been since she'd eaten anything?

She stared down at her bloody hands. They were stripped of their color in the twilight. She opened them, turned them over, sensitive to the faint stickiness that held her fingers together. That was a sensation she hadn't felt since the tomb slab closed . . .

She shook herself away from the reverie and bent to drag the jacket from the corpse. As it came loose, a little piece of metal clattered on the stone floor. Thinking it might be some kind of traveling money, Raena snatched it up.

Instead, it was a small silvery disk. She held it close to her face to examine it, smudging its surface with bloody fingerprints. They didn't obscure the pair of crossed sword blades embossed on it.

Recognition came over her in a hot rush. This was her mother's final gift. Fiana had given the hologram medallion to Raena for her eleventh birthday, the day she sent the girl away into the universe.

The last time Raena had seen the medallion was when she gave it to Gavin Sloane aboard the Arbiter. He had been attempting to rescue her from Thallian then, but instead she covered his escape and went to meet her fate.

She stared down at the corpse at her feet. There was no longer any way to tell if this was—or had been—Gavin Sloane.

It didn't matter. She slung the medallion over her head and shouldered into his coat. It hung practically to her knees. She rolled back its sleeves, then stripped his body of its weapons. Finally, she retrieved the helmet from the tomb's floor. Once she had it strapped on, she walked out into the gritty wind.

Raena opened her eyes blearily and found herself sprawled across her bunk, still naked from her shower. She sat up and rubbed her damp hair, trying to force her thoughts to clear.

This sleep thing, she thought raggedly, *is just not working out.* No more trying to exhaust herself. From now on, she was going to stay awake as long as possible.

She squinted at the clock and realized she could probably make it to lunch if she hurried.

Mykah had outdone himself with the cooking this time. The central part of the meal was some sort of cardboard-brown noodles, over which he ladled a complex orange sauce full of bite-sized pieces of a rainbow of vegetables.

Raena watched the others, studying their techniques for eating. Mykah twirled the long pasta on his fork, shoving in huge mouthfuls at a time. Haoun merely scooped up a forkful and sucked the noodles in like long skinny worms. Coni and Vezali chopped their food so that they could manage it much more delicately.

"I don't get it," Raena said as she tried to wind up some of her own pasta. "I know I've been away for a long time and a lot has changed, but why is the media still so obsessed with Thallian? I thought there would be rejoicing that the murderer had been punished, you all would be heroes for breaking the news, then interest would wane. Everyone would move on to the next scandal."

Haoun and Coni exchanged a glance. Mykah looked uncomfortably down at his plate. Raena sensed she had said something truly stupid, but she was honestly puzzled. She didn't apologize.

Coni spoke first. "You noticed that it's not human newsfolk who are calling now?"

She hadn't paid that much attention, but Raena nodded for Coni to continue.

"Humanity's attention has moved on. Maybe there's an element of embarrassment or they're disavowing him, distancing themselves from the past, but they're done with the story. Other people in the galaxy, though, it's more than morbid curiosity on their part. They want to understand Thallian, all the Thallians, and the Empire, too. They want to understand what drove humans to think it was acceptable to wipe out an entire people, to imagine they could do such a thing and no one would protest."

"Thallian was a madman," Raena said. "I thought everyone understood that."

"But he didn't act alone," Haoun reminded. "The galaxy wants to know if humans are likely to do something similar again, if another madman leads them or when someone else gets in their way. They want to know if Thallian and the Empire were an anomaly or if another of you is going to take a genocidal hatred to some other species, someone even less able to protect themselves than the Templars were, and fashion a plan for wiping them all out. If humanity is going to keep killing until they're the only species left."

"The galaxy is still afraid of *us*, all these years later?"

"They haven't had closure for very long," Coni explained. "Thallian's show trial was a long time ago, but people would have been more comfortable to see him tried again, in person. They wish they'd been able to hear his justifications from his own mouth, so they could judge him themselves. It would help if they could have heard how crazy he was."

"And they sense that someone went in and wiped out the Thallians," Raena guessed. "More indication that humans—if the assassin was human—are inherently violent and dangerous."

There was a strained silence at the table as everyone shared the understanding that Raena had just described herself.

"They think," Haoun said at last, "that Thallian's death was just one more cover-up."

"That's why I keep doing the interviews," Mykah said quietly. "Because I want the galaxy to understand that Thallian was an aberration. Those of us humans who survive in the galaxy today reject the kind of xenophobia that conceived of the Templar plague. I am not like the Thallians, and by extension, other humans are not like them."

Raena remembered Sloane's casual sale of the Templar artifacts his men had looted from the tombworld. Humans First! bigotry wasn't as dead as Mykah might have hoped, even if the terminology had fallen out of fashion. At least she'd been able to ensure that Gavin couldn't go back for any more treasures.

"I didn't know this was going to be so complicated," Raena said. "It honestly never occurred to me to try to bring Thallian to justice. I was so frightened of him that all I could think of was ending him, erasing his power over me, and his threats . . . As it was, you know I barely escaped. If Eilif hadn't turned on him at the last moment, I might still be his prisoner. Maybe, with an army, we could have swept in there and pulled the Thallians out. Or we could have all died as the ocean crashed through the domes on top of us. Surrender was never anything Thallian contemplated, at least not as long as I knew him. Suicide, though, if he could take all his enemies with him: he would have seen that as another path to glorious victory."

She looked around the table, met each of their eyes. "I'm sorry I dragged you all into this."

"I'm glad that you did," Vezali said quickly. "I'm honored to have helped you bring justice to the Thallians. Even if it's not the justice that the rest of the galaxy thinks they want. I have always felt that public executions are unnecessary, bloodthirsty spectacles. We should be better than that."

"I'm honored, too," Mykah said. "You did your part, Raena, the part only you could do. Now I'm doing mine. I've studied the galactic media my whole life. And I get to stand up for us scattered humans, show we're not all bad. I'm happy."

"I'm just along for the ride," Haoun said.

Raena laughed along with the others, glad to have gotten the joke for a change.

She wasn't ready to let the conversation slip away just yet, though. She caught Coni's eyes. "You've studied humans," she said. "Do you think we should be more closely controlled?"

"I'm continuing to monitor the situation," Coni answered. Her tone was so serious that Raena was unsure if she was joking or not. She wished she could glance away to check Mykah's reaction, but she met Coni's eyes instead and nodded.

After lunch, at loose ends, Raena threaded her way through the *Veracity*'s engine, stepping over cables and ducking under conduits. It amazed her how well the old ship ran with Vezali continually pulling it apart and putting it back together.

Imperial ships like the *Veracity* had clunky FTL drives that generated a hyperspace bubble around the ship. It made them tricky to pilot; you had to calculate the course very carefully and broadcast your location constantly to warn other ships to get out of your way. Raena didn't know exactly how all the moving parts worked, only the right sequence of buttons to push. She'd only ever learned to pilot well enough to run, not for the joy of flying like Ariel had.

Raena must have made enough noise coming through the engine room to alert Vezali. From somewhere overhead, the tentacled girl asked, "Can you bring me the mag spanner?"

Raena glanced around for the tool, located it hung neatly on the wall amidst the other spanners, and pulled it free.

Vezali leaned down from a crawlspace overhead and reached out a delicately pointed pink tentacle. Raena held the tool up and let Vezali find her own grip.

The girl hung suspended upside down, some tentacles wrapped around handholds inside the engine, others bracing her in place. Now that Raena counted them, she found that Vezali had an odd number of tentacles. The largest central one she referred to as her root. She used it mostly for balance, when she was upright, and something to sit on when she wasn't moving. Raena thought it was probably a continuation of Vezali's spine, although she couldn't say for sure if Vezali had bones or cartilage or if she was simply held upright by muscle strength—or force of will.

Raena envied the girl her flexibility of body and the ability to have more hands or legs as a situation required. She would've liked the chance to spar with Vezali, just to learn more about how the girl could move, but she wasn't sure how fragile Vezali's species might be. Raena didn't want to bully the crew into working out with her, so she respected the girl's reluctance. That didn't make her stop wishing things were different.

Vezali tinkered silently, then flipped a switch plate back into place. The *Veracity* seemed to take a breath. Then it began humming along happily.

Vezali flushed a little greener, clearly pleased.

"What will you do for fun once you understand how the engine works?" Raena wondered.

"Take apart the weapons systems. Then take apart the hand weapons. Then? I don't know. There's always the galley systems, if Mykah will let me in there, or waste disposal, or life support."

"We're gonna have to be grounded before you fiddle with *that*," Raena teased.

"Maybe," Vezali teased back. "Don't you trust me?" She reached down half a dozen tools, each in a separate tentacle. Raena gathered them all awkwardly into the crook of her arm. She took them back to the wall and began to put them away. Everything in its place, Thallian used to tell her. Raena supposed that had been meant to include her.

Vezali shifted her balance and flipped over so her tentacles could flow to the deck. "Is there something I can help you with, Raena?"

Her voice, like Haoun's, came over a translator she wore. Haoun's was a necklace, but Vezali—having no neck, per se—wore hers as a belt around her midriff. Her species didn't use their mouths for audible communication, but generated sound inside their bodies. The new translator gave her a high-pitched girlish voice, which Raena guessed must be pleasing to Vezali's auditory system, wherever it was. Otherwise, Vezali was clearly clever enough to adjust it to any pitch she wanted, even though it was based on Templar technology.

Now, though, Vezali sounded eager.

Raena knew the other girl enjoyed Raena's little technical puzzles. She was sorry to disappoint her now. "All I need today is a needle."

"I don't understand the word."

"It's a sharp sliver of metal for mending fabric."

"Let me see."

Raena retrieved her catsuit from where she'd left it by the hatchway.

Vezali examined it closely. "It can be mended," she said, "but it's going to have a scar. The fibers have broken off so jaggedly that there's no way to reweave it." She handed it back to Raena.

"I'll just have to make the scar a feature," Raena said, thinking of her own scars.

Vezali's eyestalk bobbed in an imitation of a nod. She drifted over to her tools and rummaged through them, lifting things and leaning forward to peer underneath. Finally she came up with a miniaturized awl. "Will this do?"

"Perfect," Raena said, plucking it delicately from Vezali's tentacle.

Raena found that she didn't want to return to the solitude of her cabin. Her hands still felt slightly sticky, as if from the memory of her dream.

It didn't really happen, she reminded herself. She'd had blood on her hands many times, all sorts of shades and colors of blood, but no one had come into her tomb until Kavanaugh did—and she'd let those men escape. Why, then, wouldn't this nightmare leave her alone?

She went to the lounge and settled in on one of the carpeted benches with her back against the wall. The room was quiet now, with all her shipmates amusing themselves elsewhere. She recognized that things were peaceful and wondered why that didn't make her happy.

She spread the catsuit across her lap and studied the tear. Fairly quickly she discovered that mending it was beyond her meager sewing skills. She could get holes drilled through the fabric and the floss threaded through the holes, but there was no way to make it look like an adornment rather than a sloppy patch job. In the end, she chucked the magenta catsuit into the incinerator.

It was a shame. The stretchy fabric was supremely comfortable and she loved its hideous color. She supposed, at some point soon, she was going to have break down and do some shopping. One more reason to get in touch with Ariel: she had always been so much better at that kind of thing.

In the cabin she shared with Mykah, Coni sat back from her screen. It showed Raena sitting quietly in the lounge, bent over a piece of eye-piercing red fabric.

When Coni started to monitor Raena, it had been with hazy notions of continuing her research on humans. She'd thought Raena might serve as an example of the last of the Imperials, but now that Coni had pried so deeply into Raena's Imperial record, it was clear that the little woman never actually bought into the Empire's rhetoric. Raena didn't even seem to have held an official rank. She was enlisted as Thallian's aide, but the role seemed fluid and ill-defined.

While Raena had done as Thallian ordered her, he had clearly been a loose cannon, under surveillance by his superiors even before Raena's defection showed how precariously he held his command together.

Beyond the way Thallian isolated Raena from his crew, she had been an object of ridicule—and worse, aware of it. Everyone aboard the *Arbiter* seemed to know how much she meant to their commander—and exactly what she did for him behind closed doors. It meant that, on the rare occasions that she stepped out of her commander's shadow, the crew shunned her.

Coni tried to imagine Raena's life onboard the *Arbiter*. No doubt she held herself aloof from her shipmates, as she had initially done from the crew of the *Veracity*. At first Coni had thought that Raena interacted chiefly with Mykah because she still harbored Imperial prejudice, however unspoken, against anyone nonhuman. Now, looking over Raena's life, Coni wondered that Raena was brave enough to speak to any of them at all. She had always been surrounded by humans—and for the most part, humanity had treated her shamefully.

Little wonder she preferred her own company to anyone else's.

CHAPTER 5

The crew of the *Veracity* gathered every afternoon—Galactic Standard Time—to watch the news. Everything was available online eventually, but the crew found comfort in watching the "best news team in the galaxy" run down the biggest news stories of the day.

Raena never joined them. Rarely did the news concern itself with humanity. Most news stories referenced peoples and planets and political systems she'd never heard of. Instead of troubling her crewmates with the breadth of her ignorance, Raena took her shift in the cockpit, monitoring their flight, while the others debated the new scandals of the day.

So she hadn't really been paying attention until the good-natured banter between the others fell into uneasy silence. The lack of voices caught her notice.

She hit the comm button. "Everything okay?"

"Come back," Mykah said. "Everything just changed."

A cold shiver paced up Raena's spine. She locked everything in the cockpit down so it could be left unattended, before she strode back to the lounge.

She had no idea what she expected, but the squirrel-faced creature paused on the screen wasn't it. "What's happened?"

"Mellix uncovered a flaw in the tesseract drive," Haoun said.

Raena twitched her head no, not grasping what that meant.

"The tesseract is the newest star drive technology," Vezali explained. "Every big ship built in the last five years has one. The shipbuilding cartels have really pushed the technology, creating incredible demand for it. It's revised travel times across the galaxy. "

"Mellix has drawn a pattern between the sporadic disappearances of transport ships over the past five years," Mykah explained. "They've been jumping into tesseract and never coming out."

"At first the manufacturer blamed pilot error: exiting into asteroid fields, jumping into suns. Then they accused workers of sabotage. Mellix interviewed a whistle-blower, a Shtrell engineer who was assassinated shortly after they spoke. Mellix worked through the documents the guy smuggled out—and they point to a flaw in the drive's design," Coni finished.

The four of them gazed at Raena as if they expected her to piece it together on her own.

She struggled to catch up. "How many ships are affected? If it's only ships built in the last five years . . ."

Vezali corrected her. "A lot of older ships have been upgraded. A *lot*. Maybe most."

"This news is going to seriously disrupt interstellar travel," Mykah said. "It will halt tourism, trade, shipments of food and medicine, relief efforts . . ."

"Everyone is going to be afraid to leave wherever they find themselves stranded right now," Coni said. "The whole galaxy is suddenly full of refugees, until they can find a ship with pre-tesseract technology on which to travel."

Raena sank onto the bench next to Vezali, who shifted her tentacles invitingly to make room. The galaxy will grind to a halt, she finally understood. "Is he sure?"

"Mellix is the most trusted journalist in the galaxy," Mykah said. No one contradicted his hyperbole. "He wouldn't have announced it unless he was absolutely certain."

"We were about to watch the evidence," Vezali said. "We thought you would want to see it, too."

"Yes," Raena said, touched to be thought of when they were all obviously so stunned. "Thank you. But first, before you start—*we* are okay, right? We're not suddenly going to get trapped in tesseract space?"

"We're fine," Haoun said. "We haven't been able to afford to upgrade our drive yet."

Vezali nodded her eyestalk. "The *Veracity* still has its original Earther drive. I've been hoping we could replace it, but updating the living spaces and media capabilities took precedence over the engine, for the time being."

"Thank the stars," Coni said.

Mykah jumped up to rummage around in the galley. Everyone watched him silently, puzzled by his behavior. He returned with a bottle of green on a tray with five glasses. "I get the feeling we'll want a drink to absorb this news."

"What about the gate system?" Raena asked suddenly. She didn't understand exactly how they worked, but the gates were Templar tech for the masses. When the Templars controlled galactic trade twenty years ago, the gates provided checkpoints where the Templar could track who was moving what around their galaxy. Although several different FTL drives existed, most people used to travel through the gates.

"The gates don't go everywhere you might want to," Haoun explained.

"And a lot of the new tesseract ships are too big to go through the gates," Vezali explained. "Until the technology improves to allow bigger gates, or the big ships can be re-engineered to have their drives replaced with older tech, they're grounded."

"How long is that going to take?" Raena asked. She envisioned ships lining up at shipyards, ready to be retrofitted.

"Old-tech engines of every size are going to have to be recreated practically piece by piece in factories that have switched over to something else. And how are you going to get the new engines delivered to the ships, or get the ships to the factories where the engines are being made? It will take a while to sort it all out," Haoun said.

The evidence Mellix laid out was meticulous and complex. Raena didn't understand a lot of it, but it boiled down to the fact that the tesseract drives were based around Templar technology. There was a lot of math—and experts to explain the math—for how the drives worked. The math also accounted for the times when the drives malfunctioned. Apparently, the Templar had workarounds. So far, the surviving galaxy had not discovered them.

"Fucking Templar tech," Haoun said, as he poured another round of green for everyone. "I'm amazed they got it to work once, let alone installed in all those ships."

"Getting it to work isn't the problem," Vezali countered. "Getting it to stop is a whole 'nother thing. Remember all those plague ships that arrived at their destinations after all the Templars onboard were dead?"

"You think all the tesseract ships that have been lost might show up someday?" Mykah asked.

"Who can say? They went somewhere, whether through space or in time or into another dimension. It's Templar tech. Their philosophy was really fascinating," Vezali chirped, full of enthusiasm—or catching a buzz from the green, Raena wasn't sure. "Have you read any of it?"

The conversation spun onward, but Raena leaned back against the wall, nursing her drink, content to watch her crewmates. She was amused to find she had grown rather fond of them, even Haoun with his hissing, growling voice.

Mykah moved to come sit beside her and top off her glass. "I haven't read much Templar philosophy, either," he confided.

Raena laughed. "I haven't read much of any philosophy. My education is pretty thoroughly lacking."

That left nowhere for the conversation to go, so Raena retreated into honesty. "I think this stuff is going to my head."

"It's pretty strong," Mykah agreed. "I never tried it until I waited tables on Kai. The restaurants held a party once a week, where all the waitstaff got to sample a different liquor."

"That sounds like fun," Raena said.

"Sometimes it was. Most of the time, though, it was hard work. Some of the liquors we served were pretty noxious for humans. We had to try enough of everything that we could report to our patrons what its effects would be. Warn them away from things, if necessary."

"I hadn't realized restaurant work could be so dangerous." Raena smiled at him to show she was teasing.

Mykah grew serious. "What do you think about this?" He waved his glass toward the screen. The liquor slopped close to the edge, but he caught it before it spilled.

"It's going to be bad," Raena predicted. "Without the big freighters to haul things around the galaxy, there will be shortages. Riots. Famines."

"You think?"

"I'm a pessimist." She had another sip of the green. It was bitter at first, with sweetness underneath. "Even if things don't get bad right away, there will be rationing and hoarding. People will be unhappy if they don't get all they want, or if they think their neighbors are getting more."

Mykah nodded and filled her glass again. He was sitting closer to Raena than she preferred to let people get, unless she was fighting them. Still, she didn't move back, for fear of insulting him.

"Hey!" Coni snatched the bottle away from him. "Don't drink it all, you two."

"Case in point," Raena observed.

Mykah held up one finger. "You think we ought to apply to haul food?"

The others fell silent to listen to her. Raena nodded. "It's not glamorous work, but it will be necessary in the short term. If the big ships can't do it, it's going to take a flotilla of smaller ones to get the job done. Hungry people aren't the most patient. Or peaceable."

She set her glass down. "This stuff is making me see double," she said. It was only a slight exaggeration. "I'm going to go lie down."

"Feel better," Vezali wished.

After she got back to her cabin, Raena wondered if she should have asked Mykah to make her some tea. She really didn't want to go to sleep and face her dreams, but the disorientation brought on by the green was worse at the moment.

She pulled the coverlet around her shoulders and sat up in the corner of the wall, head on her knees. That kept the bed from spinning.

It didn't keep her from dreaming.

Raena woke sluggishly. Her wrists were pinned to a chair by heavy cuffs. Cold fluid drained through a plastic tube into the back of her right hand. That, she suspected, was the mind-dampening chemical. When she tried to switch the hair out of her face, she felt the tug of something taped to her scalp. That chilled her more than anything else.

Thallian reached into her field of vision to train a lock of hair out of her eyes, tucking it gently back behind her ear. "You deserve better accommodations, my dear, but you rejected those you had."

Fear blackened Raena's vision. Then a searing, nuclear-bright flash exploded in her brain, sweeping thoughts and breath out of its path.

Raena felt her body spasm. Her muscles protested when she tried to control the convulsions. Tears of shame melted down her face.

"No mind drugs for you, my love," Thallian whispered as the torture burned itself out. "The Emperor does not want you stupid and senseless when he asks why you betrayed us."

She ignored his bitterness and swallowed hard, trying to control her voice. "What's in the tube?"

"Nourishment. Those shocks will drain you, but you're not to have food or sleep until we reach the Emperor's flagship."

"Whose order was that?"

"Mine, of course." He brushed the tears from her eyes with the thumbs of his velvet gloves. "I'm surprised you have to ask."

Silver blinded her. Again her thoughts were shattered in the attack. This time no tears escaped. Hatred stronger than she could have imagined allowed her to hold her head upright so she could stare at him throughout the shock.

He held her gaze with a smile that revealed his sharpened teeth.

"How this must amuse you," Raena said. Her only hope was that she could seduce him into releasing her from the chair, from the shocks.

"You have no idea how much I'm enjoying this," he answered. "I wish I could enjoy it more. For now, though, I'll leave you here to consider what you've done and how you might make amends. That is, if you have respite long enough to consider anything at all." The hatch slid open behind him and he slithered out.

Raena stared after him as if her gaze could melt the cell door. Around her, the room measured a scant two meters square. That bastard knew she hated small rooms. In fact, he knew more than enough to destroy her.

A brilliant flash demolished those thoughts but only stoked her hatred.

Some uncountable time later, Thallian returned to gloat. "How have you occupied yourself, my dear?"

Raena stared at his perfect black beard and envisioned the shockingly white throat beneath. "There are forty-eight electrodes threaded through my scalp."

"Very good." He trailed a gloved finger across her lips, daring her to bite him. When she did not, he pouted. "I do care for you, my dear. I designed this machine to give you no pain. The shock merely disrupts your brain waves. It does no physical damage. Your body harms itself as it fights the machine."

"So generous of you," she mocked. Knowing that the pain was self-inflicted made the next wave easier to bear. It rolled off of her, leaving only a residual ache in her muscles.

"In theory, you will never be allowed long enough to attempt escape, but I am curious to see if the voltage will indeed prevent you." Thallian bent closer to her. "Do you regret abandoning your post?"

"Not for an instant, my lord."

Thallian grabbed her jaw. His kiss tasted like carrion, like everything venomous and rotten. She felt his hand slide down to caress her windpipe.

Another shock blotted out whatever happened next. When she was able to focus again, Thallian leaned against the door, his smile so self-satisfied she yearned to slap it from his face. "If the Emperor takes you away, he will return you to me in due time. I'll have you yet, Raena, and then you won't have this chair to protect you."

Time passed, but Raena had no way to measure it, no meals or sleep to break the monotony. Left alone, her mind played tricks. Sometimes the walls crept inward, though she watched to keep them away.

For entertainment, she imagined the things she might do to Thallian, given a chance. Perhaps she would castrate him a millimeter at a time with a welding torch. Or she would mutilate his face with her knives. She hated herself while she hated him, because she had believed she loved him once.

Sometimes a med tech would come to check the needle in her hand. It occurred to her to beg them to help her overdose and escape him, but she decided against it and held her tongue. With her thoughts scrambled, Thallian could out-guess her every move. When he finally suggested the techs as an escape route, Raena only laughed at him. Her acceptance of her fate confused, then enraged, Thallian. Luckily, he grew bored with her after a while.

"Keep still," someone whispered. "The cameras will only be off a few moments more and I don't want my face flashed on Imperial channels. Bad for business."

Raena looked up through the blur obscuring her vision. A med tech was pulling the electrodes from her scalp, but none too gently. She could feel the wires tearing free of her skin. Tiny prickles of blood oozed through her hair.

". . . you doing?" she mumbled.

"Getting you out of here," a man said from somewhere behind her. It was the first voice she had heard that wasn't Thallian's in what seemed like forever. Raena couldn't remember its owner's name.

". . . 's a trap," she said in the same mumble, but already her brain was clearing. She noticed that he'd already pulled the tube of nourishment from the vein in the back of her right hand. The liquid trickled out to puddle on the floor.

She counted quickly. He didn't have that many more leads to remove. Soon she'd be free of the chair. She realized her arms were already free and flexed her fingers.

Should she kill him before trying to escape the cell? This had to be a game of Thallian's. Was there any way she could win it?

"We haven't got long," the man said, as if echoing her thoughts. "It's the middle of the night. The guard is light. Can you shoot?"

"Yes," Raena said decisively.

He set a med tech's kit in her lap, pressed the release so it bloomed open for her. Inside she saw a disassembled Stinger sporting pistol. Raena got busy putting the pieces back together.

The man finished with the electrodes. He reached past her into the bag—their hands met briefly—to pull out a roll of gauze. He wrapped it sloppily around her head.

"Leave off," Raena said. She yanked the gauze off angrily, dropping it onto the floor.

"You're bleeding."

"It'll stop."

He came around to face her finally. Raena squinted up at him: med tech uniform, new haircut, familiar muddy green eyes.

He spoke before she could admit that she really didn't know who he was. "I couldn't let him have you, Raena. I couldn't let you be taken from me like that, without a fight."

Gavin? She didn't dare say his name aloud, on the slim chance that they would actually get out of this alive. No need to help Thallian identify her rescuer. Let him wonder.

"Are you insane?" she asked instead as he hauled her to her feet.

"Quite possibly. Ready?"

She slapped the power pack to make sure the connection was tight and thumbed the pistol live. And grinned.

He slid the jammer into the lock. Raena dove past him and found herself in Thallian's office. That figured. She took out the guards with quick head shots, then waited for Gavin to come around her to unlock the door to the corridor.

As he punched coordinates into the lift control, Raena panted, "How did you get in to get me?"

"A med tech ID is surprisingly easy to get."

The lift doors opened and Raena dropped the three men inside before they could react.

"You flew in with all the other med techs?"

"No, I needed my own ship to fly us out. So I hired a friend as pilot and told Flight Control I missed the last tech shuttle. We had the right codes, so they let us land. I've been lying low onboard, trying to find out where you were being held, for the last couple of days."

Raena drew the medallion over her head and put it into Gavin's hand. He looked it over. She knew the tarnished silver disk didn't look like much, but he put it into his breast pocket anyway.

The lift halted. Raena shot the man waiting outside and slammed her fist on the doors closed button. "Why are you risking your life for me?" she asked.

"Those bastards tried to kill me with the Messiah. You should've seen me when I woke up with it stuck in my hair. I was terrified to look in the mirror."

She examined him. He did seem older than she remembered, now that she got a clear-eyed look at him. "What happened?"

"I landed backwards in it. It looks powdery, but once you touch it, it's gummy. I was practically sealed to the floor. I had to cut myself free, blind." He mimed reaching over his head to hack at his hair. "Once I finally got off the floor, it took forever for me to comb it out. I never held my breath for so long in my life." He grinned at her. "Anyway, I owed you."

"Thank you."

The elevator slowed as it reached the docking levels. Gavin checked the charge on his guns. "Let me shoot some this time."

"No promises," Raena said.

When the doors opened, an entire squadron had taken position outside, guns aimed and ready. Raena spun toward Gavin and gave him the only mercy she could. She knew what Thallian would do to him otherwise.

One shot took her down, too. Too bad the Imperial soldiers were only shooting to stun.

Raena straightened up and whacked her head against the wall. That helped her headache not at all. *All right*, she told herself. *Up. No more drinking. Find some tea.*

But her body didn't want to obey. It remembered the aches she felt after the machine had tortured her. It remembered how much she had feared Thallian.

"He's dead," she whispered to herself. She forced herself to remember the strike of the match, the small magnesium flare of it in her fingers. She remembered flicking the match away, watching it spin end over end. She remembered the sound when the flame encountered the accelerant's fumes. She remembered the smell of his body burning.

He was gone. She was safe. He was gone.

Raena rested her face against her knees and let the sobbing take her.

Later, after she heard the others up and moving around, she forced herself to get up and dress. She trailed her fingers over the mirrored catsuit that she'd bought on Kai the day she'd met Mykah and Coni. She loved the way it reflected the viewer back on himself, but today she didn't feel like being so eye-catching.

She paged through the other outfits in her closet. None of the bright colors suited her mood. She passed beyond them to the things she'd salvaged when Mykah and Coni moved into Jain Thallian's cabin.

The boy had been somewhat taller than Raena, but her heels made up the difference. He'd been slim, like his father, so that his shirts hung slightly loose on her. She stepped into a pair of black cargo pants and pulled a dark blue sweater over her head.

She wondered if she had drugged the boy, kept him imprisoned on the *Veracity* when she went to kill his father, if she could have ever tamed Jain. He had been his father's favorite clone and had insisted he go home, but she'd known from the start that that was never going to end well. She marveled at herself for missing him now.

Why, she wondered, couldn't she dream about Jain? She would have enjoyed talking to him again.

Mykah called the crew together for a late breakfast. It was simple today—some form of pressed protein sandwiched between two crisp yellow leaves. Of course, there was some unfamiliar red sauce on the side in which to dip it. Raena watched the others to see what they did before she approached her own food. Her stomach felt mutinous.

Mykah slipped a bottle onto the table in front of her as he sat down. "It's cider," he said. "It'll help with the hangover."

"Thank you," she said quietly and twisted its cap off so she could sip at it.

Mykah settled in across from her. "We've been offered some work," he said. "I'd like to take it. Mellix needs to get out of Capital City quickly. He is looking for reliable transportation."

Haoun scoffed, "His network can't organize it for him?"

Mykah and Coni exchanged glances. "Actually," Mykah started, then looked down at his sandwich, before meeting Haoun's gaze. "There have been death threats. A lot of people are unhappy about the ban on interstellar travel. They're blaming Mellix as the cause of the ban. No regular ship will take him on as a passenger, in order to protect the other passengers and crew."

"Even little ships?" Vezali asked.

"He's not sure who he can trust," Mykah answered.

"Why would he trust us?" Raena wondered. "Why should we risk it?"

"Mellix is . . ."

"He's Mykah's idol," Coni supplied. "From the university. I understand why he would risk his life for Mellix."

Mykah cut her off before she could say more. "This ship is a democracy," he reminded them. "This might be dangerous, but you've watched Mellix's work. You know how fearless he is. You know how much good he has done in the galaxy. If we can rescue him, I think . . . I feel like it's my duty to help him."

Raena got the feeling he wasn't talking to her. She tried to puzzle out why. Since the ship was a democracy, he probably didn't feel he needed her vote. It was the first time she'd seen him actually take command.

"I'm in," Haoun said. "You can't fly without me, anyway. But I grew up watching Mellix and I'd be honored just to meet him."

Vezali nodded. "Same goes for me. I'm in."

"Will you need me?" Raena asked. "It sounds like a pretty straight-forward transport job."

The *Veracity* was her home, the only home she had. She could gather her few possessions and disembark at Capital City, but she couldn't calculate the odds of work ever bringing the *Veracity* back her way. Was this where they parted company?

Mykah and Coni exchanged glances again. Then Mykah said, "Mellix is in hiding now. Getting him from the safe house to the *Veracity* is going to be tricky."

"Define tricky," Raena suggested.

"We can't dock at Capital City. All the docking slips are occupied indefinitely by ships that were grounded by the travel ban. The ships already there won the right to remain docked as long as their docking fees can be paid."

"So how is the station getting supplies in and out?"

"They're building an elevator. We will dock there, but the . . ."

"But the entrance would be the perfect place to ambush Mellix," Raena said. "Do you have another plan?"

Coni spoke up for him. "Mykah's hoping you can come up with one."

Raena sipped from her bottle of cider, closed her eyes to savor. They did have a place for her talents. Without her to slip the journalist past his would-be assassins, there was no transport job. She couldn't believe how relieved she felt to be needed.

"Of course I'm in," Raena said. "Sounds like fun."

Coni followed Raena from the galley toward her gym. "Can I tell you about my progress on your new identity?" she asked.

"Of course. Thank you."

Coni cocked her head, gazing at Raena full in the face. Humans often didn't like to make eye contact, fearing it might provoke the other party, as if there was safety in being seen but not to look. Raena, on the other hand, met Coni's gaze evenly. Her expression remained completely neutral, closed off somehow but not hostile.

"I've written the scars on your back and the place where Thallian shot you in the shoulder into your record," Coni reported. "They're now souvenirs of your work as a body guard. There are even hospital reports, if anyone digs down that far."

"Thank you," Raena said, impressed. Her expression warmed with the enthusiasm in her voice.

Seeing the little woman's happiness made the next part of the conversation even more difficult, Coni realized. For a moment, she wanted to leave things well enough alone, but she felt deeply that she needed to point the obvious out to Raena. "I started to do the same backgrounding for the scar on your face. I went back to your service records to see how you received it . . ."

"It predates my Imperial service," Raena said drily.

"That's the issue," Coni agreed. "It's very visible in your wanted poster. We can obfuscate everything else, but that scar is like a finger-print. For you to have a scar that exactly matches a twenty-year-old wanted poster . . ."

"I see." Raena nodded. "Thank you. It's going to have to come off."

Raena's face had gone blank again. Coni wondered how deeply she was upset. If she were talking to Mykah, she would ask, but Coni was still hesitant to provoke Raena.

"There are plenty of spas on Capital City. I can find you somewhere discreet that will resurface your skin without questions, as long as you pay up front."

Raena surprised her by asking, "Will you come with me? My last medical procedure was done by Thallian's family robot. Before that, it was onboard the *Arbiter*. I . . . I would feel more comfortable if someone came with me to make sure the med techs don't suddenly ID me in the middle of the procedure and arrest me for war crimes . . ."

Her voice trailed off and she met Coni's gaze again. "Please come along to watch my back."

Coni was touched. The request seemed to cross the line from being shipmates to something more intimate. It wasn't a line that Coni had been aware that she wanted to cross, until now.

"Of course," she said. "I'd be glad to."

Later, thinking about that conversation, Coni wondered about Raena's attachment to her own appearance. Coni lived closely with a human man who re-sculptured his facial hair every other day, who thought nothing of changing the color or loft of the hair atop his head. Mykah's appearance was fluid and fun for him to play around with.

Raena's appearance remained consistent throughout her Imperial records. That might have been mostly to cater to Thallian's preferences, but even after she gave up her Imperial uniform, she continued to dress in black. On the run, she often wore a cloak to cover her weaponry, but she'd worn a cape while working as a "diplomat" on the *Arbiter*. It wasn't much of a change.

Even while she was trying to hide from Thallian's bounty hunters, Raena never altered her face or attempted to disguise her height or weight. She even kept her hair long, loose, and always black.

Coni thought over the outlines of Raena's life, as she knew it: a refugee traveling with her deranged mother, bought as a slave for an arms manufacturer's daughter, enlisted by Thallian as his aide and trained to kill. Then she had the year or so on the run before she was captured, tried, and sentenced to the Templar tomb.

In all that time, Raena had nothing to call her own. Nothing except the clothes she wore and whatever she could strap on her back. Nothing, really, except the body that served as the only possession she couldn't mislay, the only commodity she could trade to keep herself alive.

No wonder she didn't want to change it. It was all she had ever had.

Coni clenched her eyes shut and ordered herself not to weep. Raena had never asked for pity, only for help.

Haoun stretched out on the heated platform that took up most of his cabin. Warmth crept into his limbs, making him sleepy, but he put the call through anyway.

Jexx answered him immediately. "Daddy!"

His daughter had gotten longer in the face and her scales were losing their rounded childish edges. Haoun ached that he couldn't be home to watch her grow.

"Hi, Baby," he said with false cheer. "What are you still doing awake?"

"Homework," she pouted. "I have to write a poem to perform tomorrow."

"When did you get the assignment?"

She hung her head.

Haoun laughed at her. "I won't keep you long, then. I just wanted to tell you . . ." His voice trailed off. He'd wanted to tell her not to worry, but clearly she wasn't worried. Was it possible she didn't know about the recall of the tesseract engines? *She was very mature for her age*, he thought proudly, *but she was still a child*.

"I'm going to Capital City," he finished.

She tilted her head and looked at him skeptically. "You called to tell me that?"

"I called to ask if you wanted a souvenir. I've never been before."

"Who are you talking to, Jexx? You're supposed to be finishing your homework." Serese appeared in the doorway behind the desk. She'd gotten heavier since Haoun left. The muscles bunched around her jaw looked strong enough to bite through metal. She was so beautiful.

"Hello," Haoun said. He hoped the pang he felt wasn't audible in his voice. "I was about to let her go back to work."

"Hello, Haoun," Serese said coldly. It was uncommon for Na'ash males to hang around their families after the eggs hatched. Serese felt that Haoun's interest in his spawn was creepy.

"I wanted to let the kids know I'm okay," he said quickly. "The *Veracity* has an old Earther drive. It's not affected by the recall."

"Good, Haoun. I'll tell the boys in the morning. For now . . ."

"Get to work, Jexxie," he said dutifully. "I expect you to be brilliant."

"Love you, Daddy!" she chirped, as Serese leaned over to disconnect them.

"Love you too, Baby," he told the empty screen.

CHAPTER 6

As Raena left her gym for the day, Coni called to her from the cockpit. "Come up front. I think I have this about finished."

"That's great news, Coni." Raena draped her towel over her shoulders and came to perch in Haoun's oversized pilot's chair. "But first: can I ask you some questions? You probably know the official story of my life better than I do."

Coni nodded. "As far as the old Imperial records were concerned, Raena Zacari was captured, court-martialed, and executed."

"Imperial procedure was to incinerate the prisoner and send her remains back home at cost to the family. Did that happen?"

Coni poked around online. Raena sat back in Haoun's chair, arms folded across her chest, content to wait. She thought of herself as fairly adept at human-centric computer systems, but Coni understood the wider galactic systems—Raena still thought of them as alien, which she knew simply betrayed her myopia. Coni could read languages Raena couldn't even identify and find virtual niches and backwaters that Raena could not. She could be a powerful ally, but Raena couldn't figure out where Coni's true allegiance rested, other than with Mykah.

It surprised Raena to discover how much of her interaction with humans had been reliant on her ability to read their emotions. Coni, with her dry way of speaking and her inexpressive muzzle, was impossible for Raena to interpret. It left her feeling continually off balance.

"I don't see anything right away," Coni said, "but I'll keep looking." Without glancing up from her screen, Coni added, "Did you have a home for them to send things to?"

"Not that the Empire would recognize as such, probably. I doubt Thallian reported to them that, before he inducted me into Imperial service, I had been a runaway slave. The Shaads would still have legally been my owners, but they couldn't have been defined as my next of kin. It doesn't matter, I guess. I doubt the Shaads would have wanted to claim my remains, if it cost another credit."

"Your life is just one unending tale of woe, isn't it?" Coni asked. If it had been Mykah saying that, Raena would have known he meant to tease her. If it had been Vezali, her new translator was sensitive enough to register shades of sympathy. In this instance, Coni spoke Imperial Standard. She'd learned it at university, while studying human sociology. She said the words clearly, in a deadpan way that Raena could only take as mocking.

Raena smiled, choosing to let the offense slide. "All the woe is over and done," she said. "With your help, I'm going to be my own free woman soon."

"Then what?"

"Hopefully, Mykah will find us some work that suits our various talents, for which we will be as well paid as when we claimed the Thallian bounty. Then we can continue to wallow in the luxury to which we're becoming accustomed."

Coni chuckled, which did interesting things to her muzzle. The amusement didn't change the expression in her purple eyes, though.

Raena thought the blue-furred girl might say something about the drunken flirting with Mykah last night, but she didn't. Raena didn't bring it up either.

Instead she said, "Thanks for your help, Coni. I couldn't do this without you."

"That's true."

"What I don't really understand is why you're going to so much trouble for me."

"I like a puzzle," she said simply. "I've never made a person before. It's both easier and not as easy as I expected."

"So you're helping me because it's fun?"

Coni snorted. "We're all helping you because it's fun."

Then I'm safe as long as I continue to provide entertainment, Raena understood. No pressure there.

"What did you do before?" Coni asked.

"Before what?"

"When you were running from Thallian."

"I got out of the Empire into the fringes of human contact as quickly as I could. I tried to stick to worlds where a lone human wouldn't attract attention. I wore Viridian gloves all the time, always paid cash, and kept my hood up. It didn't really help. The bounty was high enough to intrigue all kinds of people. So I want to try going legitimate for a change."

"Who's looking for you now?"

"No one. That's why we're not troubling to change my name."

But Raena wondered about Gavin: Would he just assume she was hiding and not bother to search for her real name?

What did it matter, really? If he sent her a message, she could ignore it. If he sent her a package, he'd have to track down the *Veracity* first and the crew was smart enough not to open anything that came their way unexpectedly. Even if Gavin showed up in person, it wasn't as if she couldn't kick his ass from one side of the galaxy to the other. He might think of himself as a big, bad man, but having served under a truly bad man, Raena certainly wasn't afraid of *Gavin*. Ultimately, he had too much self-doubt to be very dangerous. He didn't feel like the universe owed him anything, because secretly he felt he wasn't worthy of anything. Sooner or later, he would decide he wasn't worthy of Raena—or at least that she wasn't worthy of him. Probably all he wanted was closure.

"Someone you want to tell me about?" Coni asked, fangs revealed in what might have been a smirk.

"Old boyfriend," Raena said. "He might try to look me up, but he's not going to be any trouble."

"Your previous boyfriend was a lunatic," Coni pointed out.

"This guy might be, too, but he's a whole lot less savage."

"I'm sensing a theme here."

"Not so much a theme as a common denominator," Raena said.

She wondered if Coni had been trying to be friendly, offering a girlfriend's banter. Raena shook her head. She could use a girlfriend. Any sort of friend, really. Once again she reflected that she'd never really made a friend on her own, without Ariel to serve as a bridge or a buffer. Now, beyond trying to figure out human behavior, Raena had to unravel the blue-furred girl's meanings, too.

Why was it so much easier being friends with Vezali, who was even less humanoid that bipedal Coni? They didn't even speak the same language, but hanging out with the tentacled girl was very comfortable.

Raena supposed it was because they didn't have Mykah standing between them.

Luckily, Coni didn't follow that train of thought. "Let me read through all my notes one last time and I'll send the final CV back to your cabin."

"That will be perfect. It will be great to get this all locked in before we show up at Capital City."

"I was thinking that, too."

Raena wasn't sure if the next meal was a late lunch or an early dinner. Her schedule had gotten all turned around. This time, Mykah had whipped up another simple meal, some kind of scrambled vegetable protein with cubed meat. Its smell did more to set her stomach right than anything had all day.

"Raena was correct," Mykah said as they settled around the table. "There are freighters full of food stranded all across the galaxy. The Council of Worlds is calling for smaller craft to help off-load them and deliver the goods where they are needed."

"What does that mean for us?" Haoun asked.

"I'm negotiating with an Eske ship now, which was stopped at Inkeri for refueling when the travel ban went into effect. They're loaded with perishable vegetables bound for Capital City. So we can deliver those when we stop to get Mellix."

"What are we going to ship out?" Raena asked.

"What do you mean?"

"If we show up loaded at Capital City, but don't leave loaded with something, that's going to look suspicious," she explained. "There are likely to be passengers on the station who would gladly jump on the next ship out, wherever it is headed. You're going to have to come up with a plausible reason why we don't have room for them."

There was a silence, during which Raena wondered if she'd insulted them by stating the obvious. Finally, Mykah said, "Thank you."

Haoun asked her, "Why didn't we make you captain?"

"Because I'm a much better evil mastermind than I would be a captain," Raena answered.

"If you ever change your mind . . ." Mykah offered.

Raena laughed. "Don't think you're getting out of it that easily. You're doing a great job."

"Well, don't stop advising me," he said. "And I'm sorry to say I think we should probably clear out the hold so we have room for our load of veggies."

Damn, she had not considered that. "Of course you're right," Raena said. She couldn't be selfish enough to complain about it.

"I'll take a look at it after lunch," Vezali said.

Vezali surveyed the gym. It wouldn't take long to disassemble all the pieces and return the space to its previous incarnation as a hold. She could take some of the scrap she'd salvaged from dismantling the barracks and repurpose it to store Raena's mats—which were merely unused mattresses anyway. The various bars and poles and ropes were easily disconnected. Maybe an afternoon's worth of work in all. It wouldn't even need much in the way of tools.

Raena tapped at the hatch, then entered when Vezali nodded. "Can I help?"

The little woman looked . . . different somehow, Vezali thought. She hadn't had much experience with humans, never counted one as a friend before she'd met Mykah. Human faces fascinated her—so many pieces moved, their joys and discomforts laid bare for anyone to read. Raena's face was a long silvery brown oval dominated by her black-irised eyes. Today there were new shadows on Raena's face, in the hollows beneath her eyes. The smudges emphasized the gray in her complexion.

"I'd be glad for some help," Vezali said cheerfully. "Could you bring some of the extra wall panels down to build a locker for your mats?"

"Sure. How many do you want?"

"Let's start with four."

Raena went off to retrieve them. Vezali glided over to the doorway to watch her go.

There was definitely something different about the little woman today. She was dressed in black work pants and a shapeless dark blue shirt, completely different from the rainbow of eye-catching colors she normally wore. Much less form-fitted, too. Vezali wondered if it signified anything that Raena was covering her body more, since no one on the *Veracity* usually bothered with any more than a minimum of clothing.

Or maybe it meant something that Raena had raided the hoard of clothing left behind by Jain Thallian. The teenaged boy had been a bit bigger than Raena, but his clothing looked like a comfortable fit. Was Raena missing the child? Trying to emulate him?

Mykah would be glad to help Vezali interpret the mysteries of human behavior, if she decided she was curious enough to ask.

On her home world of Dagat, it was the height of insult to ask someone if they were feeling all right. The implication was that you found something in the other person's appearance that troubled you. Vezali had lived out in the galaxy long enough to understand that some people were offended if you didn't ask how they were. She wondered where Raena fell on that spectrum.

Kavanaugh so rarely had nightmares that he was completely unprepared to find himself dreaming of the night he met Raena Zacari for the first time.

Kavanaugh crept through the darkened ship with an electric torch in his hand, not sure exactly what he was supposed to be looking for. The ship hung dead in space, a drifter, but emergency life support still functioned enough that he could see his breath in the frigid air. Ice crystals formed and spun in front of him, sparkling.

Flicking from wall to ceiling to wall to floor, his torch beam caught on a pair of scuffed boots—toes pointed down to the floor—protruding from a doorway.

Kavanaugh juggled the light to his left hand and drew his pistol. Probably should've had it out all along, but he'd wanted to have one hand free to open doors. He nudged the boots with his toe. No reaction.

"Skyler, I found something," Kavanaugh said over his headset. His adolescent voice cracked and he cursed it. He'd just turned fifteen.

"Something good?" Skyler asked.

"Don't think so." Kavanaugh traced the body with his light, but he didn't need to turn the corpse over to be certain the creature was dead. It lay face down in a pool of ice-sludged blood. The back half of its head was open to the frigid air. Kavanaugh thought, I've never actually seen a brain before.

He jerked the light away, wishing he could wipe the horrific image from behind his eyes.

The beam of light flickered across the only other person in the room. A human girl hung in an impossibly tight crash web. She was smaller than Kavanaugh and painfully thin. Shadows smudged beneath her eyes and cheekbones. Her skin was an unnatural shade of gray. Ice crystals spangled the black hair that fell past her shoulders. As he watched, a faint breath swirled before her face.

"I've got a survivor," Kavanaugh said to Skyler. "She needs Doc."

"On my way," Doc answered over the comm. He'd forgotten she would be monitoring the search.

The girl's eyes fluttered open. She focused on Kavanaugh with effort. Her eyes were . . . black. Black like space. Black like they swallowed light without a reflection or a backward gleam to make her seem alive. He would have thought she was dead, except she was moving. Kavanaugh took a step back from her.

"Kill me," she begged, her voice harsh with dehydration and cold.

And then she was out again, leaving Kavanaugh alone between the dead creature and the girl, wondering what the hell had happened.

Kavanaugh opened his eyes, looking around the familiar limits of his cabin on the *Sundog*. Everything was still in its place. He took a deep breath and wondered why he was dreaming about Raena again. Did it mean anything? Should he try to get in touch with her? He wasn't sure he wanted to. His last interaction with Raena had ended with her punching him in the head.

He thought back over the dream. When Kavanaugh was a kid, Raena had traveled with them on the *Panacea* only briefly, long enough for Doc to patch her up. During that time, Kavanaugh had followed the girl around the little medical ship, captivated by her. She wouldn't tell him much about her life, but he picked up enough to know it had treated her rough. He was impressed by her courage. He'd seen his own family die in an Imperial raid and been lucky enough to stow away with Doc. Raena had had no one to rescue her.

Kavanaugh had so wanted to be the person who could make everything right for her—but Raena said she knew how her story ended and refused to let Kavanaugh involve himself.

As she was leaving, Raena asked the *Panacea*'s crew to pass a message to Ariel Shaad. That opened up the rest of Kavanaugh's life—and led to his introduction to Sloane.

His thoughts backtracked from that. The short while she'd been on the *Panacea*, he had become infatuated with Raena. He wouldn't have called it love, but she was a girl and he'd known damned few of them at that age. She was pretty, looked delicate, was scary strong and fast, and seemed absolutely fearless, except when it came to her sinister ex-boss. Of him, she seemed rightfully terrified. Fifteen-year-old Kavanaugh would have given anything in the universe to be able to protect her from Thallian.

She insisted the *Panacea* drop her off on the first rock they passed with atmosphere. That rock happened to be Barraniche. Kavanaugh remembered standing beside Raena inside the *Panacea*'s hatch, looking out at the monsoon-lashed darkness. Doc, Kavanaugh, even Skyler, all tried their best to convince Raena to come with them, to let them find her a safe world or a job with the Coalition or some kind of hiding place beyond Thallian's reach. She'd remained adamant that her fate was sealed. Thallian would find her, no matter where she went. He would kill anyone who stood in his way, then capture her and torture her. If she was lucky, he might kill her by accident. She doubted she would be that lucky.

She kissed Kavanaugh quickly, barely brushing her lips against his, and then melted into the night. Chest hurting from the chance he'd just lost, Kavanaugh stared after her. She was gone, as if the dark had swallowed her up.

He hadn't seen her again for more than twenty years, until she came out of that tomb.

After they got the gym pulled apart and put away, Raena retreated to her cabin. She found Coni had sent over the curriculum vitae as promised. Raena was amazed at the intricacy of it. Coni had created a birth record, an institutional childhood, a series of standard educational tests, and a stint as a bodyguard to a Melisizei "businessman" whose employment ended in a crash in the asteroid field off Quagan. Raena, the sole survivor, had been burned in the crash.

It looked great, but as Raena began to commit it to memory, she realized it was missing one thing: It needed somehow to connect her to Ariel and Gavin on Kai.

That was a thing she would need to discuss with Ariel. It amused Raena to think that Aunt Ariel's orphan-rescuing foundation could have helped her settle into the galaxy.

Probably, to be absolutely safe, she should contact Gavin and get him onboard with the story, too. But that would start a whole slow-burn explosion that Raena wasn't prepared to manipulate just yet. She'd call him later, when she was sleeping better and she was certain she wouldn't lose her temper in the midst of negotiations with him.

Raena waited at the Panacea's *hatch, ready to be on her way. It wasn't like she had anything to pack. She didn't own anything but the clothes she wore and her mother's medallion.*

The Panacea's *crew came out of the cockpit. Doc handed back Raena's cloak. Her fingers trailed enviously across the rich black fabric. Raena had no desire to tell her that Thallian had given her the cloak, hoping it would make her small stature look more imposing.*

"Skyler brought me this from the bounty hunter's ship, but I knew it had to be yours. Better put it on," Doc instructed. "It's raining buckets out there. Maybe I should get you an extra jacket, or . . ."

"Thanks, but I don't think you have anything that would fit me." Raena turned to the big wolf-faced creature that was Doc's companion Skyler. "When Zwack picked me up, I was wearing a torso shield I'd stolen from another bounty hunter. You didn't happen to bring that along too, did you?"

"I saw it on his ship, but left it. Too small for any of us."

Raena nodded. It had been too much to hope for. She'd probably never see one in her size again.

"Thought you might have a use for this, though." Skyler handed her one of the bounty hunter's smaller pistols. It wasn't a Stinger, the brand that Ariel's father manufactured, but it was a good knock-off.

"Thanks," she said with the flash of a smile. "That will come in handy, I'm sure."

"Cut the belt way down for you." He passed her the holster.

"Perfect. Thank you." She meant it. After a moment's pause, she said, "I guess I've kept you long enough."

Skyler opened the hatch for her.

"Be careful," Doc ordered.

Before anyone could say anything else, Raena slipped through the hatch onto the ramp, into the sideways-lashing rain.

Kavanaugh followed her outside. The storm wind twisted his hair into cowlicks. "I guess there's no way I'll ever know how this comes out."

"I told you how it ends." At the foot of the ramp, Raena pulled her cloak's hood up over her head.

"Wait." Kavanaugh caught her shoulder. "Wait, Raena, please. The future can change, can't it? Maybe it will be different, if you're not alone. Let me go with you. I could watch your back. We could head for

someplace really far away, far enough out that nobody's in charge, where nobody'd find us."

"Stop. *It doesn't happen that way. It can't.*" He will kill you, *Raena* wanted to say. He will torture you. Or make me do it. I can't watch that happen to anyone else.

She ended the conversation the only way she knew how, with a kiss. While Kavanaugh was too stunned to respond, she melted into the night.

Raena walked through the rain toward the trees she could barely see on the other side of the landing field. The saturated ground was invisible below a shaggy carpet of weeds, but as she crossed it, it felt sodden and slick beneath her boots. Terrible footing for a fight.

She wasn't exactly sure where she was or where Doc's ship was headed after this, but it didn't matter. Raena had been on the brink of death on the bounty hunter's ship, before Kavanaugh and the others had discovered her. She had hoped they could be frightened into killing her, into ending this endless flight from Thallian. But just as she was too much of a coward to kill herself, she had developed too much affection for the Panacea's *crew to really goad them into final action.*

So here she was, with the rain driving into her face, soaking through her cape. It was so cold that she couldn't stop shivering. She almost turned back to the medical shuttle behind her. She could take it all back, ask them to drop her in a city someplace or, for that matter, anywhere warm and dry. She didn't have the stomach to run right now, even to search for somewhere to sleep out of the weather. She felt so completely overwhelmed that she thought she might cry.

Then something moved amongst the trees, a shadow blacker than the night. Raena froze, but of course she must have been seen. The ship's lights were behind her as she stood in the scrubland, no cover at all unless she flung herself flat on the spongy ground.

"Raena?" *a male voice called.* "Don't be afraid. I'm not here to hurt you."

"How do you know my name?" She suddenly felt so cold that even her shivering stopped. A quick reality check reminded her that her hands were beneath her cloak.

"I'm an old friend," he said. His voice sounded strangely amused, as if he'd had this conversation before.

"I don't have any old friends," she said bitterly, inching her right hand down toward the new holster Skyler had given her.

"I'm an old friend of Ariel's, too." He stepped clear of the trees, coming toward her at a slow, non-threatening walk.

Keep coming, Raena thought. Make this easy. I don't want to do anything hard tonight.

"How is Ariel?" Raena asked, keeping the conversation alive. "Is she safe?"

"She found her way back to the Coalition, if you consider that safe."

Raena eased the new pistol free of its holster, angled the barrel toward the man. She couldn't see him clearly at this distance and through the weather, but she was certain he was human. That made the Coalition a possibility, but the Empire much more likely.

She fired off six quick shots. One of them spun him around, took him off his feet. She ran toward him, rather than back to the med ship. Who had Doc told she was landing here? Either the Panacea had betrayed Raena or she'd just shot one of their Coalition friends. Either way, the Panacea's crew didn't want Raena showing back up on their doorstep.

The man was wheezing when she reached him. His hands were empty as he sprawled in the mud, but a pair of expensive guns hung from his belt.

"I'm here to help you," he muttered as she rolled him over. He was an older man, old enough to be her father, with thinning hair and a beard that eclipsed the lower half of his face. Nothing about him looked the least bit familiar.

Raena shot him in the heart. Then she stole his guns and the belt that they hung from and ran into the woods.

Behind her, the med ship powered up for takeoff. Raena felt adrenaline course through her. She ran among the trees, looking for a deadfall or a cave or even a low-hanging branch. She had to find a defensible hiding place, in case they came after her.

They didn't.

Raena was left alone in the storm. The weight of her guns comforted her enough to raise a smile.

Raena blinked, refocusing her eyes on the screen in front of her. The curriculum vitae that Coni had prepared for her was still open.

What had just happened? Raena shook herself, stretched, trying to get the blood flowing into her stiff muscles. Had she really just hallucinated that she shot Gavin dead in the rain on Barraniche?

That hadn't happened twenty-odd years ago. She hadn't known Gavin then, hadn't met him until the night on Nizarrh. That had been, what? Months, maybe as much as a year after she'd said goodbye to Kavanaugh and Doc and the *Panacea*.

What the hell was going on?

Now that they had her life story pieced together, Raena needed to ask Coni to expedite the documents she'd need to leave the ship. If something was going wrong in her head, she needed to get herself to a real hospital and have a real doctor check her out. And when she got there, she was going to have to be able to answer questions about who she was and where she'd come from—or they were going to lock her up until they could find out.

Raena swore bitterly that no one, anywhere, ever, was going to lock her up again.

Even as she made the promise, she had doubts she'd be able to carry it through. She had trained all her life to be a dangerous weapon. If she was going crazy, maybe locked up was the safest place for everyone else to have her.

She rubbed her temples, eyes closed, alert for another hallucination to overtake her. When nothing swallowed her up immediately, she allowed herself to poke—gently—at the content of the last vision.

She remembered the elation of firing the pistol through her cloak, even if that hadn't actually happened. The cloak had gotten ruined, yeah, and she'd had to dispose of it, but not because *she* shot it full of holes.

All the same, as Raena thought about the dream, she remembered the kick of the little pistol in her hand, just exactly what one would expect from a gun that size. She flexed her fingers, remembering the texture of the grip against her palm, the resistance of the trigger under her forefinger.

Did she remember that because she'd shot so many guns growing up with Ariel? Because she'd handled so many weapons as she trained with Thallian? Or because somewhere, somehow, she really had held that same little knock-off gun and really shot that man?

And who was he? He looked like Gavin, all right, but not the Gavin she would have encountered at that point in time. She'd been, what, eighteen or nineteen? That made Gavin twenty-five maybe. Thirty, at the outside.

The man she'd shot was much older than that. Crow's feet carved in deep around his eyes. There hadn't been enough light for her to judge the color of his beard, but it made her think of the beard Gavin was wearing when Kavanaugh pulled her out of the tomb on the Templar world. That had been sandy-colored and graying, an uncared-for mess he'd grown because he was too addicted to the Dart to pay any attention to his appearance. Raena had shaved it off of him at the first opportunity.

Gavin shared similarities with the man she'd shot, but it couldn't be the same person. It wouldn't make sense for Gavin to be older in her dreams.

Maybe, she told herself, I'm taking all this too literally. Maybe it's nothing more than a dream. I've been sleeping poorly for days.

Maybe this is what I get when I decide not to sleep. Now my dreams are spilling over into my waking life, nothing more.

Still, she had pretty much exhausted the range of things she could do to sleep without nightmares. Wearing herself out, drinking herself to sleep, staying awake, going to bed: none of it had halted the parade of death in her dreams. Raena had a horror of pharmaceuticals, but it was beginning to look like nothing else would work.

When she'd been very small, her mother used to give her something called poppy milk to keep her from crying with hunger. It didn't make her sleep, but it made her limbs so heavy that she couldn't move. After that, Raena refused to take painkillers, whenever she had a choice, for anything.

Several times, bounty hunters had drugged her in hopes of keeping her docile enough to return to Thallian in one piece. One poor guy gave her RespirAll, hoping to find out why Thallian wanted her back so badly. She chuckled now as she remembered that bounty hunter's face, once the truth drug had kicked into gear and he couldn't shut Raena up.

The worst was while she was locked up in the Parrabatta Mining Prison. As an experiment, they fed her a constant diet of some horrific hallucinogen. She might not have survived it, except that one of her cellmates had been a Coalition doctor. She was a strikingly tall creature with bulbous black eyes and fins running down the backs of her arms and legs, some kind of serpentine race. Raena could remember what she looked like, but not her name. The doctor had advised Raena to swallow her own hair. Something about the proteins in the hair counteracted the poison.

The mining prison wasn't one of Raena's escapes that she was proud of. She didn't mourn the Imperial guards who died when she pierced the prison walls and all its atmosphere vented into space, but the prisoners died as well, trapped in their cells. At the time, Raena hadn't cared. Now, as a non-hallucinating adult, the prison massacre was one of the worst regrets of her life. If she could go back in time, she would save as many prisoners as she could. She would make certain that the helpful doctor got away.

Raena took a deep breath and shook her head to clear it. Wishing for time travel? Really? These dreams of the past were starting to unhinge her.

She rubbed her temples again. She needed good, black, dreamless sleep, without a horrible bloody nightmare to spit her back into the waking world afterward. There must be some nice, gentle sedative that would ease her off to solid, uninterrupted unconsciousness.

It was a huge step to take, but at this point, she couldn't remember the last time she closed her eyes without a brain-splitting nightmare. For her sanity's sake, she would turn to medicine. She simply needed to ask Mykah to find her some sleeping pills. He'd know something that was safe for humans. She'd take it for a while, give the dreams time to go away on their own.

And if they didn't, she would haul herself to the best head-shrinker in the galaxy and find out what the hell was wrong with her.

In the Thomas Allard Home for Retired Interstellar Laborers, Doc glanced over at the Dakarai struggling to breathe in the bed beside her chair. The poor guy was not going to last the night. Fluid was seeping into his lungs from breathing toxins in the engine room of the decrepit freighter where he'd spent most of his life. Doc had done her best to relieve his pain, but unless he asked her for more, she couldn't do anything else.

She cracked the seal on a new bottle of whiskey, the last Gavin Sloane had given her, and poured herself a stiff drink. It was going to be a long night, but she might as well sit vigil until the Dakarai asked her for more relief or the end came of its own accord. Either way, she was going to be up in the night to attend to him.

The hour and the darkness conspired against her and she closed her eyes to grab what rest she could. It seemed as if the dream was waiting for her.

Raena Zacari stood at the Panacea's *hatch, ready to be on her way. Doc had done her best to patch the girl up, mending bones and torn muscles, shoring up her immune system to do the rest. The girl had clearly lived a rough life, but she was broken enough that she didn't want to talk about it. Doc respected that, even while it made her heart ache to see it.*

She'd tried to talk the girl into coming with them and joining the Coalition, but Raena shot that down. She was terrified enough of the man chasing her that she would continue to run rather than put any more lives at risk. Doc had Skyler and the kid to protect now, so she couldn't say Raena made the wrong choice. She just wished they weren't dumping her off the ship in the middle of a monsoon.

Doc handed Raena the rich black cloak. "Skyler brought me this from the bounty hunter's ship, but I knew it had to be yours. Better put it on. It's raining buckets out there." The lined fabric didn't seem like enough protection from everything out there that could harm the girl. "Maybe I should get you an extra jacket, or . . ."

"Thanks," Raena said, "but I don't think you have anything that would fit me."

Skyler handed her one of the bounty hunter's smaller pistols. "Thought you might have a use for this, though."

"Thanks." The smile that flashed across her face made her almost pretty. "That will come in handy, I'm sure."

"Cut the belt way down for you." He passed her the holster. Doc stared at him, amazed that he was being so effusive. The girl must have touched his heart, too.

"Perfect. Thank you." After a moment's pause, she said, "I guess I've kept you long enough."

Skyler opened the hatch for her.

"Be careful," Doc ordered. Stupid and useless advice.

Before anyone could say anything else, Raena slipped through the hatchway into the side-blown rain.

Tarik followed her outside. Doc watched the kids talk at the foot of the ramp.

"Want me to go after him?" Skyler asked.

"You won't need to," Doc predicted. Then the girl leaned forward, brushed a kiss against Tarik's lips, and melted into the night.

The look on the boy's face, when he turned back to the ship, woke Doc from the dream. She wiped her eyes and had another belt of whiskey.

CHAPTER 7

"**C**an I talk to you for a moment?" Raena asked when she found Mykah in the galley.

"Any time," he said, turning away from the ball of dough he had been shoving into shape.

Raena sat at the table. Her hands found each other in her lap. This was surprisingly hard. She'd been scared before, too many times, but the solution had always been fairly straightforward: meet violence with violence. Pre-empt it, if you could. Thallian's motto had been strike first—and leave your opposition too shattered to return fire.

None of that served her now. This time she was choosing to surrender control. "I think there's something wrong," she said hesitantly.

Mykah poured two cups of coffee: the real stuff, from beans he roasted obsessively until the whole ship smelled burnt. Raena didn't normally touch it, figuring the caffeine wouldn't help her insomnia, but after the dreams she'd been having, maybe she should drink it until she got the medicine she needed.

"I've been having bad dreams," Raena said. Prize for understatement.

"Still?" Mykah asked. "You told me that before."

Had she? Raena frowned, trying to remember. "I've been reliving moments in my life. All out of order. It's like they were turning points. Moments when things might have gone another way for me.

But I am who I am, who I've always been, and I've only ever seen one path in my life. And that path ended with Thallian's death."

She reached a shaky hand out and grabbed the metal coffee cup, just to have something solid to hold on to. "Anyway, these dreams I'm having . . . they always end in violence. People that I like—used to like, at least—keep getting hurt in them. By me. I don't recognize them until after I kill them and wake up. Either I am younger in the dreams and I haven't met these people yet, or I haven't met them yet the way they look in the dreams. And the dreams seem so real. They're like memories of things that never really happened."

She sipped the coffee and was grateful for its bitter flavor.

"I'm not surprised," Mykah said gently. "I don't know everything about your life, but I know it's been rough. You haven't been out of the last prison six months yet. It makes sense that you've got some processing to do."

"I thought processing was supposed to make you feel better," she said hopelessly.

"Not at first." He said it with enough confidence that Raena realized she didn't know much, really, about Mykah's life before she found him waiting tables. He'd studied the media, pulled his little pranks, and it seemed like a good idea when she plucked him away from all of that to find her a crew for the *Veracity*. He had been ridiculously, uncomfortably grateful. Now that she thought about it, life couldn't have been easy for him, growing up in the aftermath of the War and the purges, a human loose in a potentially hostile universe, blamed for atrocities perpetrated by madmen.

"How do I get through it?" Raena asked. She didn't like the tone in her voice, a shade too much like begging.

"What do you want to do? Do you want some professional help?"

"Maybe. After Coni gets all the documentation for my new identity nailed down. For now, though, I just want something safe to help me sleep."

"That I can find you," Mykah promised. "Let me make a couple of calls to Capital City."

"Thanks, Mykah."

"Always happy to help."

Kavanaugh was glad to see a message from Ariel Shaad. He laughed at himself when he actually got up to find a comb before returning her call. If he was going to dream about his past, he wondered, why couldn't he dream about the last flight with Ariel?

"Thanks for getting back to me so quickly, Tarik." She was leaning forward enough that he could see down her white blouse. Her hazel eyes sparkled, but the outfit was Ariel's regular uniform. The pose didn't necessarily mean anything.

"Any time, Ms. Shaad. What's on your mind?"

"It's work-related, unfortunately."

Tarik grinned to cover his disappointment. "I need work."

"I've got a couple more kids matched up with new families, but I can't deliver them myself. I just had the damn racer upgraded with a tesseract drive last year. I'm afraid if the kids don't get to Kaluum, I'll lose the parents. I know you could make more money hauling freight, so I will make it worth your while. Tell me what the job will cost me this time."

He typed in a figure, knowing she would match it.

"Thanks, Tarik." She made a couple of strokes and he heard the chime that meant the deposit had gone through. "When can we expect you?"

"I'm in your neighborhood."

"Perfect."

There was no way to change the subject casually, so he just bulled on ahead. "What's Raena up to these days?"

"She's traveling with a gang of kids her apparent age." Ariel said it drily enough that her real feelings on the subject were hidden. That was out of character; Ariel's emotions were usually right on the surface. "Why do you ask?"

He didn't want to admit that he'd been having nightmares about Ariel's little sister. "I saw some documentary about the Thallians looting the Templar tombs."

Ariel shuddered. "You think Gavin's behind that lie?"

He wanted to say that it wasn't like Gavin Sloane to be that subtle. Instead, he said, "The credits thanked the crew of the *Veracity*."

"Yeah, that's the ship Raena's on. If you talk to her, say hi."

From which Kavanaugh understood that Ariel and Raena weren't speaking at the moment. "Wasn't planning on it. I just thought it was weird, the misdirection from a ship called *Veracity*."

"The kids might not even know the truth," Ariel said. "It's not like Raena ever tells anyone what she's really doing and why."

Kavanaugh supposed that was true. He remembered the kiss she'd brushed across his lips as she disappeared into the rain on Barraniche and wondered what it really meant to her. He shuddered.

Ariel misinterpreted it. "Is your head still ringing?"

"Nah. I'm just gonna keep myself out of arm's reach from her from now on."

"Good plan."

"See you soon," he said.

"I'm looking forward to it."

Kavanaugh broke the connection, puzzling over the hint of flirt in Ariel's tone. Was that a promise of something more, or was she just being friendly? Damned if he could figure the two sisters out.

Shipping permits were much easier to get these days, when all sorts of antique craft were being brought out of mothballs to haul food around the galaxy. Coni handled the permitting process while Mykah negotiated with the Inkeri authorities about landing.

The process was so mundane that Raena found it comforting.

She was even more interested in the things the crew wanted to order from Capital City. Coni put her to work collecting up a list, which ranged from obscure vintage engine parts for Vezali to some kind of dried worms for Haoun. Mykah, unsurprisingly, had a whole grocery list.

Raena struggled to think of anything she wanted. Clothes, probably. Something to replace the magenta catsuit? But the catalogs she paged through online didn't sing to her. She decided she could get by with wearing Jain's clothes for a while longer.

The shopping process vaguely depressed her. For the first time in her life, thanks to her share of the Thallian bounty, Raena could actually afford almost anything she could think of. Did it show a lack of imagination that she couldn't think of anything other than a new spacesuit that might distract her from her unhappiness?

She supposed it meant she ought to get a hobby.

She was glad when Haoun finally kicked her out of the cockpit so they could dock with the Eske freighter.

After the *Veracity* connected to the Eske ship, Raena showed up at the hatch, ready to drive a loader if needed. The freighter's crew ignored her. They were meter-high curry-colored rodents with black button eyes. Delicate membranous ears stuck out from their heads like wings. Since they didn't wear translators amongst themselves, there was much grumbling that she didn't understand. The way their heads turned toward her afterward made their meanings clear.

She watched them climb over the crates, securing them for transport, and wondered why she felt inclined to start something. The energy building inside her wanted an outlet.

Haoun came to stand over Raena's shoulder. The lizard towered over her, the tallest member of the *Veracity*'s crew. He didn't stand up straight often—Raena thought it wasn't all that comfortable for him—but it was always impressive when he did. If she had to guess, he could stretch to over two and a half meters tall.

She suspected his translator must translate all languages, not just Galactic Standard. She leaned back against him so she could ask quietly, "What did they say?"

"You don't want to know," Haoun's translator said. His real voice rumbled at such a low frequency that it raised her hackles.

"That's what I thought," Raena said. "Are they insulting me or all humans?"

"Does it matter?" Haoun asked. The tone of his words through the translator was honestly curious.

"Not really," she decided. "I could use some exercise."

He tilted his head down to meet her eyes. "You know there's a whole ship full of them, right?"

Raena looked back at the little stevedores. They'd gotten to work now, running crates of produce into the *Veracity's* hold. They were businesslike, as if they only wanted to get the job over.

It might be interesting to see if she could school a whole freighter full of creatures who disrespected humans, but she doubted they'd take the lesson that she intended. Besides, she was supposed to be keeping a low profile.

"Thanks for having my back, Haoun."

He laughed. "Any time you want me to be the Voice of Reason, Raena, let me know."

The *Veracity's* crew didn't gather for dinner until the hold was sealed and the *Veracity* was again underway. By then, the smell of the bread Mykah had baked had Raena beside herself with hunger. It felt good to be hungry. She was the first person at the table when Mykah rang the chime.

"Mellix is being evicted from his apartment," Mykah reported once they were all settled. "Capital City has decided it's likely to be a focus for terrorists, so all his things are going to be hauled off-world and placed in storage."

"So we're going to apply to haul away his stuff?" Raena guessed.

"Ah," Mykah said. "I hadn't yet figured out what we should haul away from Capital City."

"No ship is going to want to take his stuff, if there's a threat of terrorism," Raena pointed out. "But Capital City will be eager to get rid of it. Make them an offer, set the price high, and demand secrecy on their part."

Mykah nodded. "I'll do it tomorrow, before we land."

"Oh, now we're movers?" Haoun scoffed. "This job is getting more glamorous by the day."

After they'd cleared the meal away, the others settled in to watch the news. Raena took her shift in the cockpit. It seemed a good opportunity to watch recordings of Mellix's exposés over the years.

His primary interest seemed to be in the artifacts left abandoned across the galaxy after the plague wiped the Templars out. In some cases, Templar buildings had been gutted and repurposed, like the casinos on Kai. In other cases, Templar technology had been bent to new uses, like the tesseract drive. Mellix did a whole story on the Dart, the drug that had helped Gavin find her on the Templar tombworld. Apparently, it wasn't the only Templar chemical that had been subject to misuse.

Raena learned more about the Templars from Mellix's news stories than she had ever known before. Mostly, his work pointed up the continuing questions surrounding them. It was commonly believed the Templars were a very old people, journeying through the stars before anyone else had developed interstellar travel. No one knew where their homeworld was, although logically they must have had an origin at some point. Everyone knew where their tombworld was, although no one had been allowed to visit when the Templars were still alive to guard it. No one spoke Templar, since it was a language composed of colors, although scholars could read a few of the written texts they'd left behind.

Mellix himself was completely obsessive in his knowledge about them, but his enthusiasm inspired the viewer as well. He'd been working long enough that he must be older than he looked. His fur was a glossy chestnut that lit up nicely in the camera lights. His tufted ears rose in sensitive points above overlarge shiny black eyes. His bristling whiskers seemed permanently atwitch. He reminded her of the Eske stevedores who had taken such a dislike to her, although he was taller, and a much snappier dresser.

Most of his stories came through a tip line. Raena wondered how easy that would be to prank, to offer the journalist some juicy bit of scandal that would draw him into an ambush. She supposed he must have someone like Coni tracing back the tips. They probably weren't as anonymous as the tipsters believed.

Mellix seemed to have received every accolade possible, to the point that there had been a free museum in his honor on Capital City that displayed all his awards. That is, there had been a museum until his announcement of the tesseract flaw. After that, it had been bombed by terrorists unknown. Three docents and several tourist families had been killed. The death toll might have been much higher, except that the news of the tesseract flaw had affected the flood of tourists on Capital City. Raena found it ironic that Mellix's announcement had already saved lives.

While everything she learned was fascinating, it didn't explain Mykah's connection to the journalist. Why was he so eager to lay his life, his ship, and his crew on the line for Mellix?

Coni was in the galley making a snack when Raena found her. "Hungry?" Coni asked.

"Thirsty," Raena decided. She opened the cooler for a bottle of cider. "Could I ask you something?"

"Go ahead," she said.

Raena wondered if Coni's tone was a little guarded, but she went ahead anyway. "It's about Mykah. I get that he has some special affinity for Mellix."

"Ah," Coni said. That was an affectation copied from Mykah's speech. "And you didn't want to ask him about it?"

Actually, Raena was still trying not to be alone with Mykah, although she didn't want to admit that to his girlfriend. She had wondered if the subject of his relationship with Mellix was too private for a mealtime conversation, which was why Mykah dodged it at breakfast. Instead, she said, "I thought maybe you would be more honest."

"Mykah would be honest with you. It's just that the others already know that Mellix was his advisor at university. Mykah was the only human in his cohort. Mellix assigned them to find a societal problem, investigate it, and assemble an exposé on it for their final project. Mykah's project was on the institutionalized abuse of human sex workers. The rest of the cohort parlayed their less-controversial exposés into internships in the media. No one would broadcast Mykah's."

"Because his subjects were human?"

Coni settled down at the table and began to eat. "That's what Mykah believes," she said between nibbles. "Mellix ended up hiring Mykah for a semester, so Mykah could finish his requirements and get his degree. Together they did an exposé on chronic illness amongst migrant farmworkers. It won several awards."

Raena found it interesting to discover there was a darker side to their affable captain. "How did Mykah end up working on Kai, then?"

"He didn't want to be merely a cameraman or a research assistant. He wanted to be on camera. But Mellix warned Mykah that if he took a job in the human media, he'd be ghettoized and never find anything else. Once he turned down the few offers he got from

Earth, no one else would hire him. Until he started handling your interview requests, no one would even return his calls."

"Is that so?" No wonder he was so thrilled to be doing interviews in her place, Raena thought. Finally, he was getting the attention for his work that he wanted. She wondered if he was actually appearing in the news footage or if the nonhuman media personalities merely quoted him as a source.

Afterward, Raena sequestered herself in her cabin, sweating over every repetitive exercise she could think of. She didn't know how else to pass the time.

The longer she worked, the stronger she became—which was good. Unfortunately, the long stretches of solitude gave her too much time to mull over the false memories. As she studied their details, she began to lose certainty of what events had really happened and which hadn't.

If there were two Gavins, as in the memory of being drugged by him in the souk, she knew she could easily discount it. The other hallucinations, though, where things were only subtly out of place, were harder for her to be sure of. Maybe what she thought she remembered was wrong.

She decided she needed to start keeping a log, just so she could chart if the false memories also mutated over time.

An audio log seemed too personal, though, and she already suspected Coni monitored her. Talking to herself, even to tell her own life story, was going to raise suspicions. So Raena spent the long hours that she couldn't sleep noting things down in the code she and Ariel had used to communicate when they were kids. It wouldn't fool Coni for long, once she got interested in it, and *that* would make Raena look even crazier than talking to herself might. All the same, it entertained Raena and in a strange way, it comforted her, too.

I come by my paranoia honestly, she told herself. *It's honed by way too many years on the run.*

Still, in all the time she had been trying to escape Thallian, she had never felt the need to make a record of her existence. If anything, she had wanted to be erased as soon as the universe could arrange it.

Now, she wanted to leave some kind of record behind—in case these horrible, unraveling dreams began to happen to someone else.

"Raena's having trouble sleeping," Mykah said into Coni's shoulder as he cuddled into her in bed.

Coni wanted to say, "I know," but she couldn't figure out how to, without admitting that she had been spying on their crewmate. "Is she feeling cooped up on the ship?" seemed a safe question to ask.

"I don't know. I get the feeling that maybe she doesn't know what to do with herself, without someone giving her orders. She doesn't seem to have developed any hobbies, other than working out."

"And now you've taken her gym away."

"Yeah."

Coni shifted to take better advantage of his touch and lost the thread of the conversation momentarily.

When at last she'd caught her breath again, she said, "You know what I think?"

Mykah chuckled sleepily.

"Well, yes, that, too," Coni agreed. "I think Raena would sleep better with company."

"Are you volunteering?" Mykah wondered.

Coni laughed. "I'm volunteering you."

"Yikes, Coni, how can you say that?"

"I just thought . . . you're both human. You would fit together." She wondered over his hesitance, then asked, "You're not afraid of Raena, are you?"

"Only in bed," he answered.

Fair enough, Coni supposed. She'd seen what Raena labeled as love marks.

"I know what she's capable of," Mykah said as he flopped over onto his stomach. "I know she's been gentle with me, relatively speaking, when we spar. I'm kind of in awe of her, but I never thought of her . . ."

Coni stopped his mouth with hers. She kissed him seriously enough that she felt the conflict leave his body. She smiled and leaned back so he could meet her eyes. "If you do," she said softly, "if she needs you, I'm fine with it."

"Why?"

Coni considered the question, then decided on the simplest answer: "I like her." She didn't say, "I feel sorry for her," because she knew how Mykah felt about that.

Eventually it got late enough that Raena crawled into bed. Her muscles ached, but in a way that made her happy. She closed her eyes and prayed for oblivion to take her.

The dream got to her first.

Raena didn't know where the Viridians were leading her, but she was grateful it didn't require any more of the horrific suffocating cloth they'd used when they captured her. She walked in the midst of a pod of them to a doorway.

Beyond the door stretched a large, bright open space. Raena stepped into it, blinking, and heard the door whoosh closed behind her.

As her eyes adjusted to the light, she saw a rack of weapons in the middle of the space. She recognized staves, shields, edged weapons of various lengths and weights.

She seemed to be alone in the room—at least, nothing else was moving. She heard the sound of voices. Somewhere, above the lights, she was being watched.

She walked over to the rack and pulled out a sword, testing its heft and balance and the way it cut through the air.

Another door opened and a woman was shoved through it. She shouted in a language Raena didn't understand. The woman struggled to cover her body with her hands.

Only after Raena saw her did she realize that she was still naked herself. Nothing she could do about it now. She went back to examining the weapons.

A second door opened, and a third, then more. All the slaves were female. Raena didn't pay them much attention until animals rushed out of the final door and the screaming started.

She dropped the sword to snatch up a lance tipped with a battle-axe. She decided it was better to have reach than weight in her weapon. She would've preferred to fight nearer to the wall, but since the doors remained invisible until they opened to spit something out, the rack of weapons was probably a better thing to have at her back. She didn't want to get far from the weapons anyway, in case her halberd's haft broke.

The spectacle was a bloodbath. After a while, the screaming died down and only the sounds of eating remained.

Raena eyed the last monster standing, a giant with a glassy black carapace. Its tail ended in a dripping barb. She slashed that off, before the creature knew she was behind it.

It spun toward her faster than she would have guessed possible.

She stabbed at its eyes with the halberd. It grabbed the haft in one claw and snapped it in half.

Raena clung to the broken stick with both hands as the monster dragged her forward. At the last second, she let go, rolling beneath the creature to retrieve the discarded axe head. She jammed it upward with all her strength, hacking until it wedged into a chink in the carapace.

The creature flopped over onto its back, grabbing at her with all its claws. Raena's small size worked to her advantage. She was able to roll between the monster's legs.

She ran back to the weapons to retrieve the sword she'd discarded earlier.

The monster squealed a single high-pitched note. Raena had never been so happy when a noise stopped.

Over a loud speaker, a voice said something she didn't understand. What followed was a gabble of voices that sounded like an auction.

A pod of Viridians came to retrieve her from the field of battle. Raena considered the ichor-dripping sword in her hand, but one of the stick creatures showed her the control in its claw. Raena's fingers touched the collar around her neck. She let the sword fall.

The Viridians surrounded her. She weighed attacking them—the one with the collar's controller first—but really, she understood what was happening now. This was a slave auction. The Viridians were selling her at last. She could choose to die now, to spite them, or she could wait and see.

She was young enough to hope that whatever happened to her next would be better.

Out in the hallway beyond the arena, one of the Viridians pushed her into a tiny cubicle. After the door closed on her, she was washed, dried, and misted with perfume. When the door opened again, a Viridian handed her a heavily embroidered robe and a comb. She dressed and began to ease the tangles from her long black hair.

The pod guided her through the shadowy ship to a lavishly upholstered sitting room. A lone old man sipped from a glass with actual ice cubes in it. The Viridians surrendered the controller for her collar and faded back into the shadows.

"Hello, Raena," he said softly. "My name is Gavin Sloane."

She couldn't think of anything to say.

"I can only imagine how you have been treated by the Viridians. We are going to have your collar removed right now. You will be free after that."

"Why?"

"Because . . ." he began. Clearly the question caught him unprepared. "Because I knew you in another life. I want to spare you from being a slave."

"Why didn't you spare me from the Viridians?" she asked.

"I didn't know where you were sold to them, but I did know when they sold you."

That didn't make any sense. Raena began to wonder if she were dreaming.

Sloane slipped the collar controller into the breast pocket of his flight jacket and buttoned the flap over it. He offered a hand to her. "Let's go."

She took his leathery hand and followed him from the Viridians' ship. She found herself in an enormous spaceport. She and Sloane ascended a towering escalator to a platform where a serpentine transit car waited to rush people into the city on the horizon. Raena had no idea what planet they were on.

She had never before seen the kinds of creatures that pressed into the transit car around her. They wore feathers or scales or fur of many colors. Some were bipedal. Others had multiple legs. Some had fangs, others claws. All carried conspicuous weaponry.

She moved closer to her new owner. He smiled down at her and drew her in front of him so he could reach around either side of her to the pole that kept them from toppling over when the car glided to its first stop.

Having him pressed up against her flank made her vastly uncomfortable.

The controller to her collar was so close now. She thought she could probably snatch it from his pocket and dive out of the rapidly closing doors—but that wouldn't really gain her anything. She would still be collared. Someone bigger than her would take the controller away and then they'd own her. If she destroyed the controller or lost it somewhere, she'd still be collared and marked as a slave. Anyone could turn her in as a runaway and claim a reward. Either she'd be returned to Sloane or she'd be dragged back to the Viridians and forced back onto one of their ships to begin the process again.

She eyed the ray gun holstered near her right hand on the thigh of some kind of bipedal ogre. She could steal the gun and kill Sloane—or kill herself—but she couldn't bring herself to take the easy escape. So she waited. Eventually they would get wherever they were headed and she'd get the collar off and then she would have more choices.

The shrouded creature who owned the electronics shop led them through towering stacks of small appliances into a back room. He dug through a teetering stack of tools before he found a palm-sized demagnetizer. He clipped it to the remote first, disrupting its signal, before he snapped a second one onto the collar at the nape of her neck.

Sloane stepped back out of the blast radius. Raena closed her eyes and flinched.

The proprietor tsked. He caught the collar as it fell from her neck.

"Excellent," Sloane gushed. "Thank you." He paid the man with a handful of circuitry.

Then he grabbed Raena's arm and hauled her out of the shop. Dodging a fleet of two-wheeled scooters, he dragged her down the street.

"You're welcome," he said, grinning, as he hustled her along.

"I don't know how to thank you," she said quietly.

"You will."

And she did. When she caught him spying on her that evening while she washed the Viridians' choice of perfume from her hair, she throttled him with her towel and broke his neck. It didn't kill him, but pushing him out the airlock finished the job.

Raena rolled off her bunk. She woke when she hit the deck. Hard. Winded, she lay still a moment, waiting for sensation to flood back into her limbs. Until the shock wore off, she wouldn't know if she'd broken anything.

Pain ran warmly through her. She flexed her fingers, rolled her hands around on her wrists. Her left wrist protested, but it moved. No permanent damage done. That was lucky.

The dreams were getting worse, she thought. They were more and more detailed. Longer. And her subconscious was providing more unsavory details about Gavin than she ever wanted to know.

Thank the stars it hadn't really happened that way in real life. Ariel's dad bought her from the Viridians after the tournament. He himself never laid a hand on her. Instead, he ran her through a week's worth of tests so he could be certain of her conditioning, then he gave her as a gift to Ariel. A birthday present.

Life as a slave had not been too bad, other than understanding that her purpose was to die for the spoiled rich girl, if it ever came to that. Luckily, Ariel was well liked—and rich—enough that it never did.

Raena pushed herself off the deck into sitting up. A glance at the clock made her wince. She hoped someone else was awake at this hour, so she would have an excuse to stay up for a while.

When she stumbled into the galley, Mykah was there, stirring a pot on the stove. Before she could apologize and escape, he asked, "Another nightmare?"

"It was brutal," she admitted. "I fell out of bed to make it stop."

He came over to take her left arm gently in his hands and tested her wrist. "Are you all right?"

His concern was painful for her to hear. She extracted her arm from his hands, flexing her fingers, and went to get a drink of water. As she poured it, she thought to ask, "What are you doing up?"

"Coni's purring woke me." He laughed fondly. "I was going to fix myself a nightcap and go back to bed."

"What's in it?"

"Warm rice milk, some spices, and a healthy dose of rum."

She smiled at him through her exhaustion. "Would it be too much trouble to make two?"

"No trouble at all." He pulled the galley first aid kit from the wall and set it on the table without comment.

"It's not as bad as it looks," Raena argued as she popped the kit's lid open. "The shock of the fall was worse than the landing."

"What were you dreaming about?"

She noticed he had his back toward her. Making conversation, she understood, not fussing over her. "I was dreaming about being a slave."

She eased herself in behind the table. The kit had a tube of analgesic cream, she saw. Someone had used some of it, maybe Mykah after their sparring sessions. Raena twisted the cap open and squirted some onto her left wrist, gingerly rubbing it in.

"You were on a Viridian ship?" he prompted gently.

"Yeah. As a kid. The dream was about the tournament just before they sold me off. You've heard about their gladiator battles, where they pit a group of slaves against some monsters? They don't care what the death toll is, because they sell tickets to the battles, then auction the winner off."

"It's mostly illegal now." Mykah set two mugs and a bottle of rum on the table.

"It was probably illegal then," she answered. "It didn't stop it from happening."

He returned to the table with a steaming pan that smelled so inviting that Raena felt a little better already.

"This works best if you pour the milk into the rum, so serve yourself however much you want first."

She filled her mug halfway. Mykah topped it off with the steaming milk, poured from a height. He didn't spill a drop. After she retrieved her mug, he doctored his own.

"So you were the only survivor of the tournament you fought in?" Mykah guessed.

She nodded. "At the time, I didn't think anything about it. I was so furious at everything that had happened to me that I focused my anger on the things in the arena. Now I think: I was eleven. They put a naked child into a certain death battle, just to die for the sake of entertainment."

Mykah slid in beside her at the table. He sipped his nightcap, which reminded Raena to pick hers up. The warmth felt good, seeping through the cup into her hands.

This was weird, she thought, to be alone in the middle of the night with their captain—and his girlfriend asleep down the hall. Rather than relaxing, her senses prickled even more awake. She needed Coni to help her get her new identity documents cemented in place. One stroke of Coni's anger and it would all unravel. Raena would be revealed or worse.

She was about to make some excuse and escape when Mykah said, "Coni and I were talking about you earlier tonight." He didn't look up from his cup. "She thinks you might sleep better with company."

Raena set her cup carefully on the table. Her anger rapidly switched directions—from Mykah putting her in a potentially dangerous situation, to the fact that her crewmates were making sleeping arrangements for her behind her back.

Before she could distill her fury into words, Mykah continued. "Coni doesn't understand completely how problematic human interactions can get. Among her people, affection is disconnected from sex. They go into heat, to be crude about it, and mate without any emotional involvement. For them, it's a purely physical hunger. Anyone can fill it. She's read about humans and worked with them for several years, but she doesn't fully grasp how layered our relationships can be."

He sipped his nightcap and looked up at her. "I would be glad to keep you company, Raena, if you ever decide you want it. But I'm aware that your past is complicated and I don't want to make your life any more difficult."

Raena waited, but he seemed to be waiting for her response. She said quietly, "Is it okay that I'm freaked out by all of this?"

He clinked his mug against hers. "It's okay if you're freaked out on a whole spectrum of levels."

"Good, because I am." She had her first drink of the nightcap, which was more delicious than she'd expected. It felt like exactly what she needed.

She struggled to speak her thoughts. "I appreciate what you're offering me. And I appreciate Coni's generosity. But you know I've had spectacularly bad judgment when it comes to my commanding officers, so let's keep everything professional for now."

"I don't really command you," Mykah pointed out. "But I respect your decision."

She though he looked a tiny bit relieved.

"Why don't you head back to bed?" she suggested. "Big day tomorrow."

"Yeah, it is." He got up and put his cup and the pan in the dish-washer, but left the bottle of rum on the table for her. "Rest, if you can. We'll need you tomorrow."

CHAPTER 8

By the time she finally got back to bed, Raena wondered if she'd imagined the whole conversation with Mykah. Had he really told her that his girlfriend suggested they sleep together?

She burrowed into the pillow, deciding she would act from now on as if she had hallucinated the offer.

That was more comforting than to consider the repercussions if she acted on it.

Unfortunately, the nightcap didn't keep the nightmares at bay.

Raena hadn't really worked out a plan in advance. As soon as Thallian was up and out for the day, she forced herself out of bed. The burns striping her back screamed as she dressed. In case the wounds came open and began to weep, she put on three layers of clothing.

Then she pulled a bag of equipment—scramblers, credit chips, traveling cash in a variety of currencies—from the cupboard where she'd hidden it in case of emergency. This was the emergency for which she'd been preparing.

She had the advantage that no one aboard the Arbiter *really knew what she did, beyond keeping Thallian from molesting the rest of the crew. One would think they would be grateful for that, but not really, no. Still, the fluidity of her job description worked to her advantage. Since what she was assigned to do was so nebulous, generally no one questioned whatever she did.*

She took over a terminal in the detention monitoring office and attached a scrambler to it. It didn't matter too much if she covered her tracks, since she expected Thallian to discover her mutiny in fairly quick order, but no need to make it insultingly obvious either.

She looked over the new prisoner roster. Another human had been brought in overnight. Raena keyed in a command for him to be transferred to Ariel Shaad's cell. She ordered a pair of robots to meet her there.

As soon as the boy had been delivered, Raena let herself into the cell. She let the door close before she broke the kid's neck. Ariel shouldn't have had time to get attached to him yet.

As one of the robots incinerated his body, Raena grabbed Ariel's arm and pulled her close. "I'm arranging your escape," Raena said through gritted teeth into Ariel's ear, so she couldn't be heard over the incineration. "The cameras won't be off too much longer. I've scrambled the time signatures, so it will look like you've been ashed and he was moved in to take your place."

Raena took the box of ashes from the robot and labeled it with Ariel's name and prisoner ID number. Then she turned back to the blond girl. "Up on the stretcher," she ordered.

For a change, Ariel didn't argue. She hopped on the stretcher pushed by the second robot and sprawled face down as if unconscious. Raena had worried they would lose valuable time debating, but apparently Ariel was so eager to get off the Arbiter *that she'd decided to be compliant.*

Raena checked the scramblers on the robots, then pulled the sheet up over Ariel and opened the cell door. The robots glided forward to keep pace as she returned down the corridor.

"Lord Thallian wants this one down in his lab," she told the duty officer. "You'll find the order."

He checked his datascreen. "Wasting no time on that one," he noted.

"I don't question," Raena answered.

The man didn't hide his grimace. "Go ahead."

Raena diverted to the hangar and loaded Ariel as cargo on a hopper. Then she went off to arrange the clearance for her to take off.

When she returned to the hopper, Ariel had gotten herself up, uniformed, and armed. Raena didn't ask how that had happened. Instead, she handed over a chip. "These are everything you'll need to get out of here."

"Aren't you coming?"

"I'm going to cover for you."

She should have seen the scanner case coming. Maybe she did and chose not to duck. She didn't remember later, after it ceased to matter.

When Raena came to, it wasn't on the single-person hopper. The engines had a much deeper throb.

"Lie still," Ariel said affectionately. "I don't know if you have a concussion."

Raena realized she was sprawled on a stainless steel bench. "Who's flying?" she demanded.

"A Coalition friend. He saw us in the hangar and helped me get you aboard a shuttle."

"Can you trust him?"

"He had the right Coalition safe words."

Raena stared at her.

Ariel burst into shaky tears. "I was so scared," she confessed. "I just wanted to get out of there. I wasn't sure I could do it alone."

Raena got up painfully, took Ariel in her arms, and did not hiss when the blond girl clung to her. The sting from the burns on her back was more shocking now, when she didn't have endorphins in her blood to mitigate the pain.

Once Ariel calmed down enough to be coherent, Raena said, "You had a sidearm."

It was still holstered on Ariel's thigh. Raena accepted it, checked its charge. Then she strode into the cockpit and shot the mystery Coalition man dead before he could protest.

Ariel heard the shot and sprinted into the cockpit. She found Raena in the pilot's chair, staring at the readout from the navcom.

"What did you do?" Ariel demanded.

"I wanted to find out where he was taking us," Raena answered calmly.

Ariel wanted to shake her. "You could've just asked."

"He could've just lied."

Ariel slumped into the copilot's seat, then realized it was as covered in blood and tissue as everything else in the cockpit. "You didn't have to kill him," Ariel said miserably. She felt sick. "You don't have to kill everybody."

"You're not fourteen any more," Raena said harshly. "You should know better than to get in the first spaceship that comes along."

"But he—"

Raena cut her off. "He had the codes you knew. On a ship where Coalition prisoners are tortured." She wiped the hair back from her face angrily, leaving a bloody smear across her cheek. "A stranger on the Arbiter lured you onto a ship impounded by the Arbiter. You tell me the odds that it's being tracked."

The anger drained out of Ariel so fast that she had to lean her head on her knees. "I can't go back there."

"I will kill us first," Raena promised.

"What are we going to do?"

"Ditch this ship. Try to get out past Coalition space. I don't know. I wasn't planning to come along with you."

"I know," Ariel said. "I couldn't leave you."

"Now there's no one to cover your escape." Raena was sitting awkwardly in the pilot's chair, perched on its edge. Ariel had thought it was because she was avoiding the pilot's blood, but his chair was less gory than everything else in the cockpit because his body had shielded it.

Blood striped Raena's back diagonally from left shoulder to right hip.

Ariel gasped. "What happened to your back?"

"*Thallian set me on fire for luring him away from you last night. He knew I was protecting you. He wanted to punish me for not being clear in my loyalties.*"

"*He would have killed you if you'd stayed behind.*"

"*He's still going to kill me,*" Raena corrected. "*I just don't know when any more.*"

Ariel got up, unable to sit in this blood-covered room any longer. "*I've got to get out of this uniform.*"

"*Not yet,*" Raena said. "*I've figured out where we are. Can you get us to Clio? We'll have to find another ride from there.*"

"*Shift,*" Ariel said. Raena got up stiffly so Ariel could take the controls. "*Go see if there's a shower and wash your wounds. I'll come see what I can do to patch you up as soon as we're underway.*"

Raena was about to ghost away when Ariel called her back. She stretched one hand out for Raena's. "*Thank you,*" she said, like she'd never meant anything in her life.

"*Of course, Ari.*" Raena smiled, but in her black eyes, Ariel saw depths of fear like she'd never known.

"*We'll get away from him,*" she promised.

"*No one ever gets away,*" Raena answered.

Then she kissed Ariel and went to look for a shower.

After she was gone, curiosity got the better of Ariel. She rolled the dead man over with her boot.

He was too old to be an Imperial soldier, maybe seventy. His gray eyebrows and beard bristled, thick and full, but his hair had retreated until it left his crown bare. The hole from Raena's death shot went in above his left ear. He'd turned his head when he heard her coming.

Ariel opened her eyes, catapulted out of the dream by the realization that the dead man was Gavin. She didn't know how she'd recognized him—the shape of his nose, maybe—but she was certain she was correct.

What was the matter with her subconscious that it was rewriting history like that? She'd bopped Raena on the head with a scanner case, yeah, but she'd taken the hopper Raena had meant her to. They had gone to Clio. In fact, much of the conversation in the dream echoed what she remembered of the terrified race to get beyond Thallian's reach. Except, she knew, there had been no "Coalition man" for Raena to assassinate.

Ariel's hands shook as she reached out for a spice stick on the bedside table. She hoped it would settle her nerves.

As she opened her eyes in her cabin, Raena wondered, *What was it with killing Gavin?* It wasn't as if she had anything against him. Yeah, he'd loved her in an obsessive, possessive way, but she didn't really begrudge him that. In reality, he had been generous with her on Kai, relatively patient, and indulged her when he could figure out how. When the opportunity came for her to go off and kill Thallian, Gavin hadn't actually stood in her way, like she had feared he might.

Yes, it was true she hadn't officially broken up with Gavin, beyond running off after her destiny and not coming back. She wondered if Gavin had honestly expected her to come back after she assassinated Thallian. Other than the relatively cushy life Gavin could offer her, living on his profits from the looted Templar tombs, she wasn't sure what she was supposed to have come back to.

If she had been a different person, perhaps she could have loved Gavin with a passion equal to his own. She tried to imagine a life in which he let her come and go as she pleased, a life that felt like freedom. A life where he thought of her as an equal, not a pet or his girlfriend, not a child or a damsel he had rescued. He had rescued her, sure, she wasn't debating that, by funding the operation that opened the Templar tombs—and she *would* be forever grateful for that—but she could not continue to be that same person, to live that same role over and over: the girl who needed rescue.

For one thing, no matter what she looked like, she was not a girl. Due to the weird Templar stone in which she'd been imprisoned, her body hadn't aged a day. Outwardly, she still looked like the twenty-year-old who had been sealed up inside the Templar Master's tomb. But the imprisonment had given her time to mature, whether or not her body changed.

So the way these dreams kept ending—with Gavin showing up unexpectedly and her killing him with whatever came to hand—made her really uncomfortable. She had no real grudge against Gavin. She would be glad to have a drink with him someday, if they accidentally found themselves in the same bar and she knew she could walk away alone afterward.

It was the sort of dilemma that she supposed someone else would discuss with her girlfriend. But Coni could barely be counted a friend and Vezali, while friendly, would require such a vast amount of backstory that merely listening to the history would be too much to ask.

There was only one person who knew Gavin well enough, good and bad, to be a sympathetic listener. When this adventure with Mellix was over, Raena would have to bother Ariel with her problems.

"We'll be docking soon," Haoun said over the comm.

"Thanks," Raena answered. Time to suit up.

She pulled on another pair of Jain's trousers and swam into another of his sweaters. This one was a steely gray that she quite liked.

Then she retrieved the paste she'd made in Mykah's kitchen in the middle of the night. She'd worn something similar on Kai, but she hadn't made anything like this from scratch in decades. Unsurprising, the recipe came back to her easily. Her hands had concocted it many times while drunk in the middle of the night.

She shook the jar good and hard, before unscrewing its lid. Holding her hair off her forehead with one hand, she quickly painted her face, blotting out the scar that missed removing her eye.

She reached out to close the clothes locker when her eye fell on the coat she'd stolen from Revan Thallian, previous captain of the *Veracity*.

Raena pulled the coat on and buttoned its cuffs back. It must have been long on Revan, but it hung to Raena's ankles, with a cinched waist and a full skirt. Although it was big for her, it had enough interior structure to make her seem larger. Perfect. It wouldn't replace her long-lost cloak, but it was a decent substitute. She felt dressed for battle now.

The coat had a surprising array of interior pockets, meant to be filled with weaponry. She checked through all the pockets, making sure that Revan hadn't left any nasty surprises behind. Everything was empty and functional as his cabin had been when she commandeered it, except for the breast pocket. In it, Raena found a hardcopy photo of Eilif, Madame Thallian.

Raena strapped herself into the crash webbing, then picked up the photograph. In the picture, Eilif still looked like a young woman, slim and ramrod straight. The photographer caught her by surprise with a teacup in her hand, lifted halfway to her lips. Her smile looked genuine.

Interesting. Why did Revan have a photo of his younger brother's wife?

Raena shook her head. Anything between Revan and Eilif was undoubtedly one of the great unconsummated romances of the galaxy. Jonan would have killed them both—Eilif first—if he'd ever found out they'd cheated on him.

Would Eilif want the photo, Raena wondered, or would she prefer not to be reminded of the years she'd belonged to the Thallians? Personally, Raena was glad not to have any mementos of her own service with Jonan, beyond the ones he'd carved into her flesh.

She set the photo aside, intending to ask Ariel about it whenever they spoke next. Now it was time to get her head in the game.

Raena didn't really know what to expect in Capital City. She'd asked Mykah about its banal name, but he said that was merely the Galactic Standard translation. In every case, he said, Standard dumbed names down to their simplest components.

Mykah said the news reports from Capital City had been cautious, not wanting to panic the rest of the galaxy. He expected that people were exceptionally tense. The city occupied a moon-sized space station hung between three gates. All the older ships with non-tesseract drives had evacuated as many tourists and consular staff as possible after the tesseract announcement, but everyone left behind either had crucial governmental work to do or nowhere else to go. Everything from washing water to atmospheric filters was being strictly rationed. Very few people had enough of anything to be satisfied.

The *Veracity* planned to be in orbit long enough to transfer the vegetables out of the hold, find some sleep aids for Raena, and to get Mellix safely aboard. No telling how long that would take.

Raena hadn't told Mykah that she and Coni had made another appointment for while they were visiting the station. She touched her eyebrow, tracing the contours of her scar, but didn't allow herself to dwell on how she'd acquired it. The last thing she wanted was to drift off into the past again.

Haoun got the *Veracity* docked with Capital City's elevator without a bump.

"Nice docking," Raena told him over the comm.

"Thanks," the big lizard answered. "Lots of simulator hours went into it."

Raena laughed as she unclipped her harness and retrieved her high-heeled boots from the gun locker by the door. She buckled her boots on and decided to add one final element of Revan's clothing. Inside one of the desk drawers, she'd found a long black box. Inside that lay a half-dozen pairs of matching black gloves. They were made of Viridian slave cloth, the weave so fine that individual threads were invisible. These gloves left no fibers or fingerprints behind to be traceable. She'd worn them constantly while on the run from Jonan.

Raena chose a pair from the box and slipped them on. The fabric molded around her fingers as if it was liquid. She flexed her fingers, made a fist. Then she went out to join the others at the hatch.

"Haoun's going to stay onboard and make sure we're ready to jet," Mykah said as he handed comm bracelets around to everyone else. Vezali snapped hers high up on one of her tentacles, where it looked like a garter.

"Raena and I have some girl stuff to do," Coni told him. "Comm us when you need us."

Mykah glanced from one to the other of them. "Sure," he said, puzzled.

"I'm looking for an extra life support part," Vezali said.

Everyone turned to stare at her. "Kidding." She held up two tentacles and made a gentling motion. "I've got some siblings here I want to visit."

"How many siblings do you have?" Raena asked.

"Seventy-one, still living. Three of them are in the consular service here."

Raena nodded, keeping her face blank. One of these days, she really was going to have to do more research on her crewmates and learn what she could about their species.

Haoun joined them at the hatch. "Have fun out there and keep your heads down."

"Do you want us to get you anything?" Raena asked.

"I told my kids I'd send them some souvenirs."

"We'll see what we can find," Coni promised. "Two boys and a girl, right?" Haoun nodded.

Yeah, Raena thought, she really was going to have to learn more about her shipmates. She'd assumed everyone else was just as unencumbered as she was.

"Ready?" Mykah asked. When he'd collected a nod from each of them, he reached forward to open the hatch.

The dockmaster stood directly outside, flanked by two armored guards. He had glossy black fur and extremely sharp teeth. "Captain Chen?" he asked.

Mykah stepped forward. "That's me."

He had pulled his hair back under a black scarf and shaved his face clean so he looked bland and respectable. Watching him work, Raena finally understood why the others let Mykah be the captain: he was really good at dealing with bureaucrats. Thank the stars someone could save her from that.

More guards flanked the mouth of the elevator. They were professionals, Raena noticed, clocking their visible weapons and guessing at what she couldn't see. If they didn't have sleep grenades, the vestibule itself must be plumbed for gas.

She wondered if she could count on the authorities to protect Mellix when he tried to leave the station, or if the soldiers resented having to stand up here on a spindle in space.

When she clustered with Coni and Vezali in a little knot, Raena noticed the right-hand guard tracked her every shift in position.

Why had he picked her out as trouble? She'd dressed down. Her scars—and muscles—were covered. She wasn't armed except with a knife in each boot top, which any girl would carry. Capital City wasn't weapons-free the way Kai had been, but the permitting process was complicated and time-consuming if you wanted to carry an energy weapon. Raena hadn't wanted to test her new identity.

Mykah joined them at last, zipping his handheld into the pocket in the back of his jacket. When he shouldered the jacket on, Raena noticed the guards took a pointed interest in him as well.

Coni waited until the four of them were in the elevator car and going down before she muttered, "Even humans have rights."

Mykah took her hand and nodded toward the camera in the corner of the car.

"How many elevators are there here?" Raena asked conversationally.

"Two completed and others under construction," Mykah answered. "Both share the same train station and waiting room."

"Where's Haoun going to park while he's waiting for us?"

"They've got some complicated orbital system worked out. When we all get our business done, we contact him and he'll apply for another docking window. Then we'd better get on the ship during that window or we'll be left behind."

"What's the fine for overstaying your time slot?" Vezali asked.

"We can't afford it," Mykah promised. "So don't shut your comms off. When we get the word it's time to fly, we're going."

The elevator slowed and eased itself down the last hundred meters. Raena's ears popped as the pressure changed. More guards stood outside the elevator doors, facing another vestibule. Beyond yet another pair of blast doors, more guards surrounded a waiting area crowded with people hanging around until their appointments to leave.

Raena didn't like the look of that. If anyone found out Mellix was leaving, that waiting area would be the last opportunity to stop him. Unless, of course, they planned to take the entire elevator down. If people were that serious, there wasn't a lot she could do about it.

A sparking force field marked a walkway through the crowd. The fence would make you jump if you stumbled into it, but it wouldn't slow down a determined stampede. Raena counted eight guards, or roughly one for every five people waiting. The space was too tight for weapons that required accuracy to function. Raena glanced upward, expecting to see shock nets, but the ceiling was featureless except for inset light panels.

The crowd shifted enough that she caught a solid glimpse of one of the guards. He balanced on a short pedestal, not much more than a box. That meant that the floor was hot. They'd use it to pacify the rabble when the riot came.

She'd seen Mykah and Coni flying above the crowd in the casino on Kai, but she didn't know if Vezali could jump. Avoiding the first jolt would only leave you standing for the guards' hand weapons to bring you down. A puzzle, she thought.

"How long are we likely to be on the station, Captain?" she asked.

"We're aiming for a standard day, so nobody has to pay for accommodations in the City. We'll see if they really let us out of here that quickly."

As they explored Capital City, Raena walked on the outside of the passageway for a while. That way Coni could be closer to the displays as she window-shopped for Haoun's souvenirs. The tchotchkes didn't call to Raena, since she didn't recognize what most of them were.

Instead she watched the people. Their variety was breathtaking: feathers, fur, scales, all variety of clothing or lack thereof. The first time someone crossed to the other side of the passage to avoid her, she didn't think anything of it. By the fifth or sixth time, she started experimenting. Once she even took a half step toward someone, just to watch him skip backward like a startled cat.

"Don't start a fight," Coni scolded quietly.

"Not trying to, " Raena admitted. "Just making sure I saw what I thought I saw."

"You're really seeing it. Welcome to the galaxy-at-large."

Even humans have rights, Raena thought. She hadn't realized how tolerant the crew of the *Veracity* was. And how much more she should have appreciated them.

Coni consulted her handheld and turned down an alley that looked like all the others to Raena. It was quieter here. A variety of spas lined both sides of the passage, but business seemed to be slow as people conserved their money for food and lodging—and passage off Capital City, if they could find it.

Coni halted in front of a storefront that looked polished and sterile as an operating room. "Ready?"

"Let's get it over." Raena pushed the door open and stepped inside.

The medical robot grasped Raena's chin in one claw and turned her face gently from side to side, examining her skin in a variety of spectrums so it could see through her paint job.

"Yes, we can erase that scar without damaging your eye. Looks like you've lived with it a long time, though. It would have been easier to repair when the wound was fresh."

"I was stuck shipboard," Raena said, "until I could save the money up."

Coni was impressed by the ease with which the lie left the little woman's lips. She didn't know where Raena had gotten the scar that nearly cost her an eye, but it predated her induction into Imperial service. Receiving that scar was one story she hadn't told Jain Thallian.

Coni was still surprised that Raena had asked her to accompany her to the plastic surgeon. The little woman generally seemed so self-assured that Coni wasn't sure what about this process made Raena anxious.

The robot led Raena toward a door back into the salon. Coni followed along. Raena cast a glance over her shoulder that Coni read as gratitude.

A Shtrell nurse trotted up to intercept the big blue-furred girl. "You don't need to accompany your friend . . ."

Coni cut her off before she could insult her with a menu of treatments. "We've already run into some anti-humanism since we landed here." Coni kept moving forward. Raena loitered to give her time to catch up. "I know that won't be a problem *here*," Coni said, injecting emphasis, "but my friend was badly frightened. She'll be more comfortable if I stay with her."

The Shtrell shrugged, ruffling her feathers. "You'll need to stay out of the doctor's way."

"Of course," Coni agreed. She took the hand Raena held out to her, gave it a gentle squeeze. She wondered at herself, acting like Raena's friend. Strangely enough, she—and the rest of the *Veracity*'s crew—seemed to be the only friends Raena had, other than Ariel Shaad. Maybe it wasn't such an act.

Raena let herself be strapped into a complicated frame that would restrain her completely from the shoulders up. It reminded her of a telenovel she and Ariel watched as teenagers: people were always changing their faces, coming back into their lives as someone new whenever different actors took over the roles.

Bounty hunters had marked her. Thallian had remodeled her to reflect his dominance. The scar between her eyes predated all the others. It was the first scar, the primal one that had changed her the most. She'd thought she would never let it go, but it had—more than anything else, more than her DNA itself—trapped her in the past, tied her to the person she no longer wanted to be. The time had come to let it go.

Raena watched the nurses smooth her hair back from her face and secure it under a soft turban that stretched around her skull.

A stout little nurse that reminded her of Vezali—because she had tentacles, not hands—succeeded in distracting her while another rubbed numbing cream across her forehead and over her eyelid. No wonder they hadn't wanted Coni to see this part: it felt scary. Raena felt her eyelid drooping slackly over her eye. She could no longer blink.

The birdlike nurse came toward her with a mask full of anesthetic. Locked into the head frame, Raena couldn't pull away. One breath of that stuff knocked her out.

It was easy to remember when she got the scar. She'd been young—four, maybe, probably not as much as five. Her mother had been having a nightmare. A scream choked behind Fiana's teeth had woken Raena.

Raena stood at her mother's bedside, frightened, uncertain what to do. Fiana writhed on her pallet, breathing raggedly. Raena whispered, "Mama? Wake up," but Fiana didn't seem to hear.

"Mama?" she called a little louder. She was afraid to wake the others in the shelter, but they couldn't afford to be thrown out. Her mother had said they had nowhere else to go.

Raena saw the scream rising in her mother's chest. Lunging forward, she cupped her hand over Fiana's mouth.

Her mother woke instantly. One hand flashed upward to shove Raena away. There was something sharp in it: a broken cup, the raw ceramic edge like a knife.

Raena didn't feel the pain at first. Instead, she felt hot wetness spill into her eye. The blood blurred her vision and she started to cry. It stung.

"Hush, you idiot." The broken cup fell from Fiana's hand, forgotten. "What did you do?"

Fiana dug into her pack for a clean shirt. She pressed Raena's hand over the fabric to hold it in place while she pulled out the staple gun. When she prodded her daughter's forehead with a finger, she set the gun aside. "This is going to have to be done by hand," Fiana grumbled. "Why can't you be more careful?"

Raena said nothing.

"Honestly," Fiana hissed. She pulled out the sewing kit and her headlamp. "Come lie in my lap," she directed, patting her thigh. "Put your head here."

Raena did as she was told, still clutching the shirt to her face. It had grown soggy and chilled in her fingers.

Fiana eased the shirt away from the wound. She pressed a dry corner over Raena's eyelid and sprayed her forehead with something icy. Then she mopped the blood away.

"Hold this for me," Fiana ordered. She thrust a mirror into Raena's hand. "Watch this." Raena saw her own reflection, scared, young, smeared with drying blood.

"You nearly lost an eye," Fiana said. "You're lucky." She forced the edges of the wound apart to clean them. Raena caught a queasy glimpse of something that made her think of cheese, yellowy white in the light of her mother's headlamp.

"That's what you are," Fiana said. "Just bones. You are dead. We all are. We're all dead and we don't have the sense to lie down and stop moving. That's what they'd like us to do. They'd like all humans to lie down and be dead. They'd like to grind us up and feed us to their young."

Fiana pinched the edges of the wound back together and jammed the needle through them. Raena winced, more from the sight of it than because it hurt. Whatever the numbing spray was, it worked well.

Fiana slapped her. "Don't you move," she whispered. "This is hard enough to do as it is. You watch what I'm doing so you can do it yourself next time and you won't have to wake me up."

So Raena lay perfectly still and watched her mother's hands. She disassociated herself from the sight and did not make a sound.

It wasn't the last wound Fiana gave her, but it was the last her mother patched for her.

Raena focused her thoughts outward again with a shuddering breath. The medical robot tilted a mirror for her. "What do you think? Good as new?"

Raena gazed at her reflection and saw someone she had never seen before. Her forehead was smoothed now. They'd replanted her eyebrow to cover the new skin. Above the cheekbones, her face was now symmetrical and even. She looked, she thought, more like Eilif than herself.

"It's perfect," Coni said from where she stood against the wall. "Are you happy?"

Raena smiled at her, grateful that the blue girl had stood vigil through the procedure. "It's exactly what I wanted. Thank you."

The tentacled nurse unfastened the restraints and helped Raena to her feet. "Since you paid in advance, you're all set."

Raena nodded. She wondered if the new flesh would begin to hurt once the anesthetic wore off. She wondered if she would have anything left to remind her of her mother, since she'd given the hologram medallion to Ariel.

She wasn't sure if her reflexes would be shaky after being knocked out, but everyone seemed to be busy resetting the surgery suite or chatting with Coni. She pulled her bulky coat on with a flourish, slipping the pouch of anesthetic into a pocket set inside her left sleeve.

Coni waited until they'd gotten several blocks away before she asked, "Why did you have to steal something from them?"

Raena gave her a slight smile. "Lots of reasons. Primarily because if we buy anything like this, there will be a paper trail. And questions. I don't know if it will be safe for Mellix, but we know it's safe for humans. If he can't use it, it may help me rest when I can't sleep. But mostly because I wanted to see if I still could. I survived for a lot of years by taking opportunities when I saw them."

Coni stared at her. "What if you'd been caught?"

"I've seen you break into office buildings on Kai to disrupt a corporate treasure hunt simply because you were bored. I know you can improvise an escape."

"I'm serious, Raena. It was a stupid risk to take. You've seen how they feel about humans here."

Perspective shifted for Raena and she understood that Coni was not upset by the illegality of the theft, but about the way it would reflect on all humans.

"I don't represent my whole species," Raena promised. "Most humans can't do what I do."

"Mykah would be the first to tell you that you can't afford to think like that." Coni didn't glance in Raena's direction as she said it. "No one here sees you as an individual. They only see you as a representative. That's why the galaxy is so obsessed with Thallian. His crimes weren't his alone. They reflect on all humanity."

"All right," Raena conceded. "I will be cautious. But you didn't bring me along on this adventure to behave. I'm here because I have a skill set none of the rest of you possesses. Still, I promise to do my best to see that none of us are shamed in the process."

Coni watched Raena surreptitiously reach into the collar of her sweater. What was she doing now? Coni watched Raena's shoulders relax for a moment. Then they reset, her posture straightening like a soldier's once more. What had she done?

Ah. Coni remembered when they'd landed on the Thallian home-world and found Raena bleeding heavily from the wound in her shoulder. Thallian had apparently shot her with a shock capsule. Now Raena was touching her scarred shoulder superstitiously, reaffirming her own identity. Coni realized that Raena had checked to make sure her other scars were still in place.

Coni had known about humans since her childhood. She remembered learning about the trials and the containment camps on the news. Most of all, she remembered the dirty, ragged refugee children, who had taken no part in the Empire but still suffered for its crimes. She had wanted to help humans since those images had burned themselves into her eyes.

But, she realized at last, she didn't know how to help Raena at all. She could give her a new life. She could give her a new identity. But she couldn't erase her past and heal the places where she was broken. Watching Raena touch her scars to comfort herself, Coni realized finally that the past, however painful it might have been, was as hard for humans to let go of as it was for everyone else.

CHAPTER 9

Raena followed Coni into a toy store, where the blue girl sent Haoun photos of different toys until they agreed on something his kids would like. Raena stuck close and kept her hands clasped conspicuously behind her back, where the sales clerk could see them.

Even so, the store's cameras buzzed around her anyway. She considered waiting outside, but she wasn't convinced that having a human loitering outside the shop would improve the clerk's mood.

The toy search seemed to be winding down when Raena's comm bracelet chirped. She did go outside then, to take Mykah's call.

"The packing is almost finished," he reported, "but there are a couple of pets we'll need to bring with us."

"Pets?" Raena echoed.

"He has a trio of kiisas. Harmless fuzz balls. I'm checking with the authorities to see if we can bring them as luggage or if they need to go up with the cargo."

"Can Vezali adapt a crate for them?"

"That's a good idea. Why don't you meet her?" He sent over a string of coordinates. "She's at one of the freight warehouses, inventorying the supplies we ordered."

"Will do."

Coni came out of the shop with a small shipping cube supported by a repulsor field. "Talking to Mykah?" she asked.

Raena held out her bracelet to display the warehouse address. "He wants us to meet Vezali here."

Coni slid her handheld out of her jacket pocket and entered the address. "Got it. It's out on the rim. We'll need to figure out the transit system."

Raena followed Vezali back into the warehouse. A small heap of shipping containers was stacked to one side.

"Mostly, they're upgrades to the *Veracity*'s cameras. Coni ordered them as soon as we knew we were coming. I've got some extra filters and couplings for the engine, so we'll have some spares. Then there are Haoun's larva snacks and Mykah's groceries. And the spacesuit you wanted. Didn't we already have one in your size?"

Raena laughed. "It smells like teenaged boy."

Vezali didn't know how to respond to that, so Raena saved her by asking, "How do we get it all back to the ship?"

"Once we know what our boarding window is, I'll arrange a delivery."

"And they're timely?"

"They'd better be. If we miss our exit, they pick up the fine. So it will be there when we're ready to go."

"Perfect. Can we pick up an extra packing crate? Mykah said we'll be bringing along three kiisas."

"Hope somebody remembered to order food and litter for them," Vezali chirped.

"I'll ask. I was hoping you could adapt a crate as a cage to get them onto the ship. Something large enough that they'll have room to roam around inside. It will have to be pressurized, just in case, and have atmosphere."

"I can do that. Let's go talk to the warehouse manager and see what they've got for sale."

Raena nodded. Pieces were falling into place. Now she just had to figure out how to get the package into the wrapping.

Mykah waited for them just outside an armed checkpoint. One of the soldiers compared Raena, then Coni, to images on his handheld, before waving them on.

"What's that all about?" Raena asked.

"After the museum was bombed, they evacuated this whole segment of the station until they could get Mellix's apartment emptied. So you were right: they were ready to pay what I asked to get the job done."

"And it helped that you were human," Coni guessed.

Mykah nodded.

"Why's that?" Raena asked.

"Because they know life is cheap to us," Mykah said. "We're crazy enough to take a job like this, under fire."

It was eerie walking through the vacated corridors. Raena had never been on a station that had been so quiet. "Where is everyone?"

"Temporary shelters."

That wasn't good. "How much packing is there left to do?" she asked.

"We're getting it done," he said. Raena wasn't sure who he meant, since she had been with Coni and she knew where Vezali and Haoun were supposed to have been.

Mykah led her and Coni to the correct apartment door. He laid his hand in the lock. The door chimed happily and opened for him.

"It's Mykah," he called. "I've brought the girls."

The room was a chaos of packing crates and stacks of books. Raena remembered books from her childhood, from when her mother worried that computers were coming to life and reading her thoughts and would try to erase all knowledge encoded electronically in order to protect themselves. Books were the only comfort she had then, since they would survive the information purge. Raena remembered books as being really heavy.

"Do we need to take all this stuff?" she asked.

"Will it all fit on the *Veracity*?" Coni wondered.

"It should fit," Mykah answered. "Haoun ran the calculations."

"How many trips up the elevator will it take?" Raena asked.

No one had an answer for that.

"You'll need to talk to the authorities again," Raena suggested. "Ask what the elevator's capacity is and have them estimate how long it will take to get all this stuff up to the ship. Ask them how long we'll have to wait for a window of time that large. Maybe it will be quicker for us—and safer for them, too, since Mellix's stuff won't be sitting in a warehouse they'll have to guard—if we can dock the ship against one of the station's maintenance hatches and load it directly. Since they've already got this area evacuated, they won't have to worry so much about the safety of anyone but us."

"I'll ask."

"We'll help with the packing," Coni said.

The creature that ambled out of the back room seemed similar to the sorts of animals Raena's childhood friends kept as pets. Those were descended from squirrels from Old Earth. Raena recognized him from the news broadcasts. The trouble they were in was worse than she'd thought, if Mellix was not as hidden as she'd been promised.

"Mellix," Mykah said, "this is Raena. She'll provide security for you until we can get you out of Capital City."

Mellix made a sweeping motion with his arms and bowed. Raena inclined her head to hide her smile.

"Are you armed?" the creature asked in Galactic Standard.

Barely, she thought, but she said, "Of course."

"I'd prefer to be protected without harming anyone else," he said.

"Define harm," Raena said. "You want them stopped, but not permanently disabled?"

"Well," Mellix said, one of his hands clutching the other. "Well, yes."

"I can do that if they're within arm's reach," Raena promised. "But I'm not magic."

"You'll just need to get me from here to the *Veracity*."

"I'm figuring out how to do that now," she answered. "Customs coming in didn't seem too bad."

"We had to submit everyone's passports before they let us enter the system," Coni said. "All that waiting while Mykah talked to the dockmaster was so they could compare the info they'd been given to the people standing around."

"So I passed."

"You did," Coni said neutrally.

"Thank you."

"My pleasure."

Raena directed her next question to Mellix. "If we get you to the elevator, will Emigration Control let you leave?"

"What do you mean? Why wouldn't they?"

"Things seem tense here. Lots of armed guards, all these evacuated apartments—is that a common thing on Capital City? My guess is that the government is feeling kind of like trapped rats. If anyone wants to come here and wipe out the bulk of the galactic government, now would be the time, while everyone's stuck here. Say, if you have a cruise ship that's suddenly grounded, full of potentially mutinous passengers demanding costly food and lodging until they can make other arrangements to get home. My point is: are you sure you have permission to leave before the attack comes down? Or do they want you to be here to share the general doom?"

"Cheerful, Mykah. I like her."

"Unfortunately, I'm serious," Raena said. "Is it that they've removed everyone around here for your protection—or to make you more of a target? Not only is everyone trapped on Capital City until they can arrange to leave, if they can afford to, but now they're stuffed into temporary shelters. It seems to me that people don't have much else to lose and nowhere else to focus their anger."

No one had an answer for her.

"What should we do?" Mykah asked.

"We need to get out of here as quickly as possible, whether we have official permission to go or not."

"Let me contact Control and see what they have to say," Mykah said. "If they're ready to expedite us out of here, that will tell us one thing. If there's a delay . . ."

Raena nodded. "Another question, first: How well are they scanning things going off-world?"

"You're thinking of smuggling me off?" Mellix asked.

"Is it beneath your dignity?" she asked.

"No, it's just . . . Not many people know this, but . . . I'm claustrophobic."

"I used to be, too," Raena admitted.

"How'd you get over it?"

"Jail time," she hedged. It was an easily caught contradiction to her new identity, but plenty of security operatives puffed up their resumés to add to their mystique. Combat experience, jail time, and military service were expected parts of the package. The contradiction wouldn't raise any eyebrows if discovered.

"Oh." Mellix glanced at Mykah, who shrugged.

"She's reformed," he promised. "You can trust her with your life. I trust her with mine."

Raena hadn't thought of it like that, but she supposed that was true every time they sparred.

As Coni settled in to pack up the rest of the things in the front room, Raena moved farther back into the apartment to see what else needed to come along.

She opened a door to what she assumed was a bedroom and something gray and ankle-high bounced out. It streaked under the spare crate lid resting against the wall. "What was that?"

"Steam," Mellix said from behind her. "One of my kiisas. They're upset by all this disruption."

Raena smiled at the vast understatement.

Mellix chuckled self-consciously. "Them and everyone else."

"How do you normally care for them when you travel?"

"My assistant stays here with them."

"Do they have a crate or anything?"

"They sleep on my bed," he said apologetically. "They were born here in Capital City. They've never known anywhere else."

"Vezali's already working on something safe for them to travel in," Raena assured. "She wanted me to make sure you had enough food and litter to keep them comfortable on the ship."

"I think so. Like everything else, those things are being rationed."

The gray blur crept back to rub against Mellix's ankles. He reached down to sweep it up into his arms. The creature was roughly the size of a sun melon, mostly round, with a long thin tail that ended in a tuft. Its eyes were round as polished silver coins. It snuggled against Mellix, taking visible pleasure as he petted it.

"I'm going to start packing in here," Raena said. "Come in and let me know if there's anything you'd like me to leave out."

At last, the packing seemed to be done. They had things they couldn't fit into the packing crates they had, things Mellix regretted leaving behind, but the job was as finished as it was likely to get.

"Why don't you ask Vezali to bring our supplies here?" Raena asked Mykah. "She can hire a robot to push the cart, if she needs to."

"Why?"

"We might as well have it all in one place, rather than some in the warehouse and some here. It will make it easier to be sure we get it all to the elevator at the same time."

"All right. I was going to invite her for dinner, anyway. Mellix has a bunch of perishables that we should eat up, rather than compost."

After he called Vezali, Mykah got busy in the kitchen.

Raena sat on the sofa beside Coni. She held out the pouch of anesthetic she'd stolen from the spa. "Could you research this for me?"

Coni nodded, but didn't take it from Raena's hand. Raena set it between them on the cushion.

"Where did you meet Mykah?" Mellix asked.

Raena was surprised Mykah hadn't told him before, but probably the journalist was simply making conversation, not fact checking. "On Kai," she answered, looking up to meet his eyes. "He'd organized a free-running game and invited me to play."

"Were you working on Kai, too, like Mykah and Coni?"

"No," she admitted. "I was there with some friends as a tourist."

"Pricy," Mellix said.

Raena laughed. "One of their fathers was an arms manufacturer back in the day. My friend sold the business to the Coalition and now she's retired."

"You don't mean Ariel Shaad, do you?"

Raena's skin prickled with a sudden chill. She kept her face neutral. "You know Ariel?"

"I know of her. One of my colleagues did a feature on her work with war orphans."

"Raena is one of the beneficiaries of her foundation," Coni supplied.

"She knew my mother, back before the War," Raena said with what sounded like perfect honesty. She was curious to know if he remembered that the "first" Raena Zacari had been a slave in Ariel's family, but he didn't mention it, so she didn't either.

They had eaten the stir-fry Mykah prepared and thrown away the dirty dishes by the time Mykah was finally summoned to escort Vezali past the checkpoint. When she arrived at Mellix's apartment, she was a furious flame orange like Raena had never seen her before.

"They confiscated our groceries," Mykah reported.

"What?" Coni snapped. "Why?"

"No food into the evacuated zone, they said," Vezali answered. "They scanned everything carefully, triple-checked my manifest . . . They even took Haoun's worms."

"I heard from Control, too, on the walk back." Mykah met Raena's eyes. "Two standard days until we can get a time slot on the elevator. They absolutely do not want us to dock the *Veracity* to the outside of the station."

"I thought they were in a hurry to be rid of me," Mellix said.

"Not if it's going to inconvenience anyone," Raena said.

"We saved you some dinner," Coni told Vezali, passing her a plate. "Come and sit down and relax."

"What are we going to do for two days?" Mykah asked.

Raena had an answer for that. "You're going to take Coni and Vezali and enjoy some shore leave. Stick together, though, in case they decide to bump up our exit."

"You're going to stay here with Mellix?"

"That's what you're paying me for," she reminded. She didn't say she would be more comfortable having only Mellix to protect. She could see, from the subtle nod Mykah gave her, that he understood that.

He took off his jacket and removed a disassembled Stinger from an interior pocket. As he handed Raena the pieces, she snapped it back together. "I thought you didn't like to carry firearms," she said.

"I don't. I know how quickly one would get turned on me. Doesn't mean I'm not licensed to have one."

Raena checked the charge. "Thanks, Mykah. I feel better now."

Coni changed the subject. "I don't know if this helps or not. This anesthetic is rated safe for humans, but it's got a salt in it that's poisonous to most other life."

"Where'd you get that?" Mykah asked.

"From the spa," Raena answered.

"You went to a spa?" Mykah asked, surprised. Raena laughed, but Coni swatted at him.

"Then maybe you don't need this now." Mykah went to retrieve his satchel from its place by the door. He came back to hand her a carafe of clear liquid.

"What is it?" Mellix asked.

"Sleep drops."

Coni typed that in, already researching it. She handed Raena the handheld, so she could read the entry. It was a street tranquilizer generally considered safe for most life forms.

Mykah said, "You want to start with one drop in a cup of water. It should conk you out for a couple of hours. See how you feel afterward and then you can judge if you want to up the dosage."

"Having trouble sleeping?" Mellix asked.

Raena nodded.

"I've used it sometimes, when I travel. It's very gentle."

"Do you think it would be too strong for the kiisas? They might be happier if they can sleep through the transfer to the *Veracity*."

Mellix nodded unhappily. "I know they won't like being in the crate."

"Let me show you what I brought," Vezali said as she set her plate aside. The animal crate was a wonder. It stood a good meter high and a meter and a half long, easily the biggest of the boxes they had to bring with them. It was fitted with a water bottle, a kibble dispenser, and an enclosed litter pan.

"It even has some gravity," Vezali said. "It's probably larger than your kiisas need, but it will give them some room to roll around in, if we get held up getting off the station."

"Why don't you get it stocked for them?" Raena suggested to Mellix. "We can leave the lid off, so they can get used to it."

Mellix bustled around, doing just that.

Mykah took Raena aside. "You're sure you don't want us to stay?"

She smiled at him. "It would be good to have you at my side," she said quietly, "but I don't want to have to worry about the girls. Go have fun. Keep to the tourist areas. Busy places. Don't get lured off to visit any hot new underground clubs."

Mykah laughed. "Understood."

"Maybe it's nothing," she added.

"I hope so."

After her crewmates had finally gotten themselves out the door, Raena opened the crate that had her name on it. It only held two things: her new, very black spacesuit and several rolls of black cloth.

"Mellix?" Can we gather all your crates together in here?"

"It's going to make this room pretty much impassable."

"We can leave a walkway. Let's just get things organized so the most crucial stuff is all together in a block. I'm going to slave-cloth it all together, so we won't lose anything."

"You're going to what? I haven't heard it called that in a long time."

"What do they normally call it?"

"Viridian cloth."

"But that's what the Viridians designed it for."

"I suppose you're right."

She could see him thinking, but she refused to back down. "We were talking about topics we could tackle, aboard the *Veracity*. The others said that slavery was too big a topic for us."

Mellix noted, "You sound angry about it."

"My mother was a slave," she said. "Before I was born."

Mellix said, "The sort of slave trade the Viridians engaged in is less prevalent now than it was in the past. But there are still mining prisons and indenture systems that are tantamount to slavery. It seems like a valid subject to explore."

"Thank you," Raena said simply. She hoped he could persuade Mykah.

They rearranged and stacked the crates until Raena had built a fairly solid wall across the front of the apartment. She left a narrow passageway: big enough for Coni to get through, she told Mellix. She didn't mention that it was narrow enough to be a choke point. If he understood what she was doing, he didn't question her.

"Where are we on the station?" Raena asked. "I got all turned around coming here past the checkpoint."

"They call this the Heights," Mellix said. "Before the evacuation, it was a professional neighborhood: doctors, network executives, lawyers, media personalities." He walked over to the wall and pressed a switch. The wall shivered upward to reveal the sky beyond. Starships glittered against the stars, in orbit around the station. One of the gates was visible in the distance.

"Is that a view screen?" Raena asked.

"No, that's the view. I'm on the outside edge of the station."

"It's lovely."

Mellix let the wall drop back into place. "I'll miss my view. I wonder if I'll ever come back here again."

"Any regrets?" she wondered.

"Of course not. The shipbuilding cartels knew about the tesseract flaw for years. They've been working in secret to figure out why every so often a ship is lost, but they weren't going to reveal the dangers because too much money was at stake. Someone had to let people know the risks they were unknowingly taking for someone else's profit. Someone had to do it, even if the personal cost was high."

Raena nodded to show she agreed, but she couldn't think of anything to say that wouldn't sound patronizing. Eventually, she settled on, "Is your assistant going to be safe?"

"She's out on assignment. The network sent her away before we broadcast the tesseract announcement, so she'd be disconnected from the news."

"Probably for the best." Raena let the silence stand briefly, then said, "You might as well try to sleep. I'll keep watch."

"Thank you for this," Mellix said. "I understand why Mykah is risking so much—and Coni. They're idealists. But you seem much more pragmatic."

"I suppose I am," Raena admitted. "But the *Veracity* took me in when I had nowhere else to go. They gave me a home. I owe them for that."

"Were you with them when they went to the Thallian homeworld?"

"Yes."

He waited a moment, but when she didn't say anything more, he smiled, revealing even white teeth. "I'm going to sleep better, knowing you're here."

The station was so silent around her that it was easy to believe it was deserted. Raena kept herself moving so that sleep couldn't settle on her. She gathered Revan's coat, Mykah's satchel, and the toys for Haoun's kids and tucked them into the crate with her spacesuit.

Then she used the rolls of slave cloth to wrap the stacks of crates into blocks. The kiisas watched her, but wouldn't let her get close enough to pet them.

Eventually, she got up to fix them a dish of water. She opened the carafe of sleeping drops, dripped a single droplet onto her gloved finger, and flicked it off into the sink. Then she swirled her finger in the water dish and set it on the floor.

She poured a glass of water and put two small drops into it. That she carried into Mellix's room. She left it on the stack of books abandoned beside the bed.

When she came back out, the kiisas were tumbled over on the floor like balls of fluff. She picked them up one at time to check their breathing. Each one seemed softer than the next, like some kind of creature out of a children's story. Raena held the last one to her cheek, then tucked it gently beside the others inside their crate. She set the beacon on Coni's handheld and stood it up on its edge, so she could clip it to the side of the crate. Then she rested the lid over it, leaving it slightly askew so the kiisas could breathe.

It was late now. Raena stepped out of her high-heeled boots and put them in the crate with her crewmates' treasures. Then she shimmied into her beautiful new spacesuit, checking all the seals as she went. Once she had the boots clipped on, she messaged Haoun, just to have some company.

"Lonely?" she asked.

"Surprisingly."

"Where are you out there?"

"I'm out near the Berryessa Gate, bored out of my mind. There are only so many levels of Black Hole I can play."

Raena didn't know what that was, but she did sympathize. "Can you lock onto my signal and find me on the station? I'm curious what the place looks like from the outside."

"Flight Control probably won't like it, but sure. Let me come around." He fell silent while he eased the *Veracity* out of its parking place near the gate. Finally, he asked, "What's going on down there?"

"It's really quiet. Mykah and the girls have gone dancing."

Haoun cut across her. "No, there's a crew outside the station. It's too many for a repair crew, unless they're doing a massive overhaul. They're headed your way."

"How many?"

"Looks like thirteen. Some of them have pulse rifles slung over their backs."

Raena went back for Mykah's Stinger, which she'd left on the sofa. She pulled out one of the spacesuit's tethers and tied it to the gun, which she tucked into the back of her belt.

"How far away are they, Haoun?"

"They're almost on top of you. I'm coming! I think I can get a clear shot . . ."

"Absolutely not," Raena snapped. "Under no circumstances fire anywhere near the station."

"What do you want me to do?" he asked more soberly.

"Message Mykah. Tell him to get the girls to the elevator vestibule and stay there. I'm out for now." She switched the comm bracelet off, peeled it from her wrist, and wrapped it around her belt.

Pulling the spacesuit's gloves on, she went to wake Mellix.

She touched the journalist's shoulder. "Get up," she said quietly. "Trouble's on its way."

Mellix slung the covers back and sat up. "I don't have a spacesuit," he protested.

"You won't need one." She handed him the glass of water from the stack of books. He drank it without question. Raena took his compliance as a token of his faith in Mykah.

"Where are the kiisas?" he asked, his voice loud in the quiet darkness.

"Already packed up," Raena promised.

He finished the glass of water, handed it back to her empty. She could see his eyes already glazing over. He snuggled back into bed.

"Oh, no, you don't." Raena picked him up and carried him back into the front room. She nudged back the lid to the kiisas' crate and settled Mellix down amongst his pets. He mumbled something in protest, but she ignored him. She latched the lid down and switched on the crate's atmosphere and gravity. All the telltales blinked a happy blue. She grabbed a roll of slave cloth and muffled the lights.

Time to move fast. She pulled the spacesuit's helmet on over her head, latched it, and switched on its heads-up displays. She double-checked all the seals and toggled on the pressurization. Then she clambered up atop one of the stacks of crates. The gap between the top crate and the ceiling wasn't large enough for her to sit up in. Good thing she wasn't claustrophobic any longer.

She switched on the mask that canceled out the hiss of her breathing, so that all she could hear was the steady, solid thump of her heart. Once she was settled, she threw a book at the wall control, so she could admire the view.

She hit the wall control on the first try. The guy setting the charge outside the window jumped back when the window screen went up in front of him. He lost his purchase on the station. Lucky for him, he was tethered to the next guy in line.

That struck Raena as a good idea. Moving slowly, she unzipped another of her suit's tethers and fastened it to the box she lay atop.

An impressive number of rifles were trained on the window. Raena wasn't sure if they could see in, but she was comfortable where she was. Eventually everyone outside relaxed and stepped back into place. They reeled the initial bomber back in and he got back to work.

There seemed to be an exorbitant number of charges, Raena thought. If they were terrorists, laying down terrorist-sized explosives, this whole side of the station would be rubble, including the honor guard outside. That suggested that instead these were professionals, setting up tiny charges: enough to pop open the window while doing minimal damage to the expensive real estate nearby. Raena wondered if someone had already closed the blast doors around Mellix's apartment, sealing them in.

The pest control crew seemed unnecessarily large to capture one pacifist squirrel. Even if they were armed to take down two humans, Coni, and Vezali as well, they were still massively overstaffed. Either they didn't know the kids had gone clubbing, or they thought that Vezali's crates had been full of weapons. Either option pointed suspicion away from Capital City's Security Force. Raena breathed deep in relief. Her borrowed Stinger wasn't going to fend off the station's private army.

The crew outside all stepped away from the window. Raena spread out to hug the crate beneath her, trying to relax.

The window popped. Everything in the room got sucked out into space. There was a chaos of klaxons and debris and flashing red lights. Showtime.

Raena waited until the boxes she was strapped to rotated. Half the team had gone into the apartment. The other half waited outside, rifles at the ready. The demolition crew was already packing up their equipment and getting ready to walk back to the maintenance hatch where they'd come out of the station.

She was moving away from them fast, but it didn't take long for them to establish that the apartment was unoccupied. She watched the helmets turn in her direction.

The Stinger was a sporting weapon, meant for hunting in atmosphere. It would fire in space, but its range was limited. She waited for them to come to her. Once she began to fire, she would have no cover.

Ten soldiers. She counted them down, firing at rocket packs, guns, boots. These were just guys, doing a job. No need to kill them, if she could dissuade them. Besides, Mellix hadn't wanted her to do them any permanent damage.

Unfortunately, her initial judgment had been correct. These were professionals. Those that could returned fire.

Raena flung herself forward, changing the momentum of the crates she was strapped to. The whole set of them started to tumble.

She got the Stinger up and ready, because when the boxes came around, she really was going to have nowhere to hide.

Someone landed on the other side of the pallet. She couldn't hear him, but she felt the crates begin to spin a different way. She was ready when his helmet popped up over the edge of the crates. Too bad he wasn't.

She made a grab at his rifle, but it was tethered to his arm and she didn't have time to cut it loose before the rest of the team came at her.

Two of them fired on the crates, but missed her. She puzzled over that, then realized her matte black suit must be hard to see against the black slave cloth. They should have waited until she came around to face the lights of the station. By the time the third one figured out where she was, it was too late. He was too close for her to miss.

The last one had lost his weapon. The scorch where she'd hit it smudged the front of his armor.

She got the knife out of the top of her left boot. When he swung for her, she slashed his glove.

The low-tech attack caught him entirely by surprise. She pushed him away with her feet as he struggled to seal his suit with his off hand.

When the crates tumbled over again, Raena saw the *Veracity* swooping toward her. Haoun was aiming the cargo door toward her.

Raena scrambled to unhook her tethers so she wouldn't be crushed beneath the pallet when it landed on the *Veracity*'s deck.

CHAPTER 10

Mykah glanced down at the comm bracelet on his wrist. "Trouble," it read. "Wait in the elevator vestibule."

Coni was standing in line at the bartending machines, waiting to get them some drinks. Vezali was out on the dance floor somewhere. As Mykah stood to look for them, he saw Coni's head turn his way and knew she'd gotten the message, too. Vezali stretched two of her tentacles up to the lighting rig above the dancers in the low-ceilinged room and swung herself out of the crowd, to applause and a roar of approval from below.

"Are they okay?" Vezali asked when she reached him.

"We know Raena knows what she's doing, so we'll have to trust she has it handled," Mykah said.

"Either she had some warning or it's already over," Coni pointed out. "The message came from Haoun."

They edged their way through the packed club toward the corridor outside. Clubs, bars, and restaurants filled this part of the station, one up against the next. People desperate for a good time jammed the walkway.

"How do we get to the elevator?" Vezali asked.

"I left my handheld with Raena," Coni said.

"There's a transit hub up the way. Climb on," Mykah told Vezali. She wrapped enough of her tentacles around his torso that she could hold on. The other tentacles she curled into little spirals that she held close to her body. Vezali hid her eye against his shoulder. She seemed to weigh almost nothing.

Mykah launched himself sideways up a storefront, grabbed a railing, flung himself forward, kept moving. He'd missed this. Capital City didn't have the intoxicating heights he'd enjoyed free-running on Kai, but it had plenty of interesting things to catch hold of or jump off of. He didn't look behind, knowing Coni would keep up.

The metro platform bustled with revelers heading home. Unfortunately, once Mykah, Coni, and Vezali got onto the train, it emptied out as it drew nearer and nearer the elevator. Mykah wasn't liking the quiet, but he wasn't sure what else they could have done. They couldn't have run the whole way; taking a cab seemed like putting too much faith in a stranger. Mykah was pretty sure Raena wouldn't have done that, but he couldn't guess what she would have done.

When the train reached the terminal station, the three of them were the only people to get out. Mykah waited for the attack to come down as they passed through the echoing station, but no one accosted them.

Faced with the empty plaza outside the elevator's waiting area, Mykah realized he had no idea what to say to the guards. He couldn't very well admit that they had an exit window in two days' time and just planned to hang around until then. He wished Haoun—or Raena—had given them more direction.

Three Dagat—Vezali's people—flowed toward them across the plaza. "I told my siblings why we'd come to Capital City," Vezali explained. "Vezari is the Planetary Consul for our homeworld."

Once they got closer, one of the Dagat said in a high-pitched girlish voice, "We came as soon as we heard."

"Heard what?" Vezali asked.

"There was an explosion at Mellix's apartment in the Heights," another said.

"Oh, no," Coni said.

"Anyone hurt?" Mykah asked.

"They haven't said yet. It may have been an accident. Security hasn't blamed terrorists so far."

Coni took Mykah's hand, but didn't say anything.

Vezali introduced her siblings, but their names all sounded so similar it was difficult for Mykah to pick up the nuances.

"How did you know to come here to meet us?" Mykah asked.

"We have been monitoring our sibling to ensure zir safety."

"When you are arrested," another of them said, "we will go with you."

"Will we be arrested?" Coni asked.

"Assuredly. It is this local government's practice to blame, rather than take responsibility. If the explosion was not caused by terrorists attacking Capital City, then there is a fault in the design of the station. People are already very close to panic. Terrorists are less frightening than the station falling apart around us, because terrorists can be caught."

And who better to blame than a human, Mykah thought. He hoped Raena had gotten out safely.

Raena picked herself up off the *Veracity*'s deck and began tethering the pallet down. Haoun commed back, "All right in there?"

She ran through the switches in the unfamiliar suit until she found one that let her respond. "Thank you. I'm good. Can you find the pallet outside that contains Coni's handheld? I set its beacon for you."

"Got it locked. I can get over to it, but you're gonna have to get out there with a jet pack and push it in."

"I can do that." She found the correct locker and pulled the jet pack out.

As she was shouldering into it, Haoun added, "We're in trouble. They're threatening to scramble fighters unless we move away from the station."

"We need that pallet. Get us over to it, then stand down. We need to get Mellix onboard to sort this out."

"All right. It's coming in slightly above us."

Raena blasted out to get it. She got it turned and aimed toward the ship, tucking it inside like a ball into a pocket. She tethered it, then closed the hatch. The other two pallets would have to wait.

As soon as the atmosphere had settled, she pulled off her helmet and drew a deep breath.

"They're coming," Haoun warned.

"Stand down," Raena repeated. She opened the crate with Mellix and the kiisas. "Wake up, Sleeping Beauty," she told him, helping him to sit up.

"Where . . . ?"

"You're on the *Veracity*," she said. "We're in trouble again. The air force is on its way to accuse us of attacking Capital City."

Mellix rubbed his face with his paws. He looked faintly ridiculous in his pale blue pajamas, but Raena didn't point that out. After an enormous yawn, he asked, "I assume you have video of what really happened?"

"Haoun?" she said into the air.

"Yes," he answered over the comm. "I haven't played it back yet, but the cameras did record something."

"Good," Mellix said. "Can you put me through to Station Security?"

Raena guided him to stand in front of a screen. As Haoun made the connection, Raena leaned back against the wall beside Mellix: out of view, she hoped. He nodded like he understood her. She guessed he must be well used to dealing with shadowy figures.

"Mellix!"

"Good to see you, Commander," Mellix answered.

"What happened? There was an explosion in your apartment."

"We're sending over the video now," he said. As Haoun complied, Mellix watched it for the first time himself. "As you can see, a team of assassins attacked my apartment. Luckily, I was prepared for them. I'm now aboard the ship you arranged to remove my things from Capital City. We are in the process of collecting my possessions."

"Were," Haoun corrected over the comm. "We're surrounded by fighters now."

"Commander?" Mellix asked.

One of the kiisas bounced over, leaping up into Mellix's arms. Raena fought not to laugh. He stroked it calmly, completely at ease as he stared at the screen.

"You're safe?" the station commander asked.

"Yes. Now I'd like to collect the rest of my things and get out of your way."

"I'd like nothing more," the commander assured. "However, we have the movers who packed your things in custody."

"Whatever for?"

"They are being charged with planting the bomb that destroyed your apartment and damaged Capital City."

"You can see that they were not responsible," Mellix argued.

"We're investigating . . ."

Mellix's good-natured voice turned steely. "Of course, they will be released, all charges dropped, and escorted to the elevator for the next available window out. Or, you understand, everyone will see that they were not responsible for the damage to Capital City and there will be accusations that Station Security is not adequate to its task, in addition to allegations of a cover-up."

Raena was impressed by how easily the threat left Mellix's lips. She'd seen the companies and governments he'd faced down in the past, but now she could reconcile the amiable squirrel with the fiery journalist.

"I will confer with Elevator Security and Flight Control and find out what your window at the elevator will be."

"Thank you, Commander. In the meantime, can we continue to retrieve my possessions before they all float away into space?"

"Go ahead," the commander said. "Just be cautious flying so close to the station."

After the connection was severed, Haoun huffed, "Cautious? I was born cautious."

Raena laughed at him. But before Mellix could turn away, she said, "Thank you for keeping me out of trouble."

Mellix swept forward and pulled her into a hug. "Thank you for saving my life. Goodness. I can't believe anyone would send so many soldiers against me."

One of the kiisas launched itself at Raena. She caught it, fumbling just a little. It was buzzing as it snuggled up against her.

"Just doing my job," she assured. "Can you collect up the kiisas and clear the hold? I'll go out and gather up the rest of your boxes so we can go rescue my crew."

Raena didn't mean to fall asleep, but after she'd stowed away all of Mellix's crates, she made the mistake of sitting down in the lounge. Apparently, that was all it took.

She was a teenager, not yet fifteen. She was traveling with Ariel and her father on a sales call to Nyx. The girls spent the day shopping, Ariel's favorite pastime, looking for jet bike helmets in a mall near the city center. Ariel wanted a night-vision helmet, but it had to be stylish without being silly. That was proving to be a tall order.

Dissatisfied, they had returned to the street, headed to retrieve their rented jet bikes. Without warning, the sky platform overhead exploded. Bodies and debris rained down.

Raena dodged right as large pieces of the platform crashed onto the mall behind them. The skyscraper collapsed, spilling shattered masonry into the street. In the dusty chaos that followed, Ariel got separated from Raena.

From her hiding place, Raena watched Ariel mount up on the surviving jet bike. Ariel raced off without a look behind. Her father had been supposed to be on that platform, meeting with city fathers and an Imperial delegation. Ariel must be confirming that he had escaped the destruction.

Raena's first thought was relief that Ariel was safe. She started to jog after her mistress, then halted abruptly. She'd been left behind, abandoned like a broken toy. Ariel didn't know if she was alive or dead, but her priority had been her father, not her slave.

On Nyx, slavery had been outlawed. In order for Ariel's dad to bring Raena along to guard Ariel, he'd had to register Raena as a bodyguard instead of a possession. He'd taken off her collar. If she stayed here, no one owned her. No one could. She could only be hired, not purchased.

Free.

She'd be able to choose her own work. All she needed to do was to hide until the Shaad family returned to Callixtos without her.

The realization was so overwhelming that Raena felt lightheaded. Oblivious to the screaming and chaos around her, she sank down on a broken hunk of skyscraper to absorb her good fortune and decide how to celebrate.

A bearded old man appeared, climbing over the broken building down the street. He called her name.

Raena froze where she sat, certain that if she moved, he would see her. She stared hard at him, trying to figure out who he was, but nothing about him—from his tangled white beard to his spotted bald head— looked the least bit familiar.

As if he felt her gaze on him, his face swiveled her way. Raena watched his eyes lock onto her. A smile split his face. He looked like Death to her.

She raised her left hand to wave at him.

When he waved back, she shot him in the chest and knocked him back off the pile of rubble.

Raena opened her eyes, rubbing at the headache lodged over her right temple. Enough with the shooting Gavin dead, already. Now that she was awake, she knew that was who the old man in the dream had represented.

Enough dreams. Enough death. She had more pressing concerns now. She pushed herself up off the banquette and crossed to the comm. "What's the status, Haoun?"

"We're docked at the elevator, waiting for the crew to come up. There will be a slight delay before we can take off. Apparently some lunkhead confiscated Mykah's groceries, so they're having to find us replacements."

"Thanks to Mellix," Raena guessed.

"Exactly."

She smiled, then changed the subject. "I didn't get any chance to enjoy the view earlier, when I was working outside. Do I have time to go out for a little walk?"

"Don't see why not. I'll let you know when it's time to go."

Raena retrieved her new spacesuit from her cabin and climbed back into it. She eased the gloves on as she walked to the airlock.

It had been a while since she'd felt the need to get out for a space-walk. Now, with Mellix aboard, the *Veracity* felt claustrophobic. She *had* to get out.

Not that the journalist had been the least bit unfriendly. If anything, he'd been too friendly. The last thing Raena wanted was to be friends with anyone who asked questions for a living.

She knew she could lie persuasively. She'd spent a great deal of her life doing just that: protecting her mother, placating Ariel's father, pleasing Thallian. It was exhausting, all that lying.

She stepped into the airlock and closed the hatch behind her, waiting for the air to vent back into the ship before she opened the outer hatch. This hatch faced away from the station, out into space. The stars overhead twinkled in the blackness, their lights disrupted by the *Veracity's* energy shields.

It was so lovely out here. She masked the hiss of her breathing, then cancelled out the beating of her heart. Blessed silence enfolded her.

Raena closed the outer hatch and moved away from it. Her magnetic boots connected solidly to the *Veracity's* hull so that her hands could drift free. She felt tension evaporating from her. Too bad she couldn't just stay out here in the quiet all the time.

She sat on the hull and clipped herself down with a second tether. The stars drew her gaze.

When she and Ariel were teenagers, they used to play a game with Ariel's friends that they called Kill by Numbers. It was kind of like tag, but played in the target range. Everyone chose weapons from Ariel's father's shop, locked them on stun, then entered the range. The computer assigned each player a number—and a numbered player they were supposed to "kill." Every time someone was eliminated from play, the numbers scrambled and you got a new target. When you played the game, alliances were temporary. Truces were fleeting. The only way to end the game was to be the last person standing.

Once the game had come down to Ariel and Raena, the last two players left. Ariel tried to boss the computer, order it to end the game and let them out. Instead, the computer mobilized drones to come after them.

Ariel fired until she'd drained her gun, but there were too many drones for her to take them all down. Worst of all, the drone shots stung. Ariel was crying in anger and frustration as much as in pain when Raena turned her own gun on herself. Unfortunately, the computer didn't accept that. You couldn't win by giving up.

In the end, she'd crawled over and shot Ariel point-blank.

Afterward, Ariel told her not to worry about it, that it was only a game, but Raena never played again. She knew that, when it came down to it, there were always only two choices: suicide or murder.

These dreams with Gavin reminded her of Kill By Numbers. No matter when he turned up or what he looked like, she had his number. He had to die.

She sat for a moment longer, wondering whom she had to kill to make the nightmares stop. Killing Gavin over and over in her dreams hadn't given her any peace.

No answer presented itself. All right then, she told herself, back to work. She pulled Coni's handheld from the thigh pocket of her spacesuit and began scanning the hull. For all she knew, Mellix's assassins had had the presence of mind to bug the *Veracity* when they saw it come to the rescue. She wanted to be certain that no one would follow, wherever the *Veracity* headed next.

The others were in high spirits when she came in from her walk. They were so giddy that she wondered if they'd ever been arrested before. The volume and excitement were enough to make her really feel the difference between her age and theirs.

She cautioned them to check everything they brought on board for tracking devices: "To make sure no one is following Mellix," she said. That was enough to make them eager and cautious.

While they were busy, she slipped away to her cabin.

Some time later, Mykah tapped on her door. Raena looked up from the computer, where she had been trying to sort out her memories. She knew she couldn't have shot Gavin on Nyx—that just didn't make sense—but the dream seemed as certain as any of her memories now.

Grimacing, she forced herself to stand up, stroke her hair up into its staticky splendor, and answer the door.

"We're getting everything unpacked and put away, but I thought you would want this sooner rather than later." Mykah handed her the small glass carafe of sleep drops.

Raena felt lightheaded from relief. "What do I owe you?"

"I paid for it out of the fund for ship stores. You're covered."

"Thank you. Really. Thank you. Do you need me for anything now?" She cradled the flask delicately in her hands. "I might just take a nap."

"How long have you been up?"

"I dozed off for a moment, but other than that, since just before we originally docked at Capital City. I've lost track of how many hours that's been."

"Too long." Mykah stretched. "I caught a nap while we were in station custody, but I'm headed to bed before too much longer, too. I just wanted you to know that we haven't found any sort of trackers yet."

"Good. No harm in being paranoid, though."

"Mellix agrees. He thanks you for thinking of it. He says I ought to double your share of his network's reward to us. He thinks you've more than earned it."

Raena shook her head. "I'm glad for the work. Buy me more apples and I'll be fine."

Mykah laughed at her. "I'll make us a victory feast, after we all get some sleep."

"Perfect." Raena would have said her voice positively chirped. "Sweet dreams," she added belatedly.

"Not a problem." Mykah waved and headed off down the corridor.

Raena locked the door behind him. She found a cup in the locker by the sink and poured herself a drink of water. She had a sip, just to fortify herself, then twisted open the flask. Beneath its cap, the bottle was designed to dispense the drug a single drop at a time. You'd have to break the top off if you wanted to get a really good gulp of it.

She dripped a scant amount into her water, raised the cup to her lips, and tested the first mouthful. It tasted like shipboard water, slightly metallic, with a comforting tang of disinfectant. If she were honest with herself, she felt so greedy for a solid uninterrupted sleep that she was fully and completely willing to risk anything that might happen to her after taking an unknown drug. It couldn't be worse than being slowly driven mad by insomnia and hallucinations. She knocked the water back in one long swallow, rinsed the cup, and hung it on a hook to dry.

She dimmed the lights and undressed. She debated a shower, but decided she didn't want to sleep—try to sleep, anyway—with wet hair. She slid under her coverlet, curled around the pillow, and closed her eyes.

It took a little while for the drops to take effect. She supposed it was no surprise it didn't hit her as hard or fast as it had taken Mellix and the kiisas, but she was still disappointed. Raena tamped down on the desire to get up and have another dose. She forced herself to lie there, to concentrate on her breathing. She counted the regular deep breaths flowing in and out as a way to lull her mind.

While she fretted, sleep crept gently over her and dragged her down.

Raena sought Vezali out, just to have some company. She found the girl in the lounge, sitting on the floor in front of the screen. She had something disassembled in front of her, pieces spread out on the floor, like with like, emanating out from her in lines like rays.

"What are you watching?" Raena asked.

"Just the news. You want it off?"

"No, that's okay." Raena sank onto the banquette behind her, trying to puzzle out what the news was about.

Two Templars were standing in the Council of Worlds, addressing the assembly. Raena read the transcript below the screen, trying to make sense of it, since she'd come in the middle. Why was this twenty-year-old foot-age being shown now?

The Templars were droning on about some trade initiative. The cameras, apparently also bored, roamed through the audience, look-ing for reactions. Once again, Raena marveled at the variety of life forms in the galaxy. In her little shipboard cocoon, it was easy to for-get that the ratio on the Veracity—*two humans to three others—was rare in the galaxy.*

The camera didn't come across a single human face in all the Council of Worlds. Raena was about to ask about that—she'd thought that human-ity always had some delegates—when the date of the recording flashed across the screen. The vote had been taken earlier today.

Raena felt the world twist suddenly and was grateful she was already sitting down. How had she not known some Templars survived the plague? She had believed that the devastation was total and therefore totally unforgivable.

The video cut to a Templar shipyard. The insectile creatures crawled all over one of their massive stone ships, performing their inexplicable tasks. Two Templars met, embraced each other with their forelegs, caressing each other's faces with their antennae.

Raena closed her eyes. Was this a dream? All the other hallucinations had been moments in her own life. This was different altogether.

Something had changed. If the plague hadn't succeeded, had it even been spread? Or manufactured? Maybe it had never been conceived of? Maybe Thallian hadn't been cloned or the Emperor had been assassi-nated or the galaxy had become aware of humanity's ambitions before they posed any threat . . .

If there had never been Thallian to take her away from Ariel, had she followed her mistress into working for the Coalition? If she'd never been imprisoned, she'd never been on the run, she'd never done any of the things that troubled her dreams . . .

Who was she?

Raena felt darkness closing in around her as her mind struggled to comprehend this strange new world. Was this a place where she would want to live? What was her role here? Had this timeline always existed or had it just come into being when she noticed it? How had she crossed from the other world into this one?

"You look rough," Ariel said cheerfully, planting a kiss atop Raena's head.

Raena stared at her. Nearly thirty years after they'd met, Ariel remained stunning: graying blond hair still pulled back in a long braid to emphasize her cheekbones, blouse unbuttoned far enough to showcase the upper curve of her breasts. She'd always liked her clothes tight enough not to get in her way if she got into a fight. With Ariel's short fuse, a fight had rarely been far out of reach.

Raena felt herself starting to slip away, drowned by the novelty of everything. Her panicked gaze caught back on the screen.

There stood someone else she remembered. Take away the crumpled rust-colored suit and clean him up, but that was Outrider, the Messiah dealer she'd met through Gavin on Nizarrh. He hadn't aged a day. "Who is that?" Raena gasped.

"He's the prime minister," Vezali said, like it should have been obvious.

The shock pitched Raena out of the dream. She woke in her cabin, face down across her bunk. She sat up, gasping, and raked her fingers through her hair.

Where had Gavin been this time? Raena wondered what he had done to make her life—the galaxy's life—so radically different.

She bent forward, elbows on her knees. Why was she blaming Gavin suddenly? Maybe, if she'd waited longer, he would have followed Ariel into the lounge, given them both a squeeze, and Raena would still have found cause to shoot his head off.

She laughed, but the sound scared her.

She flung herself off the bunk and paced the small room. Whatever was going wrong with her was getting more elaborate.

Tears prickled her eyes, but she scrubbed them away. No sense in getting attached to any of these hallucinations. It wasn't like she could choose to remain there, as if some imaginary world could become a new real life for her. Once she started to think that any make-believe place could provide a haven, she was in deep, dark trouble.

She stepped through her door and moved through the silent ship. It must be night, she decided. Everyone was in their cabins asleep. For confirmation, she heard the whistle of Haoun's snoring through the bulkhead outside his room.

Once again Raena felt like she was the only person awake and alive in the universe.

She craved the feeling of Ariel's arms around her. Maybe it was time to break down and actually contact her sister.

Ariel picked up immediately, as if she'd been awaiting Raena's call. Raena wondered what time it was on Callixtos. Ariel was already braiding her hair for the day.

"You look rough," Ariel said by way of hello.

A shiver crawled up Raena's spine, but she laughed. "Can't sleep. Bad dreams."

"You, too?" Ariel sighed. "You're not dreaming about . . ." Her voice faltered at the name.

"Thallian? No." Raena realized she hadn't even thought about the fact that her former boss had been mostly absent from her nightmares. That was kind of surprising, really. If anyone's ghost could be expected to disturb her sleep, it should have been Jonan Thallian.

Before her mind wandered too far, Raena said, "I dreamed about you just now."

"A nightmare?"

"Only after I woke up." Raena smiled and told part of the truth. "It made me miss you."

Ariel smiled back. In her face, Raena saw the girl she'd fallen in love with all those many years ago. "I miss you, too," Ariel said. "You wanna come home?"

Raena shook her head. "Not yet." She paused for a breath, then plunged onward before she lost her nerve. "In my dream, the Templar plague never happened. They were still running trade in the galaxy."

Ariel's blond brows drew together. "I had a dream like that, too," she said slowly, trying to piece it together. "Only it wasn't a nightmare. It was kind of nice." She laughed a little. "I wouldn't have needed to adopt all my kids if the galaxy hadn't orphaned so many humans."

Raena let the silence spread, hoping Ariel would remember more.

"I had a ship," Ariel said slowly, trying to pull the dream images together in her memory. "All my crew were nonhumans."

"I dreamed about your ship, too," Raena said. "You had a girl in your crew. Her skin was kind of pinkish green and she had a bunch of tentacles."

"That's weird," Ariel said, gaze suddenly focused on Raena. "I dreamed about Vezali, too."

Oh, that was right. Raena remembered now. Ariel met the *Veracity*'s crew when they delivered Eilif to her. Although Raena was frustrated by the memory lapse, she didn't allow herself to get distracted from the dream.

"Vezali was sitting in the lounge," Raena said. "She'd taken apart some kind of machine. In the dream, I thought it was some kind of clock."

Ariel watched her closely now, hazel eyes wide in shock and recognition.

"You came into the lounge and kissed me on the top of the head and said . . ."

"You look rough," Ariel said. "That's fucked up, Raena. How did you know that? You scare me when you do this bullshit."

"It's not me," Raena promised. She hoped Ariel could hear the truth and despair in her voice. "I've been having these dreams a lot. They're completely freaking me out."

She waited for Ariel to echo her, but she didn't. Maybe she wasn't having a lot of weird dreams—only this one.

Ariel asked, "Are you dreaming about me very often?"

"Just a couple of times. I dreamed we were on Kai, shopping in the souk, and there were two . . ."

Ariel cut her off. "Two Gavins. One of them shot you with a little silver dart."

"And I dreamed about when we escaped from the *Arbiter*. Only . . ."

"Only there was a man who said he was a Coalition spy. That was Gavin, too." Ariel rummaged around on her desk and came up with a spice stick, which she lit. "In the dream, after you went to find the shower, I rolled the corpse over with my boot. I recognized Gavin."

"I've dreamed about him two or three times a night for the last week," Raena said. "He doesn't stand a chance." She sobered suddenly. "That's what's so horrible about it. I don't recognize him in the dreams and—"

"And you kill him?"

"Over and over and over."

"Can't think of anyone still alive who deserves it more."

"Like I said," Raena repeated, "it's freaking me out. I don't have anything against Gavin, really. I just don't want to be with him. I still sort of feel like, on some level, I owe him for my freedom." She nodded toward the spice stick in Ariel's hand. "Wish I had one of those."

"I should quit," Ariel said. She took another drag. "I should quit again," she corrected.

"You need old friends not to call you up in the middle of the night," Raena said, meaning it as an apology.

"No, I'm glad you called. Now I know not to worry about you."

Raena didn't disagree aloud, but she also didn't admit how worried she was. She took the liberty to change the subject. "You don't hear from Gavin, do you?"

"I'd say he wouldn't dare, but this *is* Gavin we're talking about. He'd dare just about any damn thing he wanted." Ariel sighed. "He hit me, after you lit out after Thallian. Luckily, Tarik had loaned me his gun, or I would've been in for a hell of a beating. As it was, I had to stun Gavin. On my *own* ship. After that, Tarik and I put Gavin out on the first populated rock we passed. Gavin went back to Kai and attacked the men Thallian's son left behind there. Kai Planetary Security called me, wanting me to pay his bail."

"And you refused politely," Raena guessed.

"Yeah, something like that. I'm pretty sure he got out anyway, though. A couple of weeks ago, someone was sneaking around here. I don't have any evidence one way or another, but I thought it was probably Gavin, coming here looking for you. That's been a while, though."

"I'm not sure I want to speak to him, anyway," Raena said. "I just want him out of my dreams."

"This is crazy, but . . . Do you get the sense that he's trying to contact you?"

Raena thought about it, then shook her head. "I don't get the feeling it's about me at all. You know how I was when I was on the run. That's what I've been dreaming about, mostly. Gavin just shows up in my dreams, and it's bang, bolt in the head. It's like some crazy kids' cartoon."

"You don't have to shoot me now," Ariel supplied.

"Wait'll you get home," Raena finished. "Yeah, that's it exactly. I just want to switch the channel off. No more shooting people I know while I sleep."

"I like this plan." Ariel crushed out the last of her spice. "Can I call and check up on you?" she asked cautiously. "Tell me if that's too much."

"No, I'd like that." Raena felt sure Ariel wouldn't abuse the privilege. "I'm just not ready to come see you yet."

"Okay. Let me know." Ariel's expression changed and she squinted at the screen. "You had your scar removed!"

"Yeah. It tied me down to my former life," Raena said. She'd forgotten it was gone. She reached up, touched her unmarred forehead. "What do you think?"

"Should've been done a long time ago," Ariel said honestly. "Did you have them all removed?"

Raena laughed. "My scars are my armor."

"So I've heard you say."

Raena picked up the photo beside her screen. "One last thing before I let you go. Is Eilif still with you?"

Thallian's wife had reminded Raena a lot of herself, of how her life might have been if she hadn't escaped him. She felt tangentially responsible for the way the woman's life had turned out, since she— all of them, really, even Eilif herself—understood that Thallian chose Eilif as a poor substitute for Raena.

"She is," Ariel said, brightening. "She's helping with my foundation, finding families for orphaned humans. She is amazing with the kids."

Surprised and pleased, Raena interrupted. "Really?"

"Really. Apparently, that connection is something she's always craved, but was never allowed to express before."

"Go figure." Raena thought of the cloned boys who had considered Eilif their mother and had an inkling of how lonely her life must have been. "Thank you again for taking her in for me."

"It's been a pleasure," Ariel assured. "Do you have a message for her?"

"I found a photo of her here on the *Veracity*. It was in the breast pocket of Revan Thallian's coat. I wondered if Eilif would want it, knowing he'd treasured it."

Ariel shuddered, but said, "I'll ask her."

The conversation seemed to have run down. "It's still the middle of the night here," Raena said. "I'm going to take some more medicine and try to go back to sleep."

"Sweet dreams," Ariel wished. "It's mid-morning here. Time to get to work."

"Love you," Raena said.

"You, too."

Raena let Ariel get the last word and powered her screen down. Then she shook two drops out of the flask onto her tongue and swallowed them dry. They tasted vaguely of saltwater.

CHAPTER 11

The dream pounced on her. One moment she was lying in her bunk, thinking about getting up for a drink of water; the next, *she was jammed inside a small black box, tumbling over and over as she fell. The fall halted sharply, as the escape pod she was riding in plowed into something that was slightly more yielding than rock. Raena was grateful for the helmet Vezali had forced on her.*

The escape pod popped back to the surface of the ocean, where it oscillated ever so gently on the waves. Hidden inside the communications console, Raena checked in on herself: nothing too banged up in the ejection from the Veracity *or the landing on the Thallian homeworld. She couldn't straighten her legs, but she could shift her arms enough to make certain the walls were not pressing inward on her. Not even slightly.*

She heard Jain Thallian moving around in the pod outside the gutted communications console. She was glad that she hadn't hit his head too hard when she'd knocked him out. It wouldn't have done for him to watch the Veracity *eject them, then leave them behind amidst a field of broken equipment. Everyone on Jain's home planet was meant to think that the* Veracity *struck a mine and exploded, all hands lost except Jain in his escape pod.*

Time dragged very slowly. Raena let herself doze.

When she roused, she wondered what was taking Jonan so long to come and get them. Surely he monitored his own system. Why hadn't he sent some minions to retrieve his favorite son? She had assumed that Jain wouldn't need to communicate with his family, that they would be eager to have him back.

Her tongue had grown dry in her mouth. She worked hard to swallow. It hadn't occurred to her to ask Mykah to stock the console with provisions for her return to Thallian.

She drifted off again, to be woken by the agony of her cramped limbs. Her head ached with thirst. How had she miscalculated?

She heard Jain moving around again. He banged on the outside of the console, trying to force it open. He sounded desperate to contact his family and find out when they were coming.

Fear shivered over her. She had no room to maneuver, no way to escape. If he ever got the panel pried open, she would be an easy target.

To get away from the nightmare, Raena turned over on her bunk. She pressed her face into the cool bulkhead between her cabin and Mykah and Coni's. *Someone behind her on the bunk muttered something, snuggling into her, nuzzling her shoulder. The warmth of that body made the nightmare evaporate. Raena breathed deep, completely at peace.*

It couldn't last, of course. Insomnia chewed at her and she couldn't find sleep again. She hesitated to flop around in bed and disturb her companion.

Climbing out was awkward, but she decided that was the kindest choice. Let him sleep. She peeled the coverlet off, tucked it behind her, and slid out of bed. In the darkness, she dressed quickly from force of habit, slipping her boots on last of all.

Then she crept out of her cabin into the Veracity's *passageway. She heard voices in the cockpit and headed that way.*

Rather than finding Coni and Haoun discussing the media coverage of the latest jetsail race, there were two humans she didn't know sitting in their chairs. They looked up at her inquiringly. "Did you want something, Raena?"

"Sorry." Raena rubbed her face. "Wrong turn. Looking for coffee."

She backpedalled quickly and retreated to the galley. Mykah bustled around in there as usual. He nodded to her, but stood out of the way as she poured a cup of coffee.

After choking down a sip of boiling liquid, she gasped, "Where's Coni?"

"Who?" He seemed shocked by the very sound of the name, like he'd never heard it before. Mykah looked at Raena, dark eyes narrowing. "Are you feeling all right?"

"No." Raena stumbled to the table, where she half slid, half fell onto a stool. Her thoughts moved around in her head gingerly, probing every cranny and crevice. How do you recognize when you're in a dream, *she wondered.* If you could smell the meat browning on the stove and taste the scalding coffee and feel the blister forming on the roof of your mouth, wouldn't that mean you were awake? *How, then, to explain the utter wrongness, the falseness, of the reality around her?*

"I just made that coffee," Mykah apologized. He brought her a cup of ice water. "I'm sorry I didn't warn you. I didn't think you were going to drink it straight down."

He has no idea, *Raena thought.* Absolutely no idea. Nothing has changed for him.

The wrongness suffocated her. She felt trapped, the way she'd felt in the tomb when the soldiers had closed the slab on her, sealing her inside, when the blackness had enfolded her like a swarm, shutting away light and sound and air, the rattle of her heartbeat in her head loud enough to drive her mad.

The worst question was: who had been in her bed when she woke up?

Raena stood suddenly, startling Mykah. She bumped the table with her hip, knocking over both the mug of coffee and the glass of water. The stool clattered to the floor behind her. She bounced off the doorframe hard—felt it, that would leave a bruise—and crashed into the wall in

*the hallway, fighting to stay on her feet, to keep moving despite the shad-
ows closing in. She had to make it back to her cabin. Who had that been
in her bed?*

*Her right hand went hesitantly to her collar. Then she yanked the neck
of her sweater open, stuck her fingers inside, searching her skin between
the shoulder and the swell of her left breast.*

*It was gone. The starburst scar where Thallian shot her with the shock
capsule was gone. He'd never taken her captive the final time. She'd never
killed him.*

That realization threw her backward. Her body jerked, jolted out
of the . . . memory? Dream? Hallucination? Insanity?

Mykah caught her as she went down. "You're okay," he promised.
"You'll be okay. Coni, come help us in the hallway."

He looked the same: same dark brown skin, same crazy topiary
hair, same concern in his eyes. But he knew his girlfriend's name
now. Raena thought: *I must be back from wherever I had been.*

Had she been dreaming? Sleepwalking? The nightmares had never
overtaken her when she'd been so certain she was awake.

Mykah eased Raena down onto the floor where she sprawled, feeling the comfortable solidity of the deck beneath her. She wished that
the world around her felt as solid. Would she slip back into the hallucination at any moment?

If she hadn't killed Thallian, was she still on the run from him?
What if he had been snuggling her beneath the blankets in her bunk?
Maybe it wasn't her cabin at all. Maybe this transport still belonged
to the Thallians. Maybe she still belonged to Jonan.

Raena felt the seizure take her limbs. Her eyes didn't close and she
didn't lose consciousness as her body beat itself against the floor. She
wanted desperately to black out, to cease thinking, to stop worrying.
Any respite would have been gladly received. She would have even
welcomed death.

"Coni!" Mykah shouted. "Haoun, Vezali, come! Now!"

Haoun appeared first, sprinting out of the cockpit. He grabbed Raena up in his arms. She felt the comforting strength of him, smelled the strange reptilian scent of him, as Coni opened Raena's cabin door. Haoun carried Raena in and set her gently on the bunk, despite the way she arced and thrashed in his arms.

The narrow bunk was empty, she noted. No extra body warmed it for her now.

Vezali slithered onto the mattress beside Raena and held her down. Her tentacles were incredibly strong, despite the velvety softness of their grip. One tentacle encircled Raena's head, holding her skull so that she didn't thrash herself into a concussion.

"What happened?" Coni demanded.

"I don't know," Mykah said despairingly. "I heard her stumble into the wall in the passageway. When I came out of our cabin, it looked like she'd grabbed a live wire or something, just galvanized. I was running toward her when she went down. Then this started."

Haoun's hands were cold on her ankles, holding her legs to the bunk. Raena was so grateful to them, to all of them, that she started to cry. Tears spilled from her eyes, rolling ticklishly down to puddle on the bed.

Gradually the seizure abated. Vezali didn't let her go, but it felt more like a hug now than being restrained, affection and support that Raena desperately enjoyed. Her body ached like it hadn't in years.

"Ka—" she managed to gasp out. It was impossibly hard to make her lips form the name, to make her tongue spit it out. It took a couple of tries to get it all out. "Kavanaugh," she said at last. "Tarik Kavanaugh. Old friend. Call him. He will help."

Coni nodded to the others and went to make the call.

Raena saw Mellix watching from the doorway and closed her eyes, embarrassed.

Mykah found the carafe of sleeping drops on her desk and brought it over. "Did you take this just now?" he demanded, staring into her eyes to gauge her recovery. "Maybe you had a bad reaction."

Tentatively, Raena nodded and wiped her face with her hands. "Take it away, will you? I'm scared of it now."

Haoun stepped back from her, then tsked at the bruises his hands had left on her ankles. "Don't know my own strength."

"It's okay." Raena gave him a smile. "I think you saved my life." She turned her gaze to include Vezali in that, too. "Can you stay with me for a little while? Until I get to sleep?"

"I'll stay with you then, too," Vezali promised. Raena felt more tears welling up in her eyes and blinked hard to hold them back.

"Do you need anything else?" Mykah asked.

"I'm afraid to take anything else," Raena said. "Can you find a way to keep me from wandering?"

"We'll see what we can do." Mykah grabbed her hand suddenly, gave it a squeeze, then followed Haoun out.

"How do you feel?" Vezali asked gently.

"Like I've been run over by a tank," Raena said. "Thank you for keeping me from snapping my own neck."

"I hadn't thought of it that way. You're welcome." Vezali withdrew her tentacles, but didn't get up off the bed. She grabbed the coverlet at the foot of the bunk and pulled it upward, passing it from tentacle to tentacle as it came, so she could tuck it around Raena, so gentle it was almost maternal. "Do you remember what happened?" she asked quietly.

"It's complicated," Raena said, then sighed. "It's been happening for a while. And it's been getting worse. It started with bad dreams. They were like I was reliving a memory—but that's not unusual for me. My memories often turn up as dreams. I think it's from spending so many years in the dark, without new input for my brain to make dreams out of. It's trained itself to keep itself entertained by picking over old memories. Anyway, my dreams started to change. They'd begin like the memories I remember, the true memories, but then something would happen. Almost always Gavin Sloane would show up, and the dream would spin off into a new, unfamiliar direction."

"That doesn't sound too awful," Vezali said kindly. "Sloane is someone you know?"

"He was the man who bankrolled the looting of the Templar tombs. He's the reason Kavanaugh found me and let me out."

Vezali bobbed her eyestalk, as if she was putting the pieces together now.

Raena felt a rush of affection for her and smiled again. "Gavin was my sort-of boyfriend before I met you all. He thought he loved me and wanted to keep me safe, but I thought that killing Thallian would be the only way I could really be safe. And as much as I like Gavin, he's so much older than I am. Especially now, since I came back from the tomb. I didn't want to be responsible for getting Gavin hurt because he'd grown old while I didn't. So I left him behind on Kai."

"And you didn't look back."

"Not until these dreams started. I like Gavin well enough. He's not a nice man and I find that kind of interesting. But my sister loved him, really stupidly loved him, and the whole triangle thing was not working out well for us. So I went my way and let them go theirs." She stopped, shook her head, and said, "There's nothing for me to go back to. I don't want Gavin taking care of me. I want to be free—on my own—for a change."

Vezali chuckled. "We've kind of gotten off the topic."

Did we? Raena wondered, but of course that had to be true. She said, "The dreams started getting more and more violent. I got so I tried to exhaust myself so I'd sleep without dreams. That didn't work, so I asked Mykah for some sleep medicine. I took it for the first time earlier tonight and dreamed that the Templars never died. This last dream was even more disturbing."

She paused, unwilling to go on.

"Did you have one just now, before the seizure?"

"I thought I'd gotten up," Raena said slowly, dreading the memory and dragging out the telling of it. She had to know, though, if it was safe to think about it again, if—by simply thinking about it—she would induce a seizure again. Better that she experiment now, here in her cabin, lying down, while she had company, than find out later when she was alone.

She forced herself to continue the story. "I thought I'd gone to the cockpit, but it wasn't Coni and Haoun I found there. There were two humans I didn't know. They knew me, though. So I went to the galley, where Mykah was cooking. But he said he was in his cabin, not the galley . . . so I don't know where I really went, or who I really spoke to."

"I understand you're upset," Vezali said in the same quiet voice, "but is the problem that you were sleepwalking? Or is there more to it than that?"

Raena thought back over what she'd said, trying to figure out why the dream had panicked her so badly. Finally she decided, "At the end of the dream, something made me check my scar." She pulled her collar down to display the starburst of scar tissue where the shock capsule had entered her shoulder.

"When I got into Thallian's city, when almost everyone was dead or had fled to the surface, Thallian shot me with a shock capsule. His robot doctor removed it while I was his prisoner, before Eilif helped me escape. Just now, in my dream, the scar was gone. I understood that meant that I'd never fought Thallian, never killed him. And I wondered if that meant he was still out there, if I was still running from him, or if he was on this ship right now. If the shuttle still belonged to him. If I still belonged to him."

Goose flesh shivered up over her, but she didn't feel a seizure coming on again. When she was sure she was safe, Raena added, "Still belonging to him: that's the worst nightmare I can imagine."

Vezali nodded. "But you're on the *Veracity* now. You're safe."

"Here," Raena said. "Now. But even though I knew that dream wasn't right, I couldn't break out of it. I couldn't wake myself up. It had all the sensory details of real life. I'm scared, Vezali. If I can't tell the difference between dreams and waking, if I'm up roaming around, interacting with the ship and people who aren't there . . . What if I'd thought I was opening a door and I opened an external hatch? What if I thought I was defending myself and I hurt one of you? I'm scared I'm going crazy."

"I'm not the expert on humans that Coni is," Vezali said, "but I've read that, usually, crazy humans don't have any idea they're crazy, right? They think they are acting in a perfectly logical way."

"Maybe," she hedged. Thallian had been the most deranged person she had ever met, and he certainly had strongly held justifications for all his delusions.

"By that logic, you are sane as long as you wonder if you're going crazy."

"Oh, good. I feel much better, then."

"Glad to help." Vezali stroked her face. "Do you want to rest?"

"Do we still have the restraints onboard somewhere?" Raena asked. "Maybe it wouldn't hurt to pin me down while I'm sleeping."

"I'll lock us in," Vezali said.

"What if I . . ."

"At full strength, I would be afraid of you," she said gently. "I think I can take you in this state, beaten up by insomnia and half asleep."

"You're probably right." Raena yawned. "Still, be careful. I would hate it if anything happened to you."

"So would I. I'll err on the side of caution." They lay quietly, but clearly sleep was afraid of Raena now. She asked, "Can you tell me a story? Something to take my mind off of all of this?"

Vezali eased a wisp of hair back from Raena's face with the tip of one tentacle. "The stories my people tell wouldn't make much sense to you," she said.

"I don't even know where you come from."

"It's called Dagat. It's mostly water, but we've built cities like mountains that climb from the ocean floor up into the sky."

"Is it lovely?"

"In its way. The skies turn a variety of colors I've seen nowhere else. I'll go home some day. When it's time to die."

Raena folded her arm under her head, gazing at Vezali's eyestalk, which was as much of a face as the tentacled girl had. "How will you know when it's time to die?"

"Someday I'll wake up and crave children. Then my body will become female and I'll find another of my kind and we'll mate. And I'll return to my home ocean to lay my eggs. I'll watch over them and protect them and eventually they'll hatch. Then my children will devour me."

Raena twitched involuntarily. Vezali caressed her face with a tentacle tip. "Mind off your troubles now?" She sounded amused.

"Things are in perspective," Raena said. "I thought you were female now."

"That's all right. I'm not offended. After I left home, I learned fairly early that most people were going to fit me into a gender construct already familiar to them."

"If it's not too personal a question, what do you consider yourself?"

"When I was younger, I fathered children. Now I'm between genders. The translator would call it gynandromorph. You can think of it as neutral. Someday I'll become female."

Raena nodded. "I've thought of you as 'she,'" she apologized. "I judged you on the pitch of your voice and I'm sorry."

"'She' is fine," Vezali said. "Some of my favorite people are she. I'm honored to have them count me in their company."

Raena smiled again. Her body ached from the seizure, from Vezali's protective embrace and Haoun's grip on her legs. She closed her eyes, but sleep would not come back.

What if she was going crazy, like her mother had?

The thought iced Raena's blood.

She didn't know much about her mother's madness. She'd been a child, trying to make sense of the only life she knew. Only after she met Ariel did she learn that all humans didn't hate all nonhumans. Ariel actually had nonhuman friends, people she loved and trusted, people who were kind to Raena, even though she was a slave.

Inside the relative normality of Ariel's circle of friends, Raena learned to recognize that her mother's rages and sobbing jags, her screaming outbursts and rabid bigotry, were not normal. Something had broken in Fiana and she never—in the ten years Raena was with her—got the help she needed.

Raena didn't know when her mother's madness had started. Fiana's parents were musicians. They'd lived a roaming life, performing wherever they could. Raena wondered about them now. She'd never known their names, but surely she could find them. Maybe they were still alive. Maybe, for that matter, Fiana was, too.

Raena thought that if she survived this—whatever it was that was happening to her now—perhaps she would look them up.

In the meantime, she would have to find her own answers. Whatever was going wrong in her head, it did not manifest like her mother's madness. For that, she was grateful.

Vezali heard Raena's breathing even out at last. Bit by bit, in twitches and tremors, the tension went out of the little woman's body. Vezali continued to hold her closely.

She thought over what Raena had said about memories and dreams. Vezali wasn't entirely sure what the distinction was. Her translator used the same word in Dagat for both. She'd ask Mykah what the difference was later. Raena was already too fragile to be upset by difficulties in communication.

Kavanaugh got a call as he was coming in to land. He concentrated on his flying, got his ship settled comfortably in its dock, and was glad to see the new parents were waiting when he and his passengers came down the ramp. The meeting between the orphans and their adopting parents was awkward, but sweet, and Kavanaugh couldn't keep the smile from his face through the exchange.

He also had been orphaned by the War. Luckily, Doc had been there to take him in, with her companion, the big wolf-faced Skyler. They'd been like parents to him, but as far as he knew, there'd never been any official connection between them. He wasn't sure how Doc wrangled the legal niceties. She might have claimed him as a slave, for all he knew, although she always treated him more like a son. He supposed he could ask her, if it really mattered. He thought of her as his parent, though not necessarily as his mother, and that had always been good enough for him.

He was interested to see that Ariel wasn't placing the kids for whom she found homes with strictly human families either. In Kavanaugh's admittedly limited experience delivering orphans for Ariel, at least one member of the adopting family always seemed to be human. Sometimes the families were just couples, but more often they were trios or other multiples, who may or may not have had nonhuman children, as well.

As jobs went, delivering orphans to their new homes was one of the better ones he'd ever taken. At least this one didn't trouble his conscience or give him bad dreams.

He had planned to shut the ship down, go into town, and see if he could find someone to share his good mood. But as he moved around the cockpit, locking everything up, he saw the message light was still on. He set it to play for company.

He wasn't sure what he had expected, but the message he heard came out of the blue.

"Mr. Kavanaugh, I'm a shipmate of Raena Zacari. She had an accident today and asked me to contact you."

Kavanaugh stepped back to the monitor and set the message to begin again, so he could make certain he'd heard that right.

The girl delivering the message was humanoid, in that her body was bipedal. Blue fur the color of Kavanaugh's favorite sky covered as much of her as he could see. A boxy black jacket covered the rest. Her eyes were an alarming shade of lavender. Her face had a muzzle sort of like Skyler's, but hers was more feline.

Of all the people in the galaxy Raena could call—and Kavanaugh didn't expect there were many—he wasn't sure why his name would come up. Last time he'd seen Raena, she laid him out flat with a single blow to the head. No lasting damage had been done, luckily, but it didn't inspire him to think she felt too fondly toward him. He certainly didn't owe her any favors.

Ariel would have been easier to find, Kavanaugh thought. Whatever was the matter, it apparently wasn't something Raena wanted to discuss with her sister.

He thought reluctantly of the shore leave he'd had planned, then reached forward to return the call. As he did so, he noticed the name of the ship. Why did *Veracity* sound so familiar?

The blue girl was picking up when Kavanaugh flashed on the documentary he'd watched about the Thallian family exploring the Templar tombs—and the avalanche Raena set to kill them. The *Veracity* was the ship that'd broken the news about the fall of the house of Thallian. These were the good guys.

"I'm Kavanaugh," he said by way of hello.

"Thanks for returning my call," the blue girl said. "My name is Coni Dottr Gounot. Raena Zacari is working with us on the *Veracity*, but she's been having a hard time lately. We didn't know her beforehand, so we don't really know if this issue is long-standing. She said that you were an old friend, that you could help."

"If you're asking me if Raena is dangerous, I would say yes," Kavanaugh said.

"We're not to that point yet," Coni said. "She hasn't been dangerous to us, but we're aware of how she can be."

"What can I help you with, then?"

"I'm not sure exactly. Raena had a seizure earlier today. She's scared."

Kavanaugh leaned closer to the screen. "Raena, scared? That is *hard* to imagine. Scared of what?"

"She's been having bad dreams," Coni said. "They're related to her memories. She's been trying to medicate herself, but despite that, things seem to be getting worse. She's started sleepwalking. The dream she had this afternoon triggered some kind of chemical imbalance and caused the seizure. Luckily, we were with her when it happened. She's strong enough that she could have really injured herself."

Or someone else, Kavanaugh realized. Hating himself but knowing there was nothing else he could say and get to sleep at night, Kavanaugh asked, "How can I help?"

"I'm not exactly sure. Raena asked for you specifically. Do you have medical training?"

"Not officially."

"We're working on getting her medical documentation so that she can get legitimate treatment. But if there's anything you can do for her right now . . ."

A stubble-bearded twenty-something human came into the frame behind the blue girl. "She's resting now," he said. "Look, I know travel isn't cheap, Mr. Kavanaugh. Raena has money of her own. I'm sure she will pay your expenses. Can you meet us at Tengri?"

"I'm not really sure what I can do for her. All I know is battlefield medicine. If Raena's having a psychotic break, you're gonna need to sedate her and get her into restraints."

"She's already volunteered for the restraints," the young man said.

That chilled Kavanaugh more than anything they'd said yet. He knew exactly how long Raena had spent locked up in that tomb. If she was volunteering for any kind of imprisonment, she must be well and truly scared.

He keyed Tengri into the navcom and read the response. "You're lucky. I'm pretty close. Thirty standard hours. I'll see you at Tengri."

"Thank you," Coni and the young man said simultaneously.

After she'd signed out of the comm program, Coni asked, "What are we going to do?"

"I've been working with Haoun. He's not as clever with the ship as Vezali is and she'll have to check our work, but we think we've modified Raena's cabin door so we can lock it from the outside. We can make sure she doesn't wander." Mykah came to sit in Haoun's oversized chair and stared out the port at the stars. "Have you got some way to monitor her in there?"

Coni stared at him, but he didn't look her way. Did Mykah know that she had been studying Raena ever since she'd come on board? Probably. He knew her well enough to guess that. Rather than ask what he knew about her spying, Coni said, "Yes, I can re-activate the old monitoring system that the Thallians ran throughout the ship. Do you want me just to monitor her, or to record her as well?"

Mykah shook his head, still staring into the distance. "I hate to spy on her," he said, his voice torn, "but we should record it. In case . . ."

He didn't say what it was he feared.

"I can clear some space and set the feed to record directly to the *Veracity*'s computer," she promised.

"Hopefully, it won't be for long." Mykah turned to face her finally, his dark eyes alive with compassion and sorrow. Coni didn't see love in them, though, not love for Raena, and for that she was surprisingly grateful. "How are you coming with Raena's identity papers?" he asked.

"I'm meeting my friend on Tengri to get the final documents," she assured. "After the money changes hands, Raena should look completely legal."

Coni wondered if she should say, "And then we can drop her off at the nearest emergency psych ward," but she didn't. As much pity as she felt for the strange small woman, Coni didn't have any illusions about what Raena had done and was still capable of doing. She might be insane and unable to sleep without company or drugs, but she was also in amazing physical shape. She could kill them all before any of them could get the gun locker open.

So busy not saying what she wanted to, Coni rushed into the next question. "While Vezali is modifying Raena's cabin, should we have her figure out a way to gas her?"

"What?" Mykah gasped. "No."

"Not like that," Coni said, exasperated. "To put her to sleep. Didn't you find some Doze gas or something in the Thallians' stores when you inventoried the ship?"

"I think so. I'll check again. Thank you. We'll have to calculate the dosage carefully for someone her size, but it's good to know we'll have a backup if things get out of hand."

He got up from Haoun's chair and came over to kiss her. Coni drew him closer and rubbed her head against his chest, scenting him.

He was smiling when he stepped away.

Coni knew she was going to ruin his moment of peace, but she said, "I don't think she can hurt herself if we knock her out."

"Who knows what it will do to her dreams?" Mykah's mouth twisted into a grimace. "Still, we won't hit her with it until I can tell her that we might. She's not a prisoner and she hasn't endangered any of us yet. Right now, all we're afraid of is her fear that she might hurt us. I want her to know we have a way to neutralize her, if we need to."

Would that set her mind at ease? Coni wondered. If Raena really was going crazy, she might find a way to turn the gas on her captors.

"She can probably calculate the dosage for herself better than we can, anyway," Mykah said.

He left the cockpit, off on his errand, so Coni turned to the computer and started to modify the system she already had in place for spying on Raena. Now she wouldn't have to worry about Haoun stumbling across her recordings by accident.

CHAPTER 12

Mellix caught Mykah in the galley as he was pulling out ingredients to begin dinner. "May I have some of that berry cordial?"

"Please help yourself," Mykah said. He stood out of the way so Mellix could retrieve a bottle from the cooler.

"Is Raena going to be all right?"

"We don't know," Mykah confessed. "We're not sure what happened. Apparently, she had some sort of reaction to the sleep drops."

"I've never heard of that happening before."

"Me, either." Torn between his loyalty to his mentor and to the woman who'd given him his ship and the life he'd always wanted, Mykah wasn't sure how much more to say.

"She is something special," Mellix said. "She seemed extremely calm when the attack on my apartment was imminent. I'm glad I didn't know how much danger I was in."

"Raena's very good at what she does," Mykah agreed. "It's just . . . she's been suffering from some brutal insomnia. We were hoping the sleep drops could help her."

"I'm sorry they didn't," Mellix said. "She seems as if she'd be a formidable . . ."

Mykah sent down the knife and stepped away from the vegetables he was preparing to chop. "You don't need to worry about Raena, Mellix. We have a couple more tools at hand to help her, if they're necessary. I told you I trust her with my life. She also trusts me with hers. We'll look after her."

Something about having Vezali at her side did help Raena sleep. Her body must have needed the time to recuperate from the seizure, but even more, her mind needed the solace of being watched over. She got a good, solid rest before the dreams ate at her again.

Raena remembered the day the transporters hired by her mother had escorted her to the chapter house where Raena was supposed to continue her fight training. They arrived at the correct address, but it was not the haven Raena expected.

Oh, the chapter house had certainly been there. In its place stood a blackened ruin, twisted girders jabbing jaggedly into the sky. The fire had been so long ago that the smell of ashes had dissipated. There was so little left of the building that the fire must have been spectacularly hot.

"That's just great," Kendra shouted. "What am I supposed to do with you now?" She pulled out her comm and called Llew back at the ship. "It's gone," she ranted. "The whole building's gone. There's no place to dump the kid."

Raena looked at the place where her teachers were supposed to be. The broken girders made her think of a forest in winter, bare trees naked amidst the snow. She'd seen an illustration like that in a children's story.

She could hear only half the conversation, but she got the sense that Llew calmed Kendra down. The woman's pacing took on a smaller circuit, slowed, then stopped altogether.

Raena couldn't have said what she wanted, even if it had occurred to anyone to ask. She didn't want to go home to her mother, whose behavior had grown increasingly erratic as she'd internalized more of the Humans First! rhetoric. Even a ten-year-old could grasp that things at home had gotten seriously dangerous. If they dragged her back, Raena promised herself that she would run away.

It wasn't as if she had any other family to which she could go. Raena didn't know her grandparents' names or have any clue how to find them—as if they'd be inclined to take in the street-rat that their lunatic child had spawned.

"Come on," Kendra said harshly, yanking Raena away from the ruins. "Let's go back to the ship. Llew's gonna see if he can find where the chapter relocated to."

But he hadn't. When she and Kendra arrived back at the docking slip, a pod of Viridians was waiting. Raena didn't recognize them. She'd led a fairly sheltered life in the strictly human moon colony. Aliens hadn't been welcome. Incoming news had been heavily censored. She'd known that there were aliens in the galaxy, but she hadn't actually ever seen any. If she'd known what these were, she would have fled.

The Viridians swarmed around her, measuring and prodding and penning her in. Finally, tired of being poked, she rounded on one.

Another whipped out a length of black cloth that coiled around her wrist and stopped her blow from landing. He yanked her hand back hard and secured it to her side as the others moved in and pinned her free arm. Raena kicked and struggled, but all too soon she was cocooned.

"Stop," one of them said over a tinny translator, "or we cover your face."

Raena couldn't tell them apart. There were six in the pod, ludicrously tall and thin, like scarecrows cobbled together from green sticks.

One tested her compliance by stroking her face with his long knobby fingers. Raena snapped at him, missing his finger by millimeters. Without another word, another Viridian wrapped the fabric over her face.

When the air wouldn't come, Raena panicked. She thrashed, lungs burning, wondering why they were killing her, what she had done.

When they sliced the binding off of her, she'd been collared and chained in the hold of a Viridian ship. In the dimness, she couldn't see the limits of the room, but she recognized the misery of all the creatures chained around her. Most of them lay still, curled up as small as they could make themselves, as if they only wanted to disappear. Like all the rest, Raena had been stripped nude, her hands manacled around the chain that held her to the deck.

Near her feet lurked a foul-smelling drain. She hoped that it was meant for waste, not for food. Not that she intended to eat anything onboard this ship. Let the slavers realize their bad investment as she starved herself to death.

Of course, she hadn't any clue about the torments they would subject her to, in order to get her to eat. She was too young to put up much resistance yet.

Gah. Raena shook herself awake, but her aching limbs were heavy and she slipped back into the dream.

She was lucky that she hadn't spent more than a couple of weeks on the Viridian ship. It wasn't really what they did to her that was the worst part, because she learned fairly quickly to comply and keep her head down and thereby escape punishment. They didn't want to permanently damage their property before they found a buyer for it, so compliance was rewarded with neglect. What scarred her were the things she saw done to the other slaves, the things that some of the slaves did to each other. She shuddered to remember them. With her hands manacled, she had been unable to block her ears.

That journey marked the death of her childhood.

Fighting her way out of the dream again, still groggy, Raena forced herself to sit up. Her limbs felt weighted. As soon as she let herself slump against the bulkhead between her cabin and the passageway, sleep overpowered her again.

Frigid water plummeted from the ceiling, beating Raena to the floor. She felt bruised, even as she forced herself to her feet, shivering, shaking her head to clear the water from her face. The Viridians marched through or over the slaves between her and the door. There was no way she could get away from them, nothing to hide behind, so she stood, black hair hanging damply over her face, wondering what she had done. Once the other creatures around her had been washed, the Viridians took them and they never came back.

The next time she got her eyes forced open, Raena pushed herself to her feet.

"What's going on?" Vezali asked sleepily.

"Bad dream. It won't let me go."

Raena paced her cabin, hoping to get her blood flowing. She splashed some cold water from the tap onto her cheeks. When that didn't guarantee consciousness, she flung herself into an icy shower. She did not want to go back into that dream.

The gelid water hitting her skin shocked enough adrenaline into her system that she felt awareness finally rushing into place. Shivering, she readjusted the water temperature and let herself indulge in the external warmth until the chill left her flesh.

She did have happy memories, she reminded herself. Chief among them was standing over Thallian's burning corpse. Then there were the days of running around with Ariel as a teenager, stealing guns from her father's factory and trading them for drugs. And seeing Kavanaugh again, after he'd opened her tomb. She'd always liked him. There was that final day on Kai, the one day when Ariel and Gavin had gotten along, before Thallian's men found them. Even some days of her childhood, learning to fight in the street and running across the rooftops and diving in the colony's deep tank and the first time she walked on the moon's surface and saw the stars overhead . . .

And the day she met Mykah and Coni, the day she'd joined them in disrupting the jet pack race, the day she'd learned to soar on makeshift wings. That was one of the best days of her life, too: when she finally envisioned a future for herself, free of Gavin and Ariel and Thallian, free of the Empire and the War and having been a slave. That was the day she began to look forward to life.

She shut the water off and set the heater to dry her body, fluffing her hair on end as she did so. She hoped it was nearly morning now, or something that the crew considered morning, because she was actually hungry. Maybe today she could do justice to Mykah's specially garnished creations.

Someone tapped on her door. "We're up," Raena called as she swam into one of Jain's sweaters. She heard the scratch of Haoun's claws as he unlocked the door from the outside.

Some of Vezali's tentacles flowed to the floor, while others stretched nearly to the ceiling. "Is it morning?"

"I hope so," Raena said.

Haoun opened the door. "Mykah has cooked up an 'escape from Capital City' feast. He offered to send a tray in to you, if you don't feel comfortable coming out to join us."

"If I come out, I want someone to be ready with a stun stick, in case I go into a fugue or something."

"Do you think any of us could take you with a stun stick?" Haoun asked skeptically.

"Sure," Raena said. "With surprise on your side."

"I can't tell if you're teasing," Vezali protested, "but since you got a pretty good night's rest, I don't think you're a danger to us. Come out."

Raena's smile felt shaky, but she didn't tell them how grateful she was for their trust.

A sudden thought propelled her across the room. Raena pulled Revan's coat out of the clothes locker. Inside one of the pockets, she found the stolen pouch of anesthetic.

Relief washed over her. She could still drug herself to sleep.

"What's that?" Haoun asked.

"I stole it on Capital City. It's the anesthetic they used on me when they fixed my face." She handed the pouch to Haoun. "Please use this to sedate me, if I fall asleep in public."

"If you're sure . . ."

"The last thing I want is for any of you to get hurt. Please help me make sure that doesn't happen."

He shrugged and tucked the anesthetic into the pouch he wore across his chest.

Mykah had gone all out for his feast. There were flower salads, nut-crusted noodles, some kind of vegetable mélange in a creamy broth, and a whole fish. Mykah had replaced its eyes with dollops of sauce.

Mellix didn't join them. Mykah said the journalist was hard at work, trying to find a safe haven for himself and his kiisas.

"Who were those guys who attacked Mellix?" Mykah wanted to know. He'd bleached his beard and carved it with channels that ran to the skin, so that dark lines striped his bright facial hair. The marks lined his face like a tiger's.

"Don't know," Raena said. "They were professionals. The rifle I saw up close was state of the art."

"Station Security?" Haoun wondered. "There were a lot of them, if they expected to escape notice."

"Somebody was paid not to notice them," Coni suggested.

"That's what I thought," Raena said. "Station Security knew that I was alone with Mellix. They'd checked Vezali's manifest, so they knew our crates were full of groceries, not weapons. And they would have known Mellix was a pacifist. Therefore a large, well-armed force was overkill for the two of us, especially if they were just going to vent our air and kill us in our sleep."

"Corporate thugs," Mykah cursed.

Raena smiled at his tone. "After we got Mellix aboard the *Veracity*, I watched him deal with Capital City's Security Commander. Mellix had him terrified. Whoever is trying to kill Mellix won't be frightened away by a little bad press."

"You think it's payback for the tesseract announcement?" Vezali asked her.

"I think Mellix probably has a number of enemies. If they aren't punishing him for something he's already done, they're hoping to prevent any more damage to their bottom line. No doubt he has a list of suspects."

After that announcement, the conversation drifted back to finding work. Their days of hauling food around the galaxy were curtailed until they could get Mellix's belongings out of the hold, but they weren't hurting for money now that the network had paid them for his rescue.

Raena listened to her crewmates talk about job prospects without offering any opinions. Many of the projects they debated were media hacks or investigative reporting, and she couldn't really help them with that anyway.

She wondered if they would voluntarily choose work that would require her skills. The more time she spent listening to them, the more she realized that though she'd met Mykah and Coni in the midst of disrupting an aerial scavenger hunt, they were intellectuals, more comfortable with nebulous questions of media control and influence than with the dirty physical work of solving anything more serious.

At this point, it didn't really matter to her. Until she was certain she would never again have a seizure and the weird hallucinations had ceased, she didn't want to be putting her own or anyone else's life on the line. She was surprised to admit to herself that she was content to simply be along for the ride, just like Haoun. She glanced up at him and smiled, but he was engrossed in the conversation.

Eventually a decision was reached and the voices trailed off. Raena turned outward from her thoughts just before Vezali asked, "Do you have anything to add, Raena?"

Raena shook her head. "Take the work that interests you. That's the benefit of being free."

Mellix bustled in at last. "Am I too late for lunch?"

The crew shifted over and Mykah brought another plate.

Raena observed, "You outdid yourself today, Mykah."

He grinned. "You deserved a feast. Haoun showed us the recording of you fighting off those soldiers. I can't believe you held them off with a single pistol."

"I've handled Stingers more than any other weapon. I know exactly what they can do. And I had surprise on my side, which counts for a lot in a fight."

"I notice you didn't kill them."

"Mellix said not to."

Mellix noted, "It would have been easier to kill them."

"It's always easier to kill," Raena agreed. "Do you have any idea who those guys were?"

Mellix heaped his plate with noodles. "Haoun tells me the *Veracity*'s cameras are too old to get really clear resolution, so I didn't get a good close look at any of them. Did you see any insignia?"

"Nothing. Not even places where it had been removed. Their gear was as new and unmarked as mine."

"They weren't bound by law either," he said. "The network checked into it, after I asked them to."

"So they're still out there, probably still looking for you," Raena said.

"Well, yes."

"You may wish I killed them," Raena observed.

"They'd only hire more," he said wearily. "They were corporate, weren't they?"

"You'd know better than me," she said.

He considered it, then said, "For the moment, there's been a suspicious dearth of news about the assault. Capital City blames terrorists. They have released footage of the exterior damage to the station and word has gone out that I'm safe and unharmed, but apparently the exterior cameras on that side of Capital City were offline for maintenance."

Mykah laughed.

"And," Mellix continued, "the soldiers on duty inside the station— the ones who were so eager to confiscate your provisions—didn't know anything was going on until the hull breach klaxons went off."

"Bribes have been paid?" Raena asked.

"Of course. But it's all a distraction from the tesseract flaw."

"There are going to be a lot of distractions," Mykah predicted. "People who are sheltering in place need their entertainments."

Mellix nodded, his mouth full of nut-covered noodles. "This is really wonderful," he said. "Do you eat like this all the time?"

Before Mykah could respond, Raena said, "All the time. He spoils us."

"You're feeling better?"

"Yes, thank you." She considered adding that Coni was right, all she had needed was some company while she slept. She glanced at Mykah, then at Vezali, but kept her thoughts to herself. Raena realized she must be feeling better if her sense of humor had returned.

After lunch, Raena retreated to her cabin. She opened up her journal and began to list the strange dreams she'd had in chronological order.

Haoun tapped on her door again. "Want a distraction?"

"Yes, please." Raena closed the journaling program she'd been scowling at. "I'm tired of my own company."

She slid over on the bed to make room for the lizard pilot, but he curled up on the floor instead. She had to agree that the bunk looked awfully narrow for the two of them to sit on. "What's going on outside my cabin?"

"Coni got in touch with your friend Kavanaugh. He's going to meet us on Tengri this evening."

"Shore leave for everyone?" Raena tried not to feel envious. It wasn't like she had anything she needed to do on the ground, only that she was feeling cooped up.

"Mellix is staying onboard. He doesn't want anyone to connect him to the *Veracity*, so he figures it's safer that no one sees him traveling with us."

"Did you promise him you'd lock me in?"

"Actually, Mykah did, yes."

"Good."

Haoun changed the subject by pulling a handheld from the pouch slung across his chest. "Coni got me some new games on Capital City. Want to play?"

"Sure." Anything to pass the time, she thought. "I'm not a great pilot, though."

"What makes you think I only play piloting games?"

Raena laughed. "What have you got, then?"

"There's one called Typhoon. It's about surviving a storm disaster. One's called Dare. It's a puzzle adventure. And there's a human game called Go."

"Your choice," Raena said. "Show me how it's done."

It felt like they played for hours, working from one of Haoun's games to the next. Raena found she was very comfortable in his company, that he actually had an amusingly dry sense of humor. The hiss of his natural voice bothered her less over time.

She stretched out on her bunk, head pillowed on her arms, so she could look over his shoulder as he played. After a while, she found her eyelids drooping.

"Do you want to rest?" he asked.

"Actually," she said sleepily, "I was thinking about having you anesthetize me, so I can try sleeping without dreams for a change."

"I left your drug with Coni, so she could research how to administer it." He climbed off the floor. Before he made it to the door, Coni opened it.

It could have been coincidence, but Raena thought not. It didn't surprise her that Coni really was monitoring her. If she had another seizure, she would probably be grateful to have someone watching over her. She looked up at Coni, but was unable to read anything like guilt in the girl's lavender eyes.

"This is a short-term surgical anesthetic," Coni said. "It's designed to wear off naturally after a set length of time. Vezali raided the Thallians' stores and put together a nebulizer and a breather, so we have a way to administer it, but we don't know how to calculate the dosage."

"I can do that, if you've got a drug description. It's just a matter of cross-referencing dosage and mass."

"I don't want to know how you can do that," Coni said.

"You know how I can do it," Raena corrected. "I could have built the dispenser, too, but Vezali's undoubtedly done a more elegant job. Do you think it will get me off to sleep safely?"

"I don't know how we will know until we test it."

"I'm game," Raena said. "But you don't have to sit up with me. Just keep an ear out."

That time, Coni did duck her head enough that Raena knew she'd been understood. She smiled at the blue girl, to show she hadn't taken offense.

As it had before, when Raena remembered how she'd gotten the scar across her eye, the anesthesia brought back a memory.

Somehow she'd let herself get stranded on Nizarrh. Imperial troops lurked everywhere she looked. The spaceport crawled with them.

Raena had been running for so long that it was hard to think of doing anything else. She was almost out of money and there seemed to be no prospect of getting more. On Nizarrh, no one walked out in its toxic atmosphere. She had no opportunity to get someone alone to rob him.

Any sort of illegal activity seemed a dangerous prospect, since she was sure that planetary detention would lead directly to Imperial custody.

Unfortunately, even legitimate ways of earning money seemed tightly controlled. Prostitution was legal on Nizarrh, but she needed a state ID card and a med card and transactions were made in the local credit, so the government could get its cut three ways.

Unless she could find someone with a ship and the skills to fly under the radar who was also willing to take payment out of her hide, she was stuck.

It didn't help that she couldn't remember the last time she slept. Sleeping space was extremely expensive on Nizarrh, as well as being carefully monitored. She'd found a couple of promising dark, vacant niches, but both times while she was scoping them out, the rightful renters had shown up. She'd gotten roused by the local constabulary after falling asleep on the lev train. She was so tired now that she was afraid she'd doze off if she walked very far.

She must have nodded over the drink she was trying to stretch out to fill the evening. Suddenly a man stood over her. He had a hunted look in his muddy green eyes, which didn't inspire her with confidence.

"You ready to get out of here?" he asked.

"That's the first time a bounty hunter has put it to me like that," she answered.

Sounding almost as tired as she felt, he said, "I'm not a bounty hunter."

"That's not the first time one has told me that.*" Raena was too tired to leap over the table and kill him. Let him come closer, she thought, fingering the stone knife she had tucked inside her sleeve.*

He rounded the table abruptly and slid in beside her, then snuggled up against her to whisper into her hair, "Coalition Command sent me. He's closing in on you. They want me to get you out first."

Goose prickles shivered up over Raena's skin. She didn't need to ask who "he" was. As much as she didn't want to be tried for war crimes by the Coalition, she also didn't want to wait around on Nizarrh for Thallian to catch her.

The man grunted, nodding ever so slightly toward the bartender. Raena peered through the long black hair that shrouded her face. Several men looked back toward her. One wore a diplomatic corps uniform.

The man from the Coalition suddenly hauled Raena into his lap. He dipped her backward and gave her a long, hungry kiss. Shocked by his behavior and terrified by the soldiers coming across the bar, Raena let herself melt into the kiss, trying to match the Coalition man's hunger as convincingly as possible. It really felt like he meant it.

"Nice," the Imperial officer sneered. "Haven't seen that dodge used before."

He thought he had her pinned down, but there were advantages to being so small. Raena slipped under the table, taking the Coalition man's gun with her as she vanished.

She started shooting from beneath the table, dropping the officer and his pair of guards as the Coalition man rolled under the table after her.

"What are you doing with my gun?"

"Mine needs charging."

Raena scrambled forward, out from under the table, alert for any more soldiers coming her way. A quartet at the entry headed over, but the other patrons provided the cover she needed as they struggled toward the door to get out of the way of the coming firefight.

The Coalition man grabbed Raena's arm and dragged her in the opposite direction. "This way. They'll have the front covered."

He was right. Raena followed him into the storeroom. He stopped to peel open the heavy round cover over a subterranean tunnel.

Claustrophobia washed over her in a wave. She found herself rooted to the scratched metal floor.

"Come on," her savior ordered. He was already halfway down the hatch into the tunnel below. "You're gonna die if you stay up there."

Feeling certain that she was going to die in the tunnel, Raena jumped down after the bounty hunter, landing nimbly on her high-heeled boots. She was relieved when he started to run, so she could run, too.

Before long, the chilly air in the tunnel improved her queasy stomach. Raena began to feel more awake, but adrenaline wouldn't keep her going forever. She'd need to make her move soon. Although the top of her head barely reached his shoulder, she knew she could take the Coalition man.

"Gavin Sloane," he said, by way of introduction. "Can I have my gun back, Raena?"

She considered giving him the business end, but she had no idea where she was or how to get out. She wasn't even sure she could find her way back to the bar. Dying alone, lost in an underground labyrinth: while it wasn't her worst fear, it ranked in the top ten. She handed the pistol to him, grip first. He jammed it back into his holster, but left the peace bonding off.

They dodged through the tunnels until the liquor and the maze had thoroughly confused Raena. Sloane halted before a trash-strewn stair.

"Just follow. Don't talk to him. He doesn't need to know who you are and you don't want to know anything about him." Sloane took the stairs two at a time, making plenty of noise. Raena followed silently.

The half-rotted door at the top squealed as Sloane shoved it aside. The smell of stale bodies rushed out of the basement at them. Raena wanted to cough, but didn't. Into the dim room, Sloane called, "Outrider?"

"Hush, my friend. The house is full now. The others are just returning from their dreams. Perhaps, if you will wait . . . Oh." A moon-faced man entered from another room, dressed in a rumpled rust-colored suit. "Nice to see you again," he said to Sloane. The pistol in his hand swiveled to point at Raena. "Who's your date?"

"Apprentice," Sloane corrected. "I thought you'd like to meet her."

Outrider lunged at Raena, raising his pistol as if to crack her temple with the barrel. Raena caught his wrist and straightened her arms, forcing the gun to point up toward the ceiling.

The drug dealer was stronger than he looked. She couldn't break his grip on the gun. Instead, he shook her off. Raena rolled to her feet, fully expecting to be shot, but he holstered the pistol instead.

"I'm not paying you double just because there are two of you," Outrider warned.

Sloane nodded roughly. A granite edge forced any trace of good humor out of his voice. *"We're ready to get off this rock. Do you want us to run this for you or not?"*

"Deliver this as we agreed and I'll pay you on the other end," Outrider said as he scuttled from sight.

"Velocity?" Raena asked. That was exactly what she needed to keep herself on her feet and running.

Sloane wouldn't meet her eyes. *"Messiah."*

The Messiah drug. Raena had thought it was a myth. Messiah had been blamed in several border systems where the planetary governments abruptly collapsed. The Empire swept into the vacuum. Often, it faced extended battles with the Coalition, which drove the Empire from one atrocity to the next in order to keep control.

Rumor pinned the governmental destabilization on a small number of terrorists addicted to Messiah. Raena assumed the drug was like Rage or Velocity or some similar kind of stimulant that fed the users with the energy or eloquence to provoke foot soldiers into attacking the government.

Curiosity pulled her farther into the room. Eight horizontal cubicles lined the walls. In each lay an ancient body, shriveled, gray, contorted. Extra skin hung off their bones as if their bodies had deflated. Their heads seemed too large for their spindly necks. Their mouths collapsed inward over missing teeth. Without exception, they lay entirely still.

She couldn't have guessed what species they were, until one of them opened an eye as she passed. It had a rheumy brown iris that was distinctively human.

When Outrider returned, he passed several swollen plastic pouches to Sloane, who stuffed them into the lining of his jacket.

Messiah users, Raena thought. *Returning from their dreams?* She didn't know enough about the drug to understand the connection, but it felt *important.* The realization jerked her awake.

She curled up on her bunk with the coverlet clenched in one fist. She felt rested now, not crazed from disgust and worry and lack of sleep. Perhaps the anesthetic had actually done the trick. As amazed as she was to admit it, Raena felt normal. Better than normal. She wondered how many nights she could drug herself to sleep before that too became a problem. She hoped one more wouldn't hurt.

For now, however, she intended to ride this rush of energy for as long as it lasted.

Questions swirled around in her head as she got out of bed. She was seated before the terminal and had opened her journal to begin taking notes on her dream before she realized that nothing weird had happened this time. The memory spooled out just as she remembered it—the despair she'd felt, the exhaustion, the rescue, Gavin's side trip—all of those had really happened in the way she remembered. No unusually aged Gavin had intruded on this dream. Nobody even got killed this time.

Curiosity got the better of her. She keyed in a question to the universal encyclopedia: What happened on Nizarrh after she left?

The answer only raised more questions. Not long after Sloane took her off-world, Nizarrh's Prime Minister went on a killing spree in the planetary parliament. The Empire took control, the Coalition attacked, and millions of people—human and other—were killed in the crossfire.

According to the official record, the Prime Minister had been driven mad by a small group of addicts found dead in a filthy basement. Without exception, the terrorists were elderly, decayed, lifeless husks. All human. The record identified them as young idealists who sold their youth to depose their own government. They'd been labeled Messiah addicts.

She followed that lead, but the information she turned up was more unsettling. Messiah was the common name of a poison that forced users to metabolize at an incredible rate, burning away their

youth and wasting away their bodies. It was blamed for the dissolution of more than a dozen non-aligned human-friendly planetary
governments during the War. What she'd seen on Nizarrh had been
no fluke. Those husks were really believed to be young revolutionaries eaten alive by the Messiah drug. She wondered if they'd ever
known what kind of chaos and death their addictions had rained
down on their homeworlds.

Banned throughout the galaxy, the Messiah drug seemed to have
disappeared after—if not at the same time as—the fall of the human
Empire. Because of that, the Empire had been accused of being the
drug's manufacturer. There was no proof either way, but for many of
the sources she read, it didn't matter.

Unquestionably, the galaxy seemed much more stable of late, its
modern representative government gliding happily along, at least
until the tesseract flaw had been revealed. Up until that point, no
one seemed to be trying to overthrow anyone—well, there must be
discontent somewhere, she was certain—but the civil wars, if they
existed, had not become galactic concerns.

Had the Messiah drug really vanished? Raena doubted that any
drug could be wiped out, as long as there were people vicious or
foolhardy or desperate enough to use it. An addict was born every
minute, as a friend of Ariel's used to say. He'd dealt Velocity to a
string of rich girls just like Ariel Shaad, leaving a trail of addicts in
his wake.

So what happened to Messiah after the War? Raena pursued that
line of questioning.

Answers were surprisingly difficult to pin down. While the drug
had been universally banned, there didn't seem to have been any
overarching strategy to wipe it out. There was never a wave of
arrests, or a drug war, or any sort of real concerted legal attack.
There also hadn't seemed to have been a huge supply network distributing the drug.

For the most part, the drug seemed to exist as a media bogeyman, except that Raena had ostensibly seen its victims. Why would Gavin have lied to her about it? Raena remembered the grim lines etched around his mouth. She wondered how he had gotten mixed up with the Messiah drug, where he had been going with the pouches he'd hidden in his coat.

She decided to take a different tack. What could she find out about Outrider, the smooth-talking pusher?

She closed her eyes and pictured him. Outrider had appeared human, except that he had been exceptionally strong. He would have been in his forties back then, lines creasing his forehead and carved around his eyes. Or he'd seemed to be in his forties, but if he used his own product, he might have actually been younger. In that case, she would never find him. He would have aged into a husk, killed by his own drug use while she'd been in prison.

She remembered the color of his hair, a foxy red that made her think of crusted blood. His hairline had receded on either side of his forehead, leaving a scraggly patch in the middle. His moon-shaped face had an unusual nose with a rounded tip. He was medium height for a human male, with his gut creeping over his belt. She decided she had a pretty good image in her head.

She wondered if he had been profiting for himself or if he had served an alien master. Had someone encouraged him to go destabilize planetary governments or was that something he did to entertain himself?

She keyed in Outrider and Messiah, but didn't come up with any information. Probably Outrider was just the alias he had used on Nizarrh. That was going to make finding him that much harder, if she needed to know his legal name.

She wondered, though, if the lack of response she found meant that he hadn't been arrested. Surely, if he'd gone to trial, his alias would have been a matter of record.

Maybe, she realized, there wasn't any record in the human-based grid because—if he'd worked for the Coalition—they had hidden his identity. She would have to ask Coni to look in the broader news grid, to see if there was information about him that the humans didn't know.

CHAPTER 13

Raena smiled to herself and raised her head. To the empty air, she said, "Coni, can I come out now? I have a question for the crew."

She fluffed up her hair, then turned her chair to face the door. Before long, Coni unlocked it and stood in doorway.

"You could just comm me," the blue girl said. "You made me jump."

"Sorry. I wasn't certain you were listening."

Coni gazed at her, inscrutable, and then said, "I'll try not to abuse the privilege."

"Thank you."

Coni led her down the passage. The crew—without Mellix—had gathered in the lounge. Raena sat on the floor with her back to the viewscreen, where they could all see her and no one would feel threatened.

"Do any of you know anything about the Messiah drug?" No one answered, so Raena continued, "During the War, a rash of planetary governments suddenly collapsed, to be replaced by the Empire. On the rare occasions the provocateurs were captured, they were publicly identified as addicts of Messiah. The galactic government, the Coalition, the Empire, and the greater majority of planets all unanimously condemned Messiah. As soon as the War was over, the drug seemed to vanish. Because of that, humanity—and the Empire—have been blamed for its manufacture and dissemination."

"Ancient history," Haoun said.

"Granted."

"What's your interest?" Coni asked.

"I met one of the pushers, while I was on the run. He appeared to be human. I can't find any record that he was ever captured or stopped. I think he may still be out there."

"What?" Vezali asked, but Coni spoke over her: "Why?"

"Because the only pusher whose name was attached to this drug was never captured. This drug was widespread during the War, at least across the Border Worlds. Governments around the galaxy condemned it and its users in the strongest terms. They were afraid of it. Then suddenly, conveniently, it was gone—without any publicly announced arrests, without any trials, without bringing down the distributors or manufacturers or rounding up more than a handful of users. It vanished, at least from human historical records."

Raena accepted the bottle of cider Mykah offered her, but didn't crack its seal yet. "If Messiah had been human-made, it must have been distributed by the Coalition, since it was primarily non-aligned governments that fell because of it. The Empire was always the first on the scene to pick up the pieces, but they were always eventually driven out by the Coalition. If the broader membership of the Coalition was involved . . ."

"There's a conspiracy," Mykah supplied for her. Raena saw a sparkle in his eye that indicated he was intrigued.

"I can't believe it just vanished," Raena said. "And humans were so ready to betray each other to annihilate the last traces of the Empire, if they had been able to hunt down the manufacturers of the Messiah drug, they would have thrown them on the fire as well."

"You want to exonerate humanity?" Coni asked.

"For a change. Can you find anything in the historical records that explains what happened to the drug?"

"I'll take a look," Coni promised.

Vezali asked, "But you don't really think a drug caused governments to crumble?"

"I don't know what the Messiah drug did, except to shrivel up its users, literally aging them to death. When I saw them, they were lying motionless on bunks in a fetid basement. It smelled like they had been there a long time. I didn't know what happened on Nizarrh after I left—Thallian captured me not long after that and I had other things to worry about—but now, looking back, the planet exploded into all-out chaos. Millions of people were killed in the crossfire between the Empire and the Coalition. I don't know that the Messiah drug was responsible for the bloodshed, but someone needs to avenge those deaths."

"This is all too theoretical for me," Haoun said. "You'll excuse me." He pushed himself back from the table and went off in the direction of the cockpit.

"Seems like a fair question to me," Coni said. "I'm off to investigate."

"I'm going to tinker," Vezali said.

Mellix came in as everyone was leaving. Mykah asked, "Have you ever heard of the Messiah drug?"

A strange expression drew his eyebrows together. "Yes, I remember it."

Raena jerked in surprise. "You do?"

Mellix chuckled, pleased at having startled her. "I'm older than I look."

That was more than a simple statement of fact. Raena wondered if he'd been in the passage, eavesdropping. If so, he knew a whole lot more about her true age than she was comfortable with.

Mellix continued, "During the Human-Templar War, Messiah was quite a source of concern across the galaxy, even though its use never spread beyond what you call the Border Worlds."

"What I don't understand," Raena said, "is how anyone connected a bunch of elderly addicts to the collapse of planetary governments."

"It's been a long time," Mellix answered. "I'm not sure I remember very clearly. But the Messiah drug was one of the things to first interest me in Templar tech."

Oh, he was full of surprises. "Why is that?" Raena asked.

"One of the few texts of theirs that has been translated into Standard is about moving through time with chemical help. The book is read as a novel—but some historians put it forth as an explanation of how the Messiah drug worked."

Raena stared at him, wondering if she'd fallen into a dream and no one had noticed. Maybe, she thought blearily, what was happening to her dreams wasn't a problem caused by a glitch in her own wiring—and that was why drugging herself hadn't fixed it. Maybe her dreams were being hijacked. Maybe they were vestiges of an attack on time.

And maybe all the hours of interrupted sleep had finally destroyed her ability to understand what he was saying to her. She wished Coni hadn't left, so she could ask for a translation and be sure she was jumping to the right conclusions.

"Raena," Mykah asked cautiously, "are you all right?"

She wasn't sure what her face was doing, but she did not feel the least bit all right. "Either I've lost my mind, or what's happening to me is starting to make sense. Would you walk me back to my cabin?"

"Sure."

Mellix watched them go without comment. Before long, Raena knew, she was going to have to decide how badly she wanted to discuss her past with the journalist.

Mykah escorted Raena back into her cabin, then said, "No points for subtlety, Raena."

She sank onto her bed. "I know. Mellix deserves better. But something he said . . . What if these aren't just nightmares I'm having?

What if someone has gotten hold of the Messiah drug and is using it to change my past?"

Mykah didn't respond.

"See, it does sound crazy," Raena admitted. "That's why I didn't want to say it in front of Mellix."

"Yes," Mykah agreed carefully, "it does sound crazy."

"Gavin Sloane was smuggling Messiah when I met him, just before I got captured the final time," Raena said. "Gavin was also the dealer in Templar artifacts who funded Kavanaugh's team and got me out of my tomb. Gavin has been in almost all of my dreams. What if he's somehow using the Messiah drug against me?"

She looked up out of her thoughts to see Mykah's expression. He stared at her as if calculating whether he could get out of her cabin before she could kill him. He didn't seem to like his odds.

"I'm sorry," she said quickly. "It is crazy. I know it is. I'm grasping at straws, desperate to get out from under these nightmares." She slid across her bunk to get her back against the wall, wrapped her arms around her knees, and tried to look even smaller and less threatening than she usually did. "Haoun told me you were meeting with Kavanaugh tonight?"

"Yes."

"Good. Tarik grew up on a tramp medical ship, working for the Coalition during the War. He's a good man. He'll help sort me out or he'll help you get me committed."

"Okay." Mykah walked over to the door at an angle that allowed him to keep from turning his back on her.

Raena didn't move. She couldn't think of anything she could say that wouldn't terrify him even worse.

Once she was alone again, she settled in to think back through all her dreams. She'd recognized as she dreamed them that the Gavins were too old to be the appropriate age for the memories they had invaded. Had there been a logical progression to his aging?

If so, what did that tell her?

Raena turned on her terminal and opened the file she was using as her log. Time to go back over her notes with special emphasis on Gavin.

He hadn't shown up at all in several of her dreams: the ones where the Templar didn't die out and the one with the wholly human crew of the *Veracity/Raptor*—and the one where Jain Thallian was going to kill her in the escape pod. But the other dreams, starting with the one of being drugged in the souk and carried away—had Gavin seemed older than he should have there as well?

She decided it didn't matter if he was coming backward from the future—her future—to mess with her. It didn't matter if she believed he was really time traveling or not, or whether she believed in time travel at all. All that truly mattered now was that she'd found something harmless she could obsess over to pass the time, to fill her mind, until sleep overtook her again.

If she didn't have something to occupy her thoughts, she understood, her mind was going to tear itself apart.

The deeper she looked into her log, the more evidence she accrued. Yes, there was a progression in Sloane's appearance in her dreams. He'd seemed only subtly older in the initial dream, the one with the two Gavins. From then on, his hair had fallen out, his face had grown more wrinkled, and his beard had become more and more unkempt. But if Gavin really was attacking her dreams, placing himself into her past, why wasn't he controlling how he appeared to her?

She lost track of time until Haoun commed her to say that they were about to land on Tengri. She slipped into the crash webbing and waited for sleep to overpower her, but it chose not to.

Not too much later, Mykah opened the door, but stayed in the hallway where he could slam his fist on the door control and lock her in, if she made any threatening moves. Raena stayed seated at her desk and didn't even think about all the ways she could overpower him.

"We're on Tengri," he said. "I'm going to take Coni out on the town, then we'll meet up with Kavanaugh. Haoun and Vezali are already gone. I came by to see if you wanted anything before I lock you in."

"Thank you, but I'll be fine." She lifted the still-unopened bottle of cider from her desk.

Mykah lingered there a moment, seeming to have more to say. Raena helped him out. "I'm sorry if I frightened you earlier."

"It's all right. It's just . . . I located the Doze gas the Thallians had tucked away to use on you, if they'd succeeded in taking you prisoner. They'd even calculated the dosage for you. I want you to check their figures for me. I don't want to give you too much."

"Did you send the calculation back to me?"

He nodded.

"I'll look it over, but I hope we won't need to go that far."

"I hope so, too."

Raena gazed at him. *Just a kid*, she thought, *and I am a lot of responsibility*. "Mykah . . . not that you need it, but you have my permission to do anything you have to, in order to keep the crew safe."

He nodded. "Have a good evening."

"You, too."

Once she was sure they were gone, she retrieved the anesthetic Haoun had left on her desk. It was probably extremely dangerous to use it without any supervision. No doubt she would regret it later, but claustrophobia had crept up on her again. She knew she was trapped in her cabin because she had asked to be—and really, everyone was safer because of it—but she wanted a way to skip ahead in time. The anesthetic wouldn't do that, but it would blot her out of the here and now.

She retrieved the breather and the nebulizer from the locker where she'd put them. Then she retreated to her bunk, where she arranged herself so that when the drug took effect, the weight of the nebulizer would pull the mask away from her face so she wouldn't overdose.

If she did overdose, she thought angrily, serves Sloane right.

As she was slipping away, she wondered what memory might come this time.

She noticed the tension in Sloane's face as his hands flitted over the controls. "What's wrong with your ship?" she asked.

"One of her old war wounds. The scanners are screwed to hell. We nearly flew through another ship back there because the computer didn't detect it as soon as it should have."

Raena sank into the copilot's chair, her stomach queasy again. "Wouldn't it make more sense to slow to normal space, so we can see what we're going to hit while we still have time to avoid it?"

Scowling, Sloane punched the sequence into the navcomputer before Raena could strap herself down. So he was touchy about his flying. Fine. As long as he didn't kill her trying to prove his skill.

An unfamiliar voice boomed over the ship's comm system. "B719, stand by for boarding."

Sloane swore and flipped switches for the rear viewscreen. The haze cleared to reveal an Imperial warship, too close to be in focus, floating behind them.

"Stellar." He caught her arm and hauled her back toward the hold. Raena let him take her wherever he wanted to go. At this point, the external airlock would have been welcome.

Overhead, the Imperial warship latched onto them with a clank.

Sloane grabbed a sonic drill from the tool nook and played it over a wall in the hallway. The bolts shook loose to reveal a hidden cubbyhole. "Get in," he ordered. "Don't break any of those bags of Messiah. One breath of that, and you'll be a hundred before you can count to five."

Cautiously, Raena set a high-heeled boot among the plastic bags on the locker floor. She clamped her eyes shut as he replaced the metal panel.

The cloying smell of plastic filled the locker and choked her. She tried to breathe shallowly though the fabric of her cloak. Darkness washed over her as Sloane turned off the hallway lights. Shuddering, she put out a hand to make sure the panel did not close in on her.

Claustrophobia was the worst. She wished she were afraid of water or rodents or fire or thunderstorms, anything other than small places. Space travel was difficult enough for her, without being forced into the lockers or tunnels or prison cells or any number of other tiny places where she kept finding herself. At this moment, she wanted to start screaming and never stop, let the terror out, but she knew it wouldn't help. The despair was even more painful than the fear.

The overhead noises intensified as the Imperials completed hauling in Sloane's ship. Then someone banged on the main hatch with the butt of a gun.

"Cool your jets," Sloane shouted as he pounded the combination into the lock.

When the hatch whooshed open, light trickled in around the panel in front of Raena. She stifled a sigh of relief. The walls remained steadfast in their original places.

"How can I help you, gentlemen?" Sloane offered.

"Surrender your passenger."

Sloane laughed. "Does this look like a pleasure cruiser?"

"What's your cargo, then?"

"I'm between shipments now, but I've got a bid in on some Yangmai holos. You know the kind." He chuckled salaciously. "Ought to be an interesting haul, if I get it."

Something metal trailed across the metal wall of the hallway. Raena twitched as the locker hummed around her. Then the pitch changed. The metal tapped on the wall to make a point.

"What's in there?"

"Wiring," Sloane answered.

She heard a gun powering up.

"Put it in a holding pattern," Sloane protested. "I'd be glad to open it for you."

He used his sonic drill to open the panel in question. All around Raena, the metal whined and set her teeth on edge. She held herself rigid. She wished she had the power to will herself to die, to vanish, to be completely erased from time and space.

"See?" Sloane asked. "Only wires."

"Lucky for you." The metal dragged over a few more panels, stopping in front of Raena.

She knew what was coming. She remembered it. Her muscles quivered with fear. Sloane removed the panel and she couldn't run. She couldn't escape. She couldn't even shift her feet, for fear of piercing one of the pouches of Messiah. The soldiers stunned her point-blank and hauled her back to Thallian and his torture machine . . .

Rather than watch the memory play out, Raena stomped down hard on a pouch of Messiah. The heel of her boot pierced the pouch, scattering the powdery drug throughout inside of the tiny locker.

Raena gulped in as much as she could. The drug slammed into her system, blotting her out instantly. It felt as if she had been flung bodily against a wall. She forgot how to breathe.

Raena leaned over the handlebars of the jet bike, wringing out all the speed she could from it. Ahead of her, a boy on another bike dodged through the spires of the skyscrapers on Kai, heading toward the spaceport. He nearly impacted one spire, then overcorrected. Raena winced. She hoped he wouldn't let his fear get the better of him. She needed him to pull it together enough to get himself safely back to his ship—so she could steal it.

Of course, he was Thallian's son, so he was used to living with a certain level of terror. The boy got the bike back under control and buzzed off in a straight line. Raena eased off her own throttle, slowing a little so she wouldn't catch him up yet.

He wove over the maze of docking slips, then recognized the one he was heading for. He sent his jet bike into a dive, braking as he descended. Raena hit the throttle again, closing the gap between them. She loosened her safety straps one-handed as she got closer, then unlimbered the stun stick she'd taken from a security guard when she stole the bike.

Holding the stick in her right hand, she sprang off the bike, spreading out in the air to slow her fall, then tucking into a ball around the stun stick to somersault until she could get her feet under her. She landed in a perfect three-point stance atop the Thallians' ship. She checked herself, noted that she had the stun stick angled just so, and grinned. Sometimes, she just loved what her body could do.

Her bike plummeted into the roof of the docking bay next door, exploding into a fireball. Debris rained down around her.

She crept to the edge of the Thallian ship in time to see figures coming out of the shadow of the ship's hatch. A man frogmarched the boy down the ship's ramp, out where she could see them both. The man's gun pointed steadily at the boy's head.

Raena leapt down behind them, between the pair and the open door of the ship. "He's mine!"

The man wrenched the boy around to face her. "No worries, Raena. I'm ready to get out of here, too."

The man reminded her of Gavin, but he was older, his face wrinkled like a crumpled piece of paper. What was left of his hair had turned the color of cobwebs.

"Who are you?" Raena said. If he killed the boy, she might never find Thallian. She dropped the stun stick at her feet and stepped over it, leaving her hands raised above her waist.

"Gavin," he said, as if that should be obvious.

"No. I left Gavin in the market with Ariel."

"That's another Gavin." He grimaced. "A younger one. I'm running out of time, Raena. Let me come with you."

"Where do you think I'm going?

"Off to Thallian's homeworld. To finish what he started."

What kind of trap was this? Who was this old man? How did he know where she was going? How had he found the Thallians' transport, when she'd had no idea where it was until the kid led her to it?

Someone had betrayed her, but she didn't have time to allow it to slow her down. She had to get off Kai quickly, before Planetary Security found her, or else she was going back to a jail cell to serve time for defending herself against Thallian's minions.

She took another step, hands still raised. "Why should I believe you?"

"I thought you'd ask how I knew where to find you," the stranger said by way of an answer. "After you left me on Kai, Planetary Security threw me an' Ariel off-world. I snuck back on and was able to figure out which ship you stole. You were long gone by then and I couldn't figure out how to track you. But now I've come back from the future for you. That's why I knew which docking slip the boy would bring you to. I even know which planet you're going to take him to."

How could he know that, when she hadn't told anyone? Whether he was Gavin or merely some kind of madman who thought he was, she didn't trust him. She couldn't. She had to contact Mykah and the crew. She had a message to deliver to Kavanaugh and Ariel. Time was steadily growing shorter before Planetary Security converged on her here.

So she launched herself at the boy, putting him out of the way with one good hard punch to the head. He sagged, dead weight in the old man's arm, while the gun kept the madman's other hand busy. He dropped the boy as Raena's elbow came round at his head. He blocked the blow with his gun, just as she had hoped. She hit it hard enough to put it out of commission.

He got one foot between hers. She let him pull her over, grabbing his jacket with both fists and pulling him down as well. She twisted enough that he took some of her weight in the fall. Once they'd landed, she darted her head forward, planting a good solid kiss on his mouth. That distracted him just enough that she brought her knee up hard and incapacitated him.

Then she scrambled backward off of him and pushed him off the ramp with the toe of her boot. He was lucky she didn't give him the heel.

She spoke into the comm bracelet on her wrist. "I'm in. I had an unforeseen complication, but it's been handled. There's a fire in the next docking bay over, so dodge the fire suppression team on your way here. The smoke will serve as a beacon for you. We haven't much time."

She hauled the boy up onto her back and carried him onto the ship. As expected, she found a cell the Thallians had kitted out for her. She locked the unconscious teenager into the restraints, then went back outside to check on things.

The old man had crawled over to his gun and was trying to get it aimed at her. Age or pain made his arm shake.

"I don't know who you really are," Raena told him, "but you'd better stop playing with me. Every time a Gavin-figure shows up in one of my dreams, I kill him."

As the words left her lips, though, the dream came apart. She woke up in her cabin on the *Veracity*, the very same shuttle that had been in her dream. She spared a fond thought for Jain, the boy who'd led her to it.

Her thoughts circled around to the Gavin-figure in his dream. What had he said? "I've come back from the future for you."

Her blood iced. Was that the proof she was looking for, the proof that Gavin really was using Messiah against her? Were the nightmares really visions from the moments when the time streams split? Maybe that was why they started as things she remembered, then warped. Maybe, if she'd been able to stay in the dream a little longer, she could have gotten a message to Gavin. Told him to leave her the hell alone.

Or, she thought grimly, maybe the insomnia had driven her insane to the point that such a theory would make even passing momentary sense to her.

Still, this was the first dream in which she had been able to talk back as a somewhat self-aware participant. The way all the other dreams had played out so far, she had always been passive, forced to endure her past and the emotions trapped there. Even when the dreams diverged from her memories of the past, the figure that represented her—both observed and inhabited—reacted to everything as the Raena of that era would have reacted, given the new set of circumstances.

The dream-Raena was trapped by the time in which she existed.

Perhaps the only active figure in any of these dreams was Gavin: choosing the moment, directing the change, god and king of the past.

Served him right to be punished repeatedly for his hubris, stupid fucker. Maybe he'd engineered it all so that she couldn't even speak up in her own defense or ask him to leave her alone. He could rape her memories, her past, and there was no way she could fend him off or tell him no, short of ending him in every timeline where their paths crossed.

Maybe it was time she stopped feeling guilty about killing him and see it as honest self-defense, a kind of unknowing triumph.

Raena no longer had any desire for suicide to stop her torment. The answer was going to have to be murder. Gavin had it coming.

Anyway, it wouldn't be the first time she'd killed someone who believed he loved her. As if she needed any proof that life had really changed for her, she honestly hoped that this time would be the last.

Kavanaugh picked the bar. He hadn't been to Tengri in a couple of years, at least, but he knew Ocho's would still be there. It would be kind to call the place a dive, but it had a trustworthy clientele, in that you could trust everyone there to mind their own business.

He got there early so he could scope the place out and find a good vantage point to wait to meet the crew of the *Veracity*.

He'd settled over a good amber ale—for old times' sake—when the human boy and the blue-furred girl came in holding hands.

He wore some kind of obnoxiously flashing shirt with an adver-
tisement for the casinos on Kai over hand-me-down engineer's
pants, all pockets and loops. She wore a boxy black jacket with
nothing under it and a star field-patterned skirt that swirled past
her knees.

They went straight to the bar for a drink. They weren't military
at all. Barely looked armed. They could have been a young couple
of school kids out for a night on the town, slumming, because
they didn't look like they belonged in a place like this. They may
have been the only people in the place who didn't look at all like
a threat.

Kavanaugh suspected he'd made a mistake assuming that anyone
traveling with Raena was in her league. He shouldn't have dragged
the kids here. Now that he saw them, he felt responsible for making
sure they got home safely.

He moved out of the shadows so they could see him when they
turned around, drinks in hand.

He watched the pair of Chameleon girls cross paths with the couple, but neither the boy nor the girl reacted. Kavanaugh knew what
to watch for, though. He flicked a coin at one Chameleon girl's bare
arm. Without flinching, she snatched the coin from the air, dropped
the wallet she'd stolen, and kept walking.

The boy scooped his wallet up, tucked it back into his trouser
pocket, and sealed the flap over it. "Thanks," he said when they
reached Kavanaugh's table. "I didn't even know it was gone. They
were that smooth."

"Glad to help," Kavanaugh said. "Go ahead and sit down." Once
they were settled and introductions made, he asked, "How is she?"

"No more seizures," Coni said.

"That's good."

"Now she's blaming someone named Gavin Sloane," Mykah
continued.

"Gavin loves her. The crazy-making kind of love," Kavanaugh explained. "He got himself addicted to the Dart, practically wrecked his health, and set about bankrupting himself, looking for her the last time. I saw how nuts he was when she left him on Kai. I can believe he has had a hard time turning loose of her. What is she blaming him for?"

"She thinks he's messing with her dreams," Mykah clarified.

"It makes more sense when she explains it," Coni said.

"No, not really, it doesn't," Mykah added.

Kavanaugh had a sip of ale to hide his smile. When he was certain of his poker face, he asked, "Messing with her how?"

"You really should talk to her," Mykah said. "It will sound crazy coming from one of us. In fact, it will sound crazy coming from her," he hedged, "but at least you'll know she means it."

"Duck," Kavanaugh told them, not a moment too soon.

He was impressed to see them do just that, dodging in opposite directions, staying low. When the creature came crashing across the table they'd just cleared, Kavanaugh caught the table's edge and flipped it upward, sending the spider thing to the floor.

The rest of the fight came piling their way. Kavanaugh left his gun holstered. "Never bring a gun to a fist fight," Doc used to tell him. Someone was going to hit you before you could get clear enough to take a shot, and then your gun would be roaming loose around the party. Never a good thing.

Kavanaugh circled around the altercation. He was amused to see the boy going over it, vaulting off one creature's shoulder, another's head, bouncing off the ceiling, using the light fixture to change direction. The blue girl was up and following him, a big grin on her muzzle.

They were a joy to watch. The girl knew how to work that skirt. The way the boy moved told Kavanaugh he had been training with Raena. Neither of the kids seemed interested in joining in the fight, though. They weren't even really running away, just stirring up trouble in pockets of the room where the brawl hadn't yet reached, all of it done for the sheer love of chaos.

Kavanaugh waded into the fringes of the turmoil and fought his way toward the door. As he expected, the kids got there first and were waiting on him.

"Let's go see Raena," he said.

CHAPTER 14

Mykah unlocked the cabin door and stood back. Kavanaugh had a flashback to opening Raena's tomb, not knowing what he'd find inside. Then he remembered that experience had only been terrifying in retrospect, after he better understood the danger he had been in. He wished he had a clue what he was in for now.

Raena was sitting up on her crisply made bed, back against the wall. She wore skintight workout clothes in a festive shade of aquamarine, so different from the black military-styled clothing he still thought of her wearing. It was hard to tell if her hair was brushed or if she meant it to look that way: sticking out from her head in odd tufts in all directions.

She looked tired, but he was struck again by how pretty she was, how very young she looked. Although her brown skin leaned toward shipboard pallor, her face was still completely smooth. She could pass for twenty, even though he'd met her for the first time almost twenty-five years ago. It took him a moment to miss the white line of scar between her eyes.

"Thanks for coming, Tarik," she said quietly. "I know I already owe you a couple of favors, but I wasn't sure where else I could turn."

"I'm not sure what I can do about bad dreams, Raena. We all have them. I can't prescribe anything for you."

"These are more than dreams." She scooted forward toward the side of the bed, dangling her feet over the edge. She was barefoot, which struck Kavanaugh as wrong. He couldn't remember ever seeing Raena without her high-heeled boots. Even when she'd come out of the tomb, she'd been wearing them.

She asked, "Where are my manners? Would you like something to drink?"

"What'd'ya got?"

"Oh, they'll let me have pretty much anything I ask for. This is the best prison cell I've ever had."

He couldn't tell if she was kidding, or if there was a darker edge of paranoia beneath her light tone.

"Would you like a glass of xyshin?" she offered. "I'm kind of in the mood."

"Sure, that sounds okay."

She didn't get up to get it or even to reach over to the comm button. Kavanaugh looked at her, eyebrows raised.

"One of the others will be along with it in a moment," she explained. "I found out by accident that they were monitoring me. I try not to abuse the knowledge, but room service is pretty quick here."

When the door opened again, a squid-like creature came waltzing in on a multitude of tentacles, supporting a bottle in one tentacle and a pair of glasses in another.

"Vezali, have you met Kavanaugh?" Raena asked politely.

"Not yet," the tentacled creature answered in a high-pitched girlish voice.

"He rescued me from a bounty hunter's ship a long time ago," Raena said. "Remember?"

The dream was very clear in his head: the way the icy crystals of his breath swirled in the stale air, the dead creature with the bashed-in skull glued to the deck by its own frozen blood, Raena caught impossibly tight in the crash web on the wall.

"I remember," he said. "I dreamed about it not too long ago."

Raena got up slowly, languorously, clearly trying not to frighten anyone, and took the bottle and the pair of glasses. She poured the drinks generously, handed one to Kavanaugh and the other to Vezali, and settled back on the bunk with the bottle.

"Stay," she said, "if you want to."

"Sure," Kavanaugh encouraged.

"Thanks." Vezali perched on the end of the bed, since Kavanaugh had the only chair. He wasn't sure how to read her emotions, but her body language didn't communicate any agitation to him. He would have said the squid-girl wasn't frightened of Raena at all.

"I had that dream, too," Raena said, sipping the sweet liquor. "Where did yours end? With me walking off into the rain?"

"Yeah," Kavanaugh said. "That's where my memories of that night end, too: when you left us. I remember how the storm roared outside of Doc's ship. I was so worried about you. Then I didn't see you again until we opened your tomb, all those years later."

Raena jumped in before whatever he'd planned to say next. "The dream kept going for me. I walked off across the marsh toward the forest. A man was waiting there. I thought he was another bounty hunter, so I shot him. When I confirmed the kill, the dead man looked like Gavin. Not Gavin as I saw him last, in my waking life on Kai, but aged. Gavin with less hair and more wrinkles. In the dream, I didn't know who he was. Once I woke up, I figured it out right away."

"Isn't that how dreams always go?" Kavanaugh asked. "They make more sense after you wake up and think them over."

"Do you remember when you opened my tomb?" Raena asked, conversationally, as if she wasn't invested in the answer. "You told me that you worked for Gavin. You said he was on a moon base orbiting the planet."

Kavanaugh frowned. Haltingly, he admitted, "I dreamed about that recently, too."

"Did your dream end when I walked out of the mountain?" Raena asked. "Or do you remember Gavin being there?"

Kavanaugh stared at her.

"You do remember that, don't you?" she prompted.

Kavanaugh confessed, "In my dream, Gavin walked into the tomb. He carried a torch pointed down at his feet, so I couldn't really see his face. But he walked straight over and hugged you, which was weird because—"

"It didn't really happen that way," Raena finished for him. "You came up to the moon with me and Gavin's security goons. Gavin didn't recognize me at first. He accused me of being an impostor, sent to fool him by Ariel or one of his ex-wives."

"How did you know Gavin was in the tomb in my dream?"

"He was in mine, too," she said. "Did yours end when we left you to take care of your men?"

Kavanaugh nodded.

"You're lucky, then. Mine ended after Gavin took me off the Templar's world. He turned his yacht around in the atmosphere and nuked the archaeological encampment from the air. He said Thallian's brother would torture your men in an effort to find me. 'This is kinder,' Gavin said. 'At least, this is quick.' I'm glad you don't remember getting nuked by Gavin."

Kavanaugh's mouth went dry. He raised the glass of sickly sweet liquor in his hand and choked down a swallow.

In the real world, Kavanaugh had gone up to Gavin's base with Raena expressly because he expected Gavin to do what she'd dreamed: wipe out the encampment, kill the men, erase all evidence that Sloane had funded the grave-robbing. Kavanaugh had been stunned and happily surprised when Sloane decided instead to bribe the men into silence. That is, he'd been happy until Thallian's men started finding the grave robbers and torturing them to death . . .

Raena sipped from the bottle of xyshin and added, "In my dream, I shot Gavin for killing you. That woke me up. In fact, I've shot Gavin almost nightly in my dreams, or I've beaten his head in, or I've broken his neck, or I've thrown him out an airlock . . ."

She shook herself, had another swig from her bottle, and said, "For a long time, all my dreams had Gavin in them. Then there were some that didn't. Those were the worst. But I talked to Ariel a couple of days ago. She'd shared some of the dreams I've had, including the day I rescued her from the *Arbiter*. In fact, all this started when I dreamed that Gavin drugged me and hauled me away from the souk on Kai. He snatched me before Thallian's men attacked, like he knew the attack was coming and wanted to get me out of the way first. Ariel had a dream exactly like that."

Vezali interrupted. "Is it normal for humans to share dreams at a distance?"

"I never heard of anyone sharing dreams like this," Kavanaugh said. "What does it mean?"

"When it was just me, I thought I was going crazy. But my insanity wouldn't cause you and Ariel to have similar dreams. How could it? I can't dream across time and space."

"You don't have any theories?"

"I have a theory, but it's the maddest thing yet. I don't want to get to it right away. First, I want you to know that I dreamed that Gavin met me at *this* ship on Kai the same day that Thallian's men jumped us in the souk."

"Wait a second. He met you at this ship after he carried you away from the souk?"

"Yeah. This was a new dream, one I had almost a week later. It's like Gavin just keeps coming at the problem in different ways . . . Anyway, in the real world, I didn't know where the Thallians had parked their ship, so I let the youngest member of the attack team go—he was one of Thallian's sons. The dream went just the way I remembered, until I found Gavin waiting at the *Raptor* when Jain and I got here.

Gavin grabbed the kid, held him at gunpoint. And in the dream, I knew if Gavin shot the kid, I would never find Thallian. I would never be able to kill him. I would have to flaunt where I was even more than having Mykah send videos of me to his kids. I would have to drive Thallian to come to me in person, after he'd exhausted all his brothers, all his sons, trying to capture me first . . ."

As if hearing the slightly hysterical ring to her voice, Raena had another slug from her bottle of xyshin. Kavanaugh noticed that her hands trembled.

"In my last dream," Raena said more calmly, "Gavin said he had come back from the future. He said that was why he knew which ship I'd be coming to, even before I knew myself. The weirdest thing was that he was really *old* in that dream. His hair had almost completely gone. His face was all crumpled up. He looked ancient, Tarik. He looked like he really had come from the future."

"It was a dream," Kavanaugh argued.

"Was it? What if it was an alternate timeline?"

He actually laughed at her. Afterward, he wondered that he had the courage, but at the time, it seemed like the only appropriate response. Everyone knew that time travel only happened in stories.

"Do you really think Gavin has a time machine?" he asked. "Where would he have gotten it? He pretty nearly bankrupted himself looking for you on the Templar world and buying off the archaeological team after we found you. He had some money squirreled away, and Templar artifacts to sell, but if such a thing as a time machine really existed in the universe, it would be extremely expensive to access. Gavin wouldn't have the funds."

"What if it was Templar tech? What if it was something your team dragged out of the tomb?"

Kavanaugh had a moment when he considered the possibility, but the truth was obvious: "Nobody knows how Templar tech worked."

"Vezali could probably figure it out," Raena said. "She can make almost anything work."

"You're flattering me," the tentacled girl said.

"That doesn't make it less true," Raena answered.

"Okay," Kavanaugh interrupted, "let's say you're right: Gavin has a Templar time machine and somehow got it to work. What is he trying to do?"

"Go back in time and rescue me. He's trying to save me from having to hunt down Thallian and his family. He's trying to keep me with him."

The stunning narcissism of that statement silenced Kavanaugh. He looked to Vezali, but she was calmly sipping her xyshin through a straw. Finally, he asked, "Why would he keep doing it over and over?"

"Because there is no happily ever after for us. I'm older now, wiser hopefully, and a lot less quick on the trigger. Unfortunately, every time Gavin freaks out one of my younger selves, she panics and kills him. That was how I dealt with pretty much everyone while I was on the run. It's amazing to me now, looking back, that I didn't kill him from the get-go on Nizarrh. Or I didn't kill you and Doc and Skyler. Or Ariel on the *Arbiter* . . . I was a frightened little girl. The only way I knew to protect myself was to do what Thallian taught me: strike first and leave your enemies too shattered to return fire."

"Wait a minute, wait a minute. If Gavin really is going back in time and trying to right things to be with you, why wouldn't he keep going to the same time? Why would he hop all around? If he'd already been in a specific time and things didn't work out, why wouldn't he keep coming back to the same point in time? Why wouldn't he keep redoing the same moment until he got it right?"

"Maybe he can't. Maybe he can't interfere with himself. Or maybe, once he's dead in a certain timeline, he can't come back from the dead. He's erased on that timeline, going forward."

Kavanaugh had another drink. Damn, he hated the hyper-sweet kids' liquor. He wasn't sure why he'd let her suggest it. If they were going to be imagining Gavin as a time-traveling super villain, Kavanaugh really wanted to be drinking something much stronger. And probably more bitter.

"You know this all sounds crazy, right?"

Raena clenched her teeth in a smile. "It *is* crazy. It's *making* me crazy. But that doesn't make it less real."

"All right. So let's say Gavin has a time machine. He's traveling back in time to rescue you. Why is he concentrating on the window of time between when you ran away from Thallian until you got off of Kai? Why doesn't he buy you from the slavers before Ariel's family gets you?"

"Actually, he tried that. I was eleven. I strangled him after I caught him peeping at me."

Kavanaugh was so aghast that it took him a moment to come up with another question. "Why doesn't he go back to your childhood?"

"I don't know, Tarik. I'm trying to figure this out from inside the middle of it. Maybe he can only go to times and places that he knows something specific about. Gavin knows when I was born—he'd seen my birth record—but he would have had to find my mom, who was in hiding with a group of Humans First! terrorists. We were always on the move. I never went to school. I don't even know where all we lived before my mother sent me away. I couldn't go back in time and find myself. Did you ever tell him about dropping me off on Barraniche? The where and when of it? He knew when you opened the tomb, so he could be there. He knew when the attack was coming on Kai, so he could head it off. He knew when he'd rescued me from the *Arbiter*, so he could show up a little earlier than he had the last time and spring me. Ariel probably told him when her dad bought me from the Viridians. "

"So, wait . . . If Gavin is really changing the past, wouldn't our present be wiped out? Wouldn't we all be switched over to a new timeline and continue on there? Why would we remember how things used to be at all?"

"I think you and I and Ariel, we're all continuing on our original path. I think the dreams signal when something is being changed, when time splits off from the track we're on."

"Why would we dream about them?"

"I think they're like bubbles in the stream of time. I think that when the dreams wake us, the bubbles pop. Time has been changed, but we're snapped back to our original lives. And the new timeline goes on with our mirror selves in it, none the wiser."

"We need to be drinking more," Kavanaugh groaned.

"The whole crew probably needs to be drinking more," Vezali said. "This is starting to make a scary amount of sense."

"It is?" Raena asked, surprised.

"Coni and Mellix have been researching the Messiah drug. What you're describing is how it was theorized to have worked."

"What's the Messiah drug?" Kavanaugh asked.

"Coni probably knows more about it than I do," Raena told him.

"Mellix knows the most," Vezali corrected. "Maybe he'll meet us in the galley and tell us about it."

There was a moment of awkward silence, then Vezali added, "If you fall asleep, Raena, we'll hustle you back in here."

"I appreciate it."

"So you *want* to be locked up?" Kavanaugh asked. That might have been the most difficult thing he'd been asked to believe yet.

"I don't want to hurt anyone. I was sleepwalking the other day and it freaked me out. I want them to keep me from doing any harm to them, myself, or the ship."

Mykah opened the door from the outside. "Come on down to the galley so Mellix and Coni can fill us all in."

Mykah had put the coffee on. The warm smell of it filled the room as it brewed. Raena took the center of the bench along the wall. Kavanaugh slid in beside her. She was amused. He was always more comfortable with his back against a wall, even if it meant sitting next to a serial murderer who had sleepwalking hallucinations. Being a veteran was funny that way.

"Anyone hungry?" Coni asked. "I bought moon cakes while we were out."

"I love those," Raena said, surprised. "I haven't had them in ages."

Coni took a tray from the cooler and brought them to the table. Then Mykah added a handful of mugs and the coffee carafe. Everyone settled in.

"Everything you told us earlier about the Messiah drug seems to be true," Coni told Raena. "It appeared during the Borderlands War, after the human Empire started trying to expand into Templar trade space. The drug appeared on planets where the local government had collaborated with the Empire. Several times, the governments fell, to be replaced by the Empire, and eventually overthrown by more, ah, open-minded Coalition governments."

"Meaning: nonhuman?" Raena asked.

"Yes. From what I can uncover, only humans were ever accused of using the Messiah drug and they mostly—though not always—used it against other humans. Which is what led to the theory that humans were manufacturing and distributing it."

"Humans in league with the Coalition?"

"Well, that's what I wondered, too. As you said, it doesn't make sense for the Empire to be involved, since it seemed to have worked exclusively to their detriment. In the aftermath, the Empire made a convenient scapegoat, because they weren't around to defend themselves. The drug seems to have vanished about the time that the Empire fell, and besides, why would you trust the word of a government that was known to have intentionally unleashed a genocidal plague? The timeline is exceedingly muddy, though. From everything I can find, Messiah's usage declined before the final days of the Empire, though, long before Thallian was identified as spreading the Templar plague."

Raena took one of the moon cakes and bit into it. It was every bit as sweet and perfect as she remembered. She had lost track of meals, since she'd been locked in her cabin. Had she eaten anything since Mykah's post-Capital City feast?

Mykah poured her some coffee and, after a sip, Raena dragged her thoughts back to the conversation. "Have you been able to connect Messiah to the Templars?" she asked.

Coni's lips stretched into something that might have been a smile, but Mellix answered for her. "You're not the first person to suggest that—there are several pharmacological theorists who proposed it—but beyond the novel I was telling you about, there's no evidence to support a Templar connection, other than the timing. The drug disappeared almost exactly the same time as the Templars began to die out."

"And Outrider was never found, was he?" Raena asked.

Kavanaugh interrupted. "Who is Outrider?"

"I met him through Gavin on Nizarrh," Raena said. "Gavin had been sent by Coalition Command to bring me in—that's what he said, anyway—but first he had an errand to run. He took me through the tunnels under the city to a warehouse where extremely elderly humans were lying in little cubbies. Outrider was very proud of his crop of Messiah junkies."

"What was Gavin doing?" Kavanaugh wondered.

"Working as a courier for Outrider. I'm not sure where Gavin was supposed to deliver the drug. He could have been smuggling it on the side—that wouldn't have been out of character—or it could have been meant to go to Coalition Command, along with me."

Kavanaugh said, "I can't deny the smuggling, but I never pictured Gavin as a drug runner. What happened to the shipment?"

"I don't know. Gavin said that when Thallian's minions boarded his ship, they confiscated the drug when they captured me. I don't know where it went from there."

"Sloane was pretty vocal about his disgust for drug users when we were younger. I'd always thought he stayed away from chemicals, until Ariel told me about accidentally hooking him on the Dart."

It was Vezali's turn to jump in. "What's the Dart?"

"It's a Templar drug," Raena explained. "I'm not sure how *they* used it, but apparently it makes human brains focus. Users determine the project they want to accomplish and, as long as the drug stays in their systems, they arrange their whole lives in such a way as to achieve the goal."

"That's a good summation of it," Mellix said.

Raena stared at him. She realized she'd just told the journalist that she was captured by Thallian during the War. She had completely blown any cover story she might have been trying to hide behind.

Mellix's whiskers twitched into a smile that was meant to be reassuring. "We can talk later. For now, get me up to speed on the Messiah drug."

"Wait," Mykah said. "First: Humans can take a Templar drug?"

"I'm told our physiologies are very similar," Raena said, all business again. "I don't know how true that is."

"So your man Sloane has a history of abusing Templar chemicals?" Mellix said.

Raena nodded. "He had the connection to Outrider and Messiah, although I don't think he could have afforded to use it back then—and Ariel gave him a taste for Templar-made drugs while they were together, before I got out of prison."

"Well, it's not a smoking gun," Mellix said, "but it is an interesting set of coincidences."

"Isn't it?" Raena said. She turned to Coni. "Vezali said you had figured out how the Messiah drug works."

"Not entirely," Coni said. "I've been able to read some of the trial transcripts, but there are fewer declassified documents than I expected—and there weren't many trials to begin with." She sneaked a moon cake off the tray and took a bite, chewing meditatively before she went on.

"Messiah addicts claimed that they could travel back in time. They believed they could change the past, but since those changes didn't carry through to accepted modern-day reality, their assertions were discounted as hallucinations." She took another bite of cake, licked her teeth, and said, "And yet, in our agreed-upon reality, the governments they were working to overthrow did actually fall. Not because of anything the terrorists did objectively in the real galaxy, but because the victims apparently had bad dreams that drove them mad. The victims made bad decisions, or fatal mistakes, or in a pair of cases, became dangerously violent on live news feeds."

"It doesn't make sense," Mykah protested. "The drug users didn't do anything except trip out on the past. How could that cause other people to freak out and destroy their own governments?"

"Exactly so," Coni said. "It makes no sense to us."

"Which makes it sound exactly like Templar tech," Mellix pointed out.

No one raised any exceptions to that truism, so Coni continued. "Every legitimate government in the galaxy—continental, planetary, interplanetary, all the way up to the Council of Worlds—fell over themselves to condemn the drug and its users, because they knew there is no defense against it. How do you defend against something happening somewhere else because of strangers you've never been in contact with? Everyone recognized the Messiah drug as exceptionally dangerous to those in positions of power, even if they never touched the stuff or personally knew anyone who did. They couldn't prove any connection between the handful of users they captured alive—and most that they found were already dead, used up by the drug before they were discovered. But when your government is being brought down by insanity from within, searching for the nest of dying oldsters responsible for destabilizing it was never the chief priority. Damage control from within got far more attention."

"How do you track a drug when there's no connection between its users and its victims?" Raena asked.

"Exactly," Coni said. "Try as they might, they caught no manufacturer, no distribution network, no organized crime, none of the usual players in the culture or dissemination of a drug. All they had was a number of destabilized Empire-friendly governments and a bunch of old, dried-out, dead humans, who were bio-identical to younger freedom fighters. And the name Outrider."

Raena set her coffee down before she spilled it. "They caught him?"

"No. They had descriptions of him, but never physical proof of his existence. No video recordings. No DNA evidence. Apparently, he never traveled anywhere, never touched anything, never left a record of himself anywhere that could be tracked or duplicated or stuck on a wanted poster. They never caught sight of him. They never even identified his species, although it was widely assumed he was human. He is the ghost at the heart of the mystery. Where did he come from? Why did he go? Where did he get the supply of the drug that he peddled?"

"I saw him," Raena confessed, "in one of my dreams. He was serving as the Prime Minister of the Council of Worlds."

"Did you hear his name?" Mellix asked. "His real name?"

She shook her head. "It was a dream in which the Templar were not wiped out. That weirded me out sufficiently that I lost track of pretty much everything else. And to make it hyper-realistic, the Templar had come to the Council of Worlds for no more exciting reason than to propose some new trade plan. Vezali and I watched them on the news."

Vezali's coffee cup hit the table's edge with a loud crack.

Raena looked at her and smiled. "You remember that?"

"I thought it was a hallucination," she said. "There was a blond woman, with a white shirt and her hair like this." She used a tentacle to mime a braid hanging over her shoulder.

"You remember meeting Ariel on Callixtos?" Raena asked, waiting until Vezali nodded. "She remembered you from her dream, too."

"Not to theorize about someone else's hallucinations," Mellix said, "but that could be evidence that Outrider was working with the Templar and they rewarded him with a position of power."

"Now you're *all* talking crazy," Kavanaugh said. "It doesn't matter if the Templar hired some human Quisling to pimp their drugs to fuck up governments during the War. It happened decades ago. The damage is done. What does it matter to the galaxy now?"

Raena laughed. "Oh, Tarik, you're on the *Veracity*. We solve historic atrocities and see that the perpetrators are brought to justice."

"You're mocking us," Mykah accused, actually hurt.

"Never," Raena said. "I fully expect you to find Outrider, so that he can take responsibility for his crimes."

"But why am I here?" Kavanaugh asked. "I mean, it's all a fascinating thought game, but . . ."

"I need your help tracking down Gavin. If he's using the Messiah drug to mess with my past, that means the drug still exists in a useable form. It means the galaxy is in danger. Destroying me, that's micro scale. But what if a couple of the bigger planetary governments fell? What if humans provided a convenient scapegoat once again? What if there's another galactic war—and this time, the galaxy doesn't choose to stay its hand? What if they all band together to wipe humanity out? What if humans don't actually have rights after all?"

Silence followed Raena's litany. She reached calmly forward and helped herself to a second moon cake, spilling its powdery coating across the table in a trail like the arm of the Milky Way.

"How does the Messiah drug work?" Haoun asked.

"I've been researching it," Mellix explained. "It's similar to the Dart, except that instead of moving around in the world of the living, fixated on finishing your project, Messiah addicts lie down somewhere that their bodies won't be disturbed. Then the drug knocks their spirits, ghosts, souls, whatever you choose to call them, loose from their flesh and lets them move back—only backward—in time. They can only go somewhere within the span of their own pasts, not back before they themselves were born. And the farther back they go, or the more often they go, the more of their own life energy they burn up. That's what makes them appear to age so quickly."

"But how does it work?" Mykah asked. "What does it allow them to do in the past?"

"They can only make minor changes. As soon as they interact with someone in the past and change things, then a bubble forms in the river of time. It's like knotting a new string onto an old one. The original string continues on as before, but there's a split where the new timeline is added to the old one. Sort of like branches on a tree."

Raena asked, "Can Messiah users see what changes progress from the alterations they make?"

"Only for a brief period of time. Then the participants in the new reality develop autonomy and move forward beyond the time travelers' influence and control. Eventually something happens that jolts the time traveler's consciousness back into his flesh in this universe."

"So Gavin never gets to enjoy rescuing you?" Kavanaugh asked Raena.

"As far as I've seen, Gavin never stands a chance."

Coni dragged the conversation back to the addicts. "Its effects on the body are so brutal, why would anyone use the drug more than once?"

Mellix grinned. "Raena, you'll excuse me for speaking frankly?"

"Please do."

"Sloane has been affecting your dreams for how long?"

"I was looking at my notes earlier. It's been about a week."

"And has he driven you to do anything dangerous yet?"

"Other than the night I was sleepwalking and had the seizure, no. My judgment has been impaired, though." She meant: I've admitted more in front of you than I ever intended, but she didn't confess that now. Instead, she said, "The others would be a better judge of my behavior."

"Well, now that I know what you've been going through," Mykah said, "I think you've held it together remarkably well."

"Exactly," Mellix said. "For the revolutionaries to bring down the planetary governments, they would gang up on some functionary, a president, say, or a prime minister. They would research everything about that person's life and then would take it apart in his or her dreams. And the dreams didn't need to be limited to once a night, since every addict in the team could attack every single night. Eventually, the target's sanity would be so broken that the Messiah users could attack during the day, any time the target closed his eyes."

No one bothered to point out how this sounded exactly like what Raena was experiencing.

Kavanaugh said, "I don't understand why Gavin would do this to you. Isn't his whole goal just to get in bed with you? Brainwashing chemicals aren't hard to find, if you know what you're looking for. Why would he go through all this trouble when he could just find you and dose you?"

"I think he was trying to find me for a while," Raena said. "However, except for our trip to Capital City, I haven't been off this ship since we were on Callixtos. I haven't had a legitimate identity since the Emperor had my death certificate forged. I didn't want anyone to pick me up on some civilized world before I could prove I belong in this galaxy here and now. Gavin couldn't get to me, because I wasn't anywhere he could get."

She knew Mellix was watching her face, but she didn't look up to meet his eyes.

"What makes you think Sloane will be hard to find?" Kavanaugh asked. "All he wants is you back, right? Maybe he's just waiting for you to call."

"I don't have any idea how to reach him," Raena said. "Sounds like he burned Ariel badly enough that I didn't ask her. I checked the directories, but all the Sloane Incorporated stuff, they're all just dead ends. He has vanished from the news grid."

"I've got a couple of old addresses for him," Kavanaugh offered. "One of them might work, or at least forward to him. But if not, what are you going to do?"

"I don't know," Raena said. "He's burning himself out fast, if the way he's been aging in my dreams is any indication. He's going to get really desperate, soon. I think he's already been trying whacky things like killing Thallian so that the plague didn't get disseminated and the Templar didn't die, or killing the Emperor so that the plan was never hatched. In those futures, humanity sticks to its little segment of the galaxy and does not mix."

She licked the flour off of her fingers, then added, "If we don't find him and his cache of Messiah before it kills him, then that stuff will be loose in the galaxy. So time is short, people."

"What do you need us to do?"

"Finding Gavin is priority one."

CHAPTER 15

Raena retreated to her cabin with Coni and Vezali. "I need your help," she said. "If Kavanaugh can reach Sloane, what do I say to him that will get him to agree to see me?

"What do you want to say to him?" Vezali asked.

"What the fuck do you think you're doing?" Raena grimaced at the shrill edge to her voice and added more quietly, "I don't think that's going to get me what I need."

'You're a pretty good actress," Coni said, and again Raena wasn't sure if there was condemnation or praise in her voice. "Can't you just sweet-talk him?"

"I'm not sure I could pull it off," Raena admitted. "I want to explode at him when I see him. If I lead him on first, that might make it worse over all. He could decide the ultimate fuck-you would be to send the Messiah drug out of our reach into the galaxy, where it can do the most possible harm. More than I want him to stop messing with me, I want to protect the galaxy from another all-out war. And I want Gavin to lead us to Outrider, if that's possible. I want to know what his deal is."

"I'm not entirely clear why you think Outrider is involved," Vezali said. "You've only seen him once in your dreams—"

"Twice," Raena corrected.

"And once in real life, more than twenty years past, right? That doesn't guarantee he's still alive, especially if he was using his own product, or that he's peddling it again. You've dreamt about the Templar still being alive. Not everything you dream is true."

Raena nodded, point taken. Still, she had a real sense that this thing was bigger than just one man's obsession with a woman he couldn't keep.

"If Outrider's not involved," she conceded slowly, "where did Gavin get the Messiah he's using?"

Coni said, "His men were looting everything but the bodies from the Templar tombworld, right?"

"You think Kavanaugh's team found a crate of Messiah in one of the tombs?" Raena asked.

"We know the stone preserves whatever's stored inside it, correct? Maybe there isn't a new source for the drug at all. Maybe there's only one very old source."

Raena tried to picture the day Gavin opened a Templar casket, expecting to find jewelry or sculpture or something else beautiful, and instead found pouches of gummy white chemicals. How had he recognized the Messiah for what it was?

Then she remembered him telling her about waking up on the floor of his ship, stuck to the deck by the Messiah the Imperial soldiers had spilled around him. She remembered how he told her that he'd held his breath for the longest time, terrified of inhaling the drug as he cleaned himself up.

"How would he know how to take it?" she wondered aloud. "Were there how-to directions in the old transcripts?"

"It was supposed to be vaporized before it could be inhaled," Coni said. "Among the few pieces of evidence they collected in the past were some of the vapor machines."

"Did they look Templar-made?" Vezali asked.

"No. They were really simple contraptions, almost childlike. Anyone could make or operate one."

"The perfect bait," Raena said. "Make it simple and put it in the hands of fanatics willing to die to drag down their planetary governments. I don't suppose there was ever any indication where the vaporizers were made?"

"Actually, each surviving one was different. They all seemed to have been cobbled together on the planets where they were found."

"So someone somewhere was teaching potential clients how to make their own vaporizers," Raena guessed.

Vezali followed that thought up with, "It's possible the instructions are still floating around somewhere, waiting to be found."

"Yes," Coni said. "I didn't find them as I researched, but it's possible."

"In all the hives of addicts they uncovered, did they ever find Messiah itself? If they had, is the chemical signature online?" Raena asked. "Maybe someone is synthesizing it again."

"No. That is one of the weirdest things: in every case when a den of addicts was captured, all traces of the drug were gone. It was as if someone—maybe Outrider—tidied up and left only the bodies behind."

"Did anyone ever survive their addiction?" Raena asked. "You said some of the junkies had been captured alive . . ."

"They're all dead now," Coni reported. "I checked. The way the drug works, it burns through the body, disrupting cell replication. The addicts don't just look old, their bodies stop repairing themselves. They aren't aged because the drug has eaten up all their time—although that was a theory for a while, until the autopsy evidence came in—they're aged because they are destroyed at a cellular level. All of the addicts located alive quickly succumbed to diseases associated with extreme advanced age in humans."

Raena tried to sum it all up. "Okay. So Gavin found some Messiah drug, helpfully identified in Imperial Standard, in a Templar tomb, alongside a set of easy-to-follow instructions on how to use it and a machine for making it ingestible."

"That seems far more likely than this mysterious barely-identified pusher who comes out of nowhere after all these years of anonymity carrying a universally banned substance that he shares with your ex-boyfriend, just so Sloane can mess with your head." Coni spoke so quickly that her words tumbled over each other. "This Outrider guy is used to bigger game boards than one man's bedroom."

Not insulted, Raena asked, "What if Outrider worked for the Templar? What if he was only the front, and they handled all the manufacture and distribution of the Messiah? As the plague was taking them down, they put the last of their supply into their tombs. Maybe Outrider was supposed to come and get it, but he couldn't get the slab open? Or he was afraid to come and fiddle with the tombs, just like Thallian was."

"But how would he know that your Gavin found the drug?"

"I've always thought of him as a spider, sitting in the middle of his web. He'd know when any of the strings twitched somewhere."

When Raena finished, silence filled her cabin.

"Okay," she said. "That sounds crazy, even to me. Forget I suggested it."

Vezali pointed out, "None of this gets us any closer to what you're going to say to Sloane if we can reach him."

"True. Do you have a suggestion?"

"Could you tell him you've been thinking about him? Tell him you have been rethinking how things ended, that you'd like to see him?"

Raena smiled. "That would be perfect. I'll feel better if I don't have to lie to him."

Secretly, she was entertained that it took the one of them without complicated companionship issues to come up with the simplest solution.

Kavanaugh went back to the *Sundog* and left a couple of messages for Sloane. He wasn't sure how successful any of them would be for eliciting a response, but so far, that was all he'd been called upon to do.

He pulled out the octagonal Templar box that was his only souvenir from his days robbing graves for Gavin Sloane. When he touched the box just right, its top irised open in the most elegant way possible. Inside it coiled the lock of black hair as long as his leg.

When Raena walked out of that tomb, her hair had been crazy long. Sloane asked Kavanaugh to build her a bathtub. The only thing Raena wanted in the whole galaxy, after twenty years of imprisonment, had been a bubble bath. As soon as she got her hair washed, she hacked it all off with a knife. Kavanaugh snuck in later and collected this lock as a memento.

Kavanaugh wondered if she'd had the *Veracity* outfitted with a tub, then laughed aloud at himself. That was an inappropriate direction for his thoughts to zoom off into. Clearly, he'd been alone much too long. For all he knew now, Raena had hooked up with the girl with all the tentacles.

Yeah, that train of thought was an improvement, he chided himself, shifting uncomfortably.

He touched the silken hair, uncertain why he'd kept it. Originally, he'd told himself that it was evidence to give to Ariel, a way to prove that her sister was still alive. In the end, he hadn't needed any proof.

Yet he still kept it.

He thought back to finding Raena on that bounty hunter's ship twenty-five years ago. She had looked so fragile then, like a doll made of spun glass. All he'd wanted to do had been to cradle her in his arms, to protect her from the bad men in the galaxy.

After that, she'd run away from Doc's ship, run toward Gavin, and gotten captured by Thallian. In the end, she got sentenced by the Emperor to be imprisoned in her tomb. Pretty much, the bad men had lined up to take a swing at her.

When Kavanaugh broke her out of that tomb—and after he'd gotten over his immediate, overwhelming fear of her—those protective feelings had come rushing back. He still wanted to take care of her. And by then he knew that the bad men in the galaxy included Gavin Sloane.

So what was Kavanaugh doing here, now? Still yearning to protect Raena?

This time, he realized, was different. This time, she had actually asked for his help.

He knew what she was. He knew when he'd found her the first time that she had killed the bounty hunter who had been frozen to the deck, although even now Kavanaugh wasn't entirely sure how she'd done it. He'd seen the security footage of Raena killing Thallian's henchmen in the souk on Kai. He knew she'd gone to the Thallian homeworld and killed every Thallian there, boy and man. She was a killer who wouldn't hesitate to kill again, to protect herself or those she considered her friends.

But she wasn't the first killer Kavanaugh had met, only the first he'd befriended. Twice now that he knew of, and probably more times that he didn't, Raena had passed up opportunities to kill him. He supposed that was because she counted him amongst her friends.

It wasn't much to base a friendship on, he knew, but judging from the life she led, Raena probably didn't know how to make real friends. Not with humans, anyway. She seemed to be doing a good job cobbling together a surrogate family out of the gaggle of aliens on the *Veracity*.

The *Veracity's* crew were all kids, though. Kavanaugh understood then that Raena had called on him because, when she confronted Gavin Sloane, she didn't want hackers, games players, and media pirates to watch her back. She wanted an adult. A soldier.

He looked down into the octagonal box at the black coil of hair and wondered over it: Raena had been brave enough to go alone into a whole nest of Thallians, but she wanted backup when she caught up with Gavin Sloane. Was she afraid she'd lose her nerve when it came to someone for whom she had actually professed love? Or was she afraid she wouldn't be able to stay her hand if she needed to?

He wasn't sure how he felt about watching Raena kill Gavin, if it came to that. Gavin had pushed his way into Raena's head—and Kavanaugh and Ariel's heads, too, tangentially. That casual defilement required some response. As far as Kavanaugh was concerned, Raena had the most right to make it. Kavanaugh felt violated, though, and angry enough to want a piece of justice himself.

He supposed the only way he would ever know how the story spun out was to go along for the ride.

Mykah tapped on Raena's door. "Am I welcome?"

"Always," she called. "Come in. You'll have to sit on the floor unless you brought a chair." She and Vezali sat on the bed, while Coni had her desk chair.

"The floor is fine." Mykah came in and left the door open behind him. "Are you hungry? I made naan and hummus."

"Now you really are spoiling me." Raena accepted one of the bottles of ale he handed around, but joined him on the floor to attack the warm flat bread.

"I realized you didn't get to eat on Tengri, like the rest of us," Mykah said. "So this is my apology for that—and for doubting you earlier."

She looked up from the piece of naan she was swiping through the bean dip. "Mykah—all of you—I . . . Well, I had a long time to come to terms with my past. When I was in that tomb, there was nothing else to do. I know you have discovered piecemeal, after you took me in, what I have been capable of. I am determined not to be that person I was any more, but you have every right to be afraid of her. These nightmares have tested me, but more than anything else, they've reminded me to be grateful how much my life has changed." She smiled at him, at all of them. "No apologies are needed."

She tasted Mykah's hummus and swooned for effect. "This really is the best thing I've ever eaten."

Before too long, drawn by the laughter, Haoun came in to join them, followed by Mellix and the kiisas. Steam settled into Raena's lap, purring, as she leaned back against her bunk and listened to the crew enthuse about their adventures on Tengri. Mykah told about Kavanaugh and the Chameleon girls. Coni told about the bar fight at Ocho's. Vezali had gone to a restaurant where you caught your own fish from a pond.

Raena was so comfortable and relaxed that it was easy to forget that she had a clingy ex-boyfriend somewhere in the galaxy who had been attacking her sleep for days on end. Knowing that she was not going crazy after all had changed everything. The sense of weight being lifted from her made her practically giddy.

"What do you plan to do, after we find Sloane?" Mykah asked.

"Oh, are you coming along?"

Mykah looked pointedly around the room at the others, before he spoke. "You took us out of our lives and gave us all this," he gestured around vaguely at the ship and the others, and then paused uncomfortably. "Plus, you know . . . you're one of us. We can't have you facing off another homicidal ex-boyfriend. Alone. Again."

Raena laughed, embarrassed and touched. "I wasn't going to volunteer you. Both Kavanaugh and I have been affected by it. He knows Sloane much better than I ever did. Together, we'll have to persuade him to turn over any Messiah he has left and connect us with Outrider, if he's still alive."

"And then Mellix and I will do an exposé on the Messiah drug."

Mellix met Raena's gaze and said, "Please. The galaxy needs to know about this."

"The galaxy needs to be protected from it," Raena corrected. "Stopping its spread is going to have to take precedence over the story. If you can accept that, I would be honored to have you along."

"Agreed," Mellix said.

Raena breathed out, feeling her chest unhitch. She was relieved to have them back her up.

Eventually, before she was ready, all the long hours, violent nightmares, and stress snuck up with her. Her head dropped forward suddenly, jolting her unpleasantly out of her contentment.

"Thank you all for coming in tonight," she said sleepily, cutting across Haoun's account of his winnings for the evening. "I hate to throw you out, but . . ."

The general exodus was more seemly than she might have expected.

"You, too," she told Steam, trying to nudge it up.

Mellix bent down to scoop the kiisa into his arms. "They're a pretty good judge of character," he told her.

"Thank you." She offered him a smile.

Mykah finished gathering the dishes and then paused in the doorway.

"Yes," Raena said, before he could ask. "Lock me in tonight. We haven't heard if Kavanaugh reached Gavin yet. I don't want to take any chances."

"I'm sorry," he said as he closed the door.

Coni waited in the galley to help Mykah clean up from the impromptu party.

He smiled at her as he came in with his arms full. She rinsed the ale bottles while he loaded the dishwasher. "I really thought she'd gone crazy," he admitted.

"So did she. But it's a good measure of how much she's changed that she asked for our help, then told you to protect us however you needed to."

"Don't tell me you weren't frightened of her."

Coni shrugged. Now that she thought about it, she realized she hadn't been particularly afraid. She had been observing Raena since the free-running game on Kai. No doubt she could be lethal—the Thallians were proof of that—but in every other instance where she had a choice, Coni had seen Raena choose to stay her hand.

Mykah was case in point. Coni had expected the little woman would be grateful for his company, but she hadn't rushed to drag him into her bed. Coni had read enough of Raena's history to appreciate that sort of restraint was new for her.

"It's going to be morning soon," Coni said.

"We'd better get to bed, then." Mykah took her hand and pulled her along after him.

The message chime rang, stirring her out of a deep, restful sleep. Raena gathered the coverlet around her bare midriff and scooted over to the computer to respond.

"I got through to Gavin," Kavanaugh said. "I told him you were trying to contact him."

"Did you get a look at him?"

"No. He just typed in a reply."

"What did he say?"

"He agreed to meet you." Kavanaugh shrugged. A string of numbers ran across the bottom of the screen.

"Thanks, Tarik. I'll give the coordinates to Haoun. Do you want to come along?"

"Yeah," he said. "It'd be good to see Sloane again. Do you have space for me on the *Veracity*?"

"I'll ask Vezali to knock a cabin together for you." She smiled, ran a hand through her hair and made it stand up on end. "It'll be good to have you at my back."

Raena waited to talk to Mellix until everyone was gathered for breakfast. She wanted the crew there as a check on her temper, because if she was sure of one thing, it was that you didn't threaten Mellix.

Mykah had made some kind of sweet porridge full of cubed fruit. Raena let everyone begin to eat before she asked, "Mellix, do you know who I am?"

Haoun and Coni stopped bickering over a catamaran race to listen.

The journalist looked up from his bowl to meet her eyes. "Yes," he said. "I researched you last night while everyone was on shore leave. You were supposed to have been executed by the empire."

Raena nodded.

"Some kind of Templar tech kept you alive?" he guessed.

"Yes. I was imprisoned just a hair over twenty years alone in a cave on the Templar tombworld."

"You've never been charged with the assassinations you committed in the name of the Empire."

Mykah started to defend her, but Raena cut him off. "No. I was punished for crimes against the Empire. The woman who was wanted as a war criminal is legally dead."

Mellix switched subjects abruptly. "Is there more to the story of finding the Thallians?"

Raena said, "Yes."

"Is Jonan Thallian dead?"

"Yes. Every Thallian responsible for spreading the Templar plague is dead."

"Then I don't think we need to threaten each other," Mellix said.

"Mellix . . ." Mykah started again.

"I wasn't planning to threaten you," Raena told the journalist. "You're not as afraid of death as I am of being revealed."

The journalist's whiskers twitched. "Mykah, I am a guest in your home. I owe my freedom to your crew and my life to Raena. I am not planning to reveal her to anyone. She wanted to make certain we understand each other. I think we do."

"I just want to live my life and do some good in the galaxy," Raena said.

"We all support that," Haoun said. They clinked their coffee mugs together to toast the idea.

CHAPTER 16

As Kavanaugh predicted, Gavin was eager to see her. He encouraged her to come with all speed. To her relief, the nightmares stopped.

After the initial message, all communications to Sloane went unanswered. They didn't know if they were walking into a trap, whether Outrider would be there, if there were other addicts than Sloane involved.

Raena forbade the others to come along. "You can monitor us," she suggested, "but Kavanaugh and I will have less to worry about if we go alone."

"Are you planning to kill Sloane?" Coni asked.

Raena looked to Kavanaugh before answering.

"I'm not planning to kill him," Kavanaugh said. "That's not to say he doesn't deserve it."

"If he's aged as fast in real life as he has in my dreams," Raena added, "killing him won't be necessary."

Just in case, though, Raena came to the meeting armed. She was glad to have Kavanaugh to watch her back.

Stinger in her hand, she stepped warily though the apartment's door. The room made her think of the featureless designer-furnished hidey-hole where she and Gavin lived on Brunzell. As it had there, all the furniture here came in a spectrum of shades of dirt, while the walls were an inoffensive tan. No one who had decorated this room ever intended to spend time in it.

The room was unoccupied except for a figure lying on an oversized leather couch. A chocolate brown blanket swathed it from chin to feet. She didn't recognize its shriveled monkey face.

It stuck a withered claw out from under the blanket. "You came," it croaked.

"Gavin?" She said it like she wasn't sure, but she was. It was all true. He had been killing himself with the Messiah drug. Somehow, to the very last minute, she had hoped he was not. She had hoped she'd been wrong. She slid the Stinger into its holster. Clearly, it was unnecessary.

"Is this another dream?" he asked. "I've been trying to see you for so long . . ."

"This is real, Gavin. I'm really here."

"Still so pretty," he said. He closed his watery greenish brown eyes, as if he couldn't fend sleep off any longer.

"Dammit." All the rest of her life, Raena had only recognized two states: dead or not a threat. This frail old man fit comfortably into neither category. She turned to Kavanaugh. "Is he too far gone?"

Kavanaugh checked Sloane's pulse and breathing and listened to his heart. "He's dying," Kavanaugh reported, "but not this minute. Soon. If you scare him, his heart's liable to stop."

Raena nodded. She knelt beside the sofa on a carpet that looked like fat round worms writhing over each other. It was soft beneath her knees, expensive and welcoming.

She studied Sloane. His skin was so dry that it looked clouded over, paler than paper. Brown splotched his face and scalp, irregular patches that looked like death spreading across his skin. His hair had almost completely vanished. A wiry green vein pulsed sluggishly at his temple.

"Was it worth it?" Raena asked.

Sloane's eyes fluttered open. He smiled, but what teeth he left had gone shades of yellow and brown like the furniture. "Very worth it," he echoed. "You're here."

"But I hate you for what you've been doing to me," she said quietly.

"I'm sorry about that," he wheezed. "But you already hated me."

She cut him off. "I left you, Gavin. I didn't hate you."

He chose not to argue. "I thought going back into the past would be easy. I'd just tell myself, 'Leave Kai a few days early,' or 'Get your ship fixed before you head for Nizarrh,' or 'Don't take the elevator on the *Arbiter*.' But it doesn't work that way. Whenever I caught my own eyes, the timeline would break. I'd get kicked out of the trance before I could say anything."

"But the first dream, the one where you drugged me on Kai . . . ?"

"I had to kill myself to get you," he wheezed. "I didn't want to do that more than once."

"Do you know how many times I killed you, Gavin? Shooting you or bashing your skull in or kicking you out the airlock . . . It was awful to wake up with those images in my mind, even if I hadn't really done those things."

"Nothing to feel guilty for, then." He chuckled, but it broke off into a ragged cough.

Kavanaugh put a glass of water in Raena's hand. She held it for Gavin to get a sip.

"You were magnificent," he said. "My avenging angel. I tried going to Thallian's world ahead of you, killing him before you could get there. Then you arrived in the escape pod with Thallian's son—and Thallian's clones didn't come to the surface to get you because I'd already drowned them all. I'm not sure what happened after that. Maybe the shielding prevented you from contacting the *Veracity* to rescue you. Maybe you banged on the secret panel until the boy let you out. Whatever it was, you were both dead by the time I located you."

Raena frowned as something not quite a memory flickered through her mind. She remembered waiting, trapped inside the gutted communications console, until she was past thirsty, until she was racked with cramps, until she was starving. Then Jain, under the same stress, broke into the console. She'd had no room to maneuver, no leverage, and no way to escape. He only had to hit her until she couldn't see any more. She opened his throat with her teeth. They had died covered in each other's blood, lying in each other's arms.

Raena shuddered. She had struggled to subscribe to Ariel's philosophy: life was a game. Ariel believed you could sometimes control the bumpers. Raena had always felt that, while occasionally you might be able to slow your fall, the game was inherently rigged. Gravity always won: eventually you always had to take the drop, plunge down that hole. In the meantime, you slammed around, trying to assume some kind of control over the path of your life.

It was horrible to discover how easy it was for someone who claimed to love you to purposefully crash into you, tilt you out of your true trajectory. And to do it over and over and over again.

Raena hadn't thought she could feel horror any longer, but she felt it now. How could someone who claimed to love her proceed so cheerfully to warp her life like this?

Because his love, like Thallian's, was a lust for possession. It didn't see her as real or autonomous. It didn't grant her free will, except the will to submit. She was an object in the game, not its subject and certainly not its player. She was the prize to be won, but no one cared what the trophy thought about moving from one shelf to another. Its job was to stand still and settle for the pleasure of being admired.

"How could you do this to me?" she whispered.

"I was trying to rescue you," Gavin protested. "I knew your life had been absolutely hellish, from the moment it started until the day you set Thallian on fire. I wanted to spare you."

She sat back on her heels, hands balled into fists on her thighs. She tried to keep in mind what Kavanaugh had said about scaring Sloane to death, but she wanted to hurt him so badly it made her tremble. "Gavin, by what right did you decide my life was hellish?"

"You were orphaned. A slave. And Thallian . . ."

She interrupted the tirade. "It's my *life*, Gavin. It made me who I am. I don't want to have it taken away from me. I wouldn't want to change any of it. It's mine. It's all I have. How fucking dare you?"

"It's made you the woman I love," he argued, "but I wanted to save you."

"It's made me the woman you can't have," she corrected. "You wanted to improve me."

He gaped at her, then offered her a lopsided grin. She might have fallen for it once, when they were both younger, but now she was too enraged.

"Did you ever win me?" she demanded.

"I don't know," Gavin said. "I was only aware when the past begins. Once the split occurs, things get blurry."

"You're lying," Raena accused. "You know very well what happens. The Messiah lets you stay in the moment, doesn't it? But making a change is really hard, which is why the drug is so addictive. You have to keep going back, keep trying to make the change you want to see."

He shook his head, but didn't meet her eyes.

"As far as I've seen, you mostly got killed," Raena told him. "I didn't recognize you. I was paranoid and broken. There was no way I could trust you. So I killed you, over and over and over and over. It was awful, Gavin. It had to stop."

"Is it too hard to kill someone you love?" he asked.

"You were killing me, chipping away at me like that. That wasn't hard at all, was it?"

"You didn't answer my question."

"You didn't answer mine, either. But I don't love you, Gavin. I can't. I stopped believing I might the night you had the argument with Ariel about what made my being her slave any different than my being Thallian's aide. I can't forgive you for hurting her like that. I'm not sure I ever loved you, the real Gavin Sloane. I never really knew you, until you got me out of that tomb. All the affection I felt for you in those years of darkness, the whole relationship I lived in my imagination before you freed me from that tomb: that makes it hard to wake up with the image of your blood on my hands, time and time again."

"It was hard for me, too," he protested.

"Did you ever stop to think about what the Messiah drug did to the addicts' targets, back during the War? Did you care what you were doing to me, in the galaxy here and now?"

He smiled at her. "You're strong," he said. "You're young. You always survive."

The hair stood up on the back of Raena's neck. In other words, he didn't care what he did to her.

Kavanaugh stepped in before she hit him. "Where did you get the Messiah drug, Gavin?"

"It was in the stuff your team hauled out of the Templar tombs. There were three crates of it, like the Templar had been warehousing it. I can't understand why they stored it there—there were Templar storehouses across the galaxy much more centrally located—but they must have thought nothing was as secure as their tombs. Since they allowed no one on their tombworld as long as there were Templar alive to guard it, no one could discover they were the ones destabilizing the border governments. Humanity made the perfect scapegoat, which must have amused the bugs endlessly."

"Where's all the Messiah now?" Raena asked.

"I sold it back to the pusher." He coughed, a horrible wet sound that wracked him until he was bent double.

Raena rubbed his back, trying to calm him. When he had settled back at last, she asked, "You sold it to Outrider?"

He nodded. "He'd gone all legit, lying low, working as a pharmacist, so you can imagine how surprised he was to see one of the old runners getting back in touch. Took a while for him to believe what I had."

Raena's heart plummeted inside her. She couldn't begin to envision the damage that crates of Messiah could do, wild in the galaxy. The worst scenarios she could envision were probably nothing as bad as what was to come. Her first inclination hadn't changed after all these years; there was danger ahead and she should run. But where could humanity run to? If the whole galaxy banded together and blamed humanity for the havoc this drug could do, there would be no defense. No safe hiding place. Humans were scattered across the galaxy now. They had no central government, no army, no place to hide. They were too vulnerable. They would be hunted down, rounded up, and exterminated.

Gavin fumbled at the black rubber bracelet hooked around his left wrist. With difficulty he managed to tug the prongs out of the socket and pull the thing off. He held it out to Raena.

"What's this?"

"Tracking program. I bugged the crates before I let them out of my sight. All of the packets have tracers, too, in case Outrider decided he didn't like my packing job and re-crated everything."

She took the bracelet and handed it to Kavanaugh. "Thanks, Gavin. We'll check it out."

"There's more." He pointed a trembling finger at a twist of metal on the shelf near the dining table. "Camera. I got footage of Outrider. So he can be identified. And my computer has the contact codes for him."

Later, maybe, she'd be stunned by the layers of Sloane's betrayal of the pusher, but now she was simply grateful for it. They still had a long way to go to capture this guy.

"What did he pay you?" she asked.

"He showed me how to build the vaporizer. He told me how to use the drug. And then he made a huge anonymous donation to the Shaad Family Foundation."

That was the name of Ariel's charity, the one that bought human kids out of slavery and found them homes. Raena was horrified by the sick irony of Outrider, future assassin of the human race, helping Ariel save its children for the coming slaughter.

"Why?"

"Because Ariel deserved something out of this. This damned drug taught me what it was like to love someone who couldn't love me back. I finally felt sorry for her."

"Did you hear all that?" Raena asked the comm bracelet on her left wrist. "We need to go after Outrider *now*, before this stuff hits the galaxy."

"Yes," Coni said. "Mykah's on his way over to get the tracker."

Kavanaugh said, "I've hired a med transport to get Gavin onto the *Veracity*."

"Are we taking him with us?" Raena asked.

"We can't leave him here to die alone."

Raena met Kavanaugh's eyes.

"All right, I can't leave him here," Kavanaugh corrected. "I will nurse him on the *Veracity*."

"If you could get him to the Templar tombs," she suggested, "you could keep him alive—"

Gavin fastened a bony hand on her arm. "You're not shutting me in there. I don't want to stay alive. I got nothing to live for in this universe. I fucked everything up so badly . . ."

"Look, Gavin, I don't pity you. You made your choices. I didn't bewitch you. I didn't ask for you to obsess over me. I owed you for getting me out of that tomb, but we tried living together and it didn't work."

As she talked, Kavanaugh moved around the apartment, gathering clothes and medicines—liquid for his cough, lotion for his thin skin, painkillers for his twisted joints. Raena put what food Gavin had into a cooler. There wasn't much. Apparently, Gavin had barely attended to the minimal needs of his body while he lay on the sofa, chasing dreams.

"Why don't you love me?" he asked quietly.

Raena turned to regard him, the sad, shriveled old thing.

"Gavin," she said thoughtfully, "you don't even like yourself. For a long time, I didn't like myself either, but being locked up alone for so long changed that. Maybe we could have had a chance, being broken together, but I want more from life than that. I'm willing to be alone until I can find someone who respects who I am and what I've been through—and doesn't want to take that away from me or change me to make himself more comfortable."

"I've given up everything for you," Gavin argued. "I spent a fortune and wasted years to rescue you from that tomb. Now I've wrecked my health and used up the rest of my life . . ."

"Did I ask you for any of that?" she said quietly. "You chose to make those sacrifices—and I respect the power of the emotions behind those choices. But they don't obligate me to anything."

How, she wondered, could he know so much about her life, all the details, all the turning points, and not understand her at all?

"If I was looking for someone to give me every material thing I could possibly want in the galaxy," Raena said, "I would still be with Ariel. If I wanted to feel lives in my hands, I could have stayed in the Imperial Diplomatic Corps. All I want now is freedom, Gavin. I want to belong to me. We might have been friends some day, if you'd just given me some space."

"Being friends was not enough."

"Did you ever think that it was so hard to change things because they weren't supposed to be changed?"

"See, that kind of negative thinking is why I adore you," Gavin purred.

After Kavanaugh got Sloane delivered to the *Veracity*, Coni had seen him settled comfortably in Raena's cabin. She was already prepared with her surveillance system to interview Sloane as extensively as she could, teasing out all the details of the drug and its dealer.

Raena shifted into the cabin Vezali knocked together for her in the hold. It was configured more or less like the cell the Thallians had meant for her when she first came aboard the ship. The room wasn't elegant or very comfortable, but it would do.

The *Veracity*'s crew differed on whether they would release the interviews with Gavin to the media or if they'd take the recording straight to the Council of Worlds and screen it for the government first.

The crew seemed to understand that chasing Outrider was more dangerous than anything Raena had gotten them into yet. They could easily be accused as pawns in the dissemination of the Messiah drug, or worse, as terrorists working toward the overthrow of the galactic status quo. Since Mellix was with them, public opinion could swing either way. There were still powerful forces out there, looking to do Mellix in.

Even Mykah was torn. He had the sense to be afraid to confront a pusher who knowingly dispensed a drug that would kill not only its users but hundreds, thousands, millions more who had nothing to do with it or him. If Mykah had had any kind of official government contacts, anyone with a paramilitary troop who could have captured Outrider in his place, then he would have gladly stepped aside.

In the end, Mellix persuaded the crew that they had a duty to the truth. Raena made it Mykah's job to ensure the journalist survived the confrontation.

Kavanaugh contacted Outrider, posing as an old war buddy of Sloane's—which was true, if the pusher cared to check. He delivered the Humans First! rant Raena wrote for him. Outrider agreed to come to Verwoest to discuss how he could aid Kavanaugh's work.

Nursing Sloane fell to Kavanaugh. He was the only one who had any idea what to do and, anyway, Raena refused to spend much time with the old man. She didn't see why Sloane should get what he wanted. She was not going to forgive him.

So Kavanaugh and Sloane talked over the past. Kavanaugh finally told the older man how much he had looked up to him, how grateful he was for all the times Sloane bailed him out of trouble, all the adventures they'd had when they were young.

Sloane mostly listened. He drifted in and out, sleeping a lot of the time.

When Mykah rang the dinner chime, Kavanaugh came out to find Raena already in the passage.

Doc would tell her, Kavanaugh decided. Doc believed in regretting the things you did, not the things you didn't. "You should go and sit with him," he told Raena.

Her face was unreadable. "I've said everything I have to say to him."

"He has things he needs to say to you."

She considered that. "I don't promise to like them," she said finally.

"Fair enough."

Raena let herself into her former cabin as Kavanaugh went on to dinner.

Raena pulled her desk chair over to the bed and let its magnetic feet seal to the deck. The sound woke Sloane.

"Really here?" he asked.

"Yeah. Kavanaugh said you had something to tell me."

He chuckled. It was a weird, dry, alien sound. "Not gonna apologize to you," he said. "Didn't apologize to Ariel, and I shot her."

"I'm not going to apologize to you either, Gavin."

"I expect no less."

He closed his eyes and seemed to drift off to sleep again. Raena watched his face and tried to see the man who'd kissed her on Nizarrh, back when she was young enough to believe there might be such a thing as love at first sight. In her tomb, she'd convinced herself that he'd come onto the *Arbiter* to release her from Thallian's torture machine because he had loved her, not because losing her to Thallian had hurt his pride, or because the Coalition had offered him a bounty for her.

How to explain his desecration of the Templar tombs for her? Gavin had paid so many bribes, bought so much equipment and dragged it out to that rock, hired the men—but why? He hadn't expected to find her alive. Why would he do all that for her corpse?

He couldn't have really loved her, Raena told herself. Before she came out of her tomb, he hadn't ever spent an entire day with her. He picked her up on Nizarrh and lost her to Thallian's men, then freed her briefly on the *Arbiter* before she was captured again. Then he'd spent all the years of her imprisonment learning as much about her life as he could . . .

She couldn't understand it. All her life, Raena thought she'd loved people—her mother, Thallian, Sloane—only to find that she'd been wrong. She'd mimicked love, sensed how they wanted her to feel, but in the end, love was just ashes in her hands.

She didn't mean to start crying, but when the tears filled her eyes, she didn't move to wipe them away.

Sloane opened his eyes again. Without a word, he held his withered and trembling hand out to her.

Raena wove her fingers around his.

As if that was what he had been waiting for, Gavin's breathing began to lengthen out. The exhalations grew longer. The intervals between breaths grew longer still.

Raena thought about calling for Kavanaugh, but there wasn't anything more he could do. Sloane seemed at peace at last.

Raena thought she understood Ariel a little better now. Sloane could pull the grandest gestures, then follow them with petty cruelties. He could make you feel like the center of the universe, then say the most heartless things. Kavanaugh and Ariel both loved him, so he hurt them time and time again. And they forgave him time and time again. Maybe that was why he couldn't love them back.

When Kavanaugh came back to check on them, Raena said, "He's gone."

"I thought it was getting close. You okay?"

She offered him a smile. "I'm sorry I hit you on Kai. I didn't want Ariel to have to face Thallian again. I didn't want anyone to be able to follow me. I thought I was going to my death, but that it would be worth it, if I could take Thallian down. I was angry and scared, so I lashed out at you. It wasn't fair and it wasn't right. I'm sorry."

Kavanaugh gazed at her. So many thoughts left shadows on his face, but all he said was, "Thank you."

Raena nodded. "Leave me alone with him a little longer."

After Kavanaugh left her, she sat with Sloane's body, thinking over the good times. It didn't matter what Sloane had done or why, only how it made her feel. There had been that kiss on Nizarrh, when every fiber of her body lit up. There had been the crazy escape from her cell on the *Arbiter*, when she would have done anything to thank Sloane for getting her out of Thallian's torture machine. There had been the night on Brunzell, when Raena made love to Sloane for the first time, searching desperately for a reason to live.

Now Gavin Sloane was just one more corpse in the army of corpses on Raena's conscience. As selfish and misguided as Gavin had been, he had given her the tools to make it right in the end.

She went to get a tarp from Vezali's stores, then brought it back to her cabin. She lifted Gavin's body and set it carefully in the middle of the tarp, tucked in the edges around him, and bundled him up. Then she carried him back to the cell where she had been staying.

It was quick to gather her few things and return them to her cabin. Then she placed Gavin's corpse on the cell's bunk, secured him with the restraints, and left the room. Once the door was locked behind her, she rerouted the room's life support. It should refrigerate him effectively until they knew whether they'd need to turn over his body for evidence of the Messiah drug's return to the galaxy.

Outrider didn't make himself difficult to meet. Still, Raena didn't like the warren of buildings through which they walked on Verwoest. There were too many shadows, too many alleys, too many nooks in which someone could hide. If she had been traveling through this neighborhood alone, she would have drawn her pistol.

Kavanaugh had point, while she and Mykah hung back. Somewhere behind them walked Haoun, Coni, and the journalist Mellix. Since they couldn't pass for human, they were pretending to be unaware of the first trio. Since he was the fastest, Mykah was supposed to run away at the first sign of trouble and bring the law if he could.

"We're here," Kavanaugh said softly.

The door looked as decrepit as everything else around them. There was nothing special about it, except for the scarred palm lock installed outside. Kavanaugh put his hand on the lock and let it ID him.

After the door ground open, a voice said, "Come in, Mr. Kavanaugh." The room inside was as shadowy as the one in which Raena had first seen the Messiah drug, all those decades ago. This one did not yet reek of unwashed bodies, but Raena was certain that would come in time, if Outrider had his way.

"Show me your payment first," Outrider said from somewhere in the room.

Mykah put the case on the floor and nudged it open. A pile of Templar artifacts glimmered in the dim light.

"Tell me again how you found me," Outrider said, not moving from wherever he stood. Raena wondered if he was really in the room with them, or if it was a speaker.

"I worked for Gavin Sloane," Kavanaugh said. "I led the team he'd hired to open the Templar tombs. We rediscovered the Messiah drug in one. I didn't know what it was, but Sloane did."

"How is old Sloane?"

"Dead." Kavanaugh managed to say it coldly, without a hint of the fury Raena knew he felt.

"Did he get what he wanted?"

"In the end, yes. That's why we're here."

Shadows shifted in the back of the room, but not clearly enough that Raena could make out a target.

"The media said the tombs were looted by the Thallians."

Raena was glad she'd persuaded Mykah to shave his beard to distinguish himself from the man in the documentaries.

"The Thallians were there, too, after Sloane packed us up and we left," Kavanaugh said. "Some of their men died there."

"Did you set the booby trap on the Templar Master's tomb?"

"I did," Raena said. She wore Revan Thallian's coat, which hid the fact that her boot heels were so tall, and a wide-brimmed hat of Coni's that shadowed her face. "I'm also the one who released the video of the Thallians on the ground there. No evidence remains to connect Sloane to the tombs any more."

The shadow moved a little closer. It moved strangely, reminding Raena again of a spider, sidling forward, halting. "Your voice is familiar," Outrider said.

"Don't know how that can be."

Someone darted in from the side, snatching at her hat. Raena heard him coming a half second before he touched her. She turned toward the sound and grabbed the outstretched wrist.

She heard Mykah and Kavanaugh moving behind her, going separate directions. She spun inside her assailant's reach. He was stronger than she expected and she couldn't get him off balance.

He knocked the hat from her head with his free hand. Their eyes locked. He was still a puffy, slightly overweight human with thinning red hair and bloodshot eyes.

"You haven't changed a bit," Raena said.

"Nor have you."

She got the stone knife out of her sleeve sheath, into her free hand, and stabbed it hard into his arm as he brought the pistol up from his thigh holster. He didn't drop the gun, so she twisted the blade, sawing its jagged edge against what she thought was bone.

Shots were exchanged behind her, but Outrider didn't flinch. Raena couldn't afford to either. She exerted all her strength to keep his gun pointed away from Kavanaugh and Mykah.

"Stun doesn't work," Kavanaugh said grimly. "That was point-blank."

"I'm okay," Mykah said, but he didn't sound it. He obviously hadn't gotten out like he had been supposed to. Raena wondered if they had been locked in, if this had been a trap from the start.

Outrider tangled his foot between Raena's. She used his shift in balance to kick up hard over her shoulder. Her boot heel took out one of his eyes. That revealed what she should have suspected as soon as she realized he hadn't aged: Outrider wasn't human. Something writhed inside his skull, mechanical worms crawling over each other in a hypnotic clockwork motion.

"He's an android," Raena said. She spun sideways, flinging herself into a flip that launched her away from his grasp. He still had the gun, though, and that was a problem. She drew her own Stinger and dropped into a crouch.

He helpfully shot at her from his new position. Raena nudged her pistol out of stun with her thumb—the motion was second nature—and fired at the android's gun, rather than at his body. As she'd expected, the gun was less well shielded. It exploded, raining burning plasma everywhere.

She shut her eyes tight, but the flash and the resultant fire still burned bright inside her eyelids. She rolled sideways, and aimed blind at the place where the android had been.

And then the fight stopped being a sequence of events that followed logically in her mind. Kavanaugh fired off wildly from behind some kind of cover, which allowed Raena to see there were two sources of fire coming back his way. She launched herself at the nearest one, nothing like a plan in her head.

In the end, they collected pieces of all three Outrider androids, enough to prove that Outrider had not been human—or at least that he wasn't any longer. The pieces kept reaching out for one another, trying to reassemble themselves into one working copy. Raena made sure Mellix got some good footage of that. No one doubted it was Templar tech.

She sorted out the best of the Outrider heads and wrapped it and one hand—separately—in some of her Viridian slave cloth. As she'd hoped, the pieces went quiescent once they no longer sensed each other directly.

Mykah had been shot, but he would live. Luckily, Kavanaugh had plenty of experience dealing with battlefield wounds and got him stabilized enough that Coni could get him safely to the hospital.

Haoun searched the rest of the building and located one crate full of the Messiah drug. The others were nowhere to be found. Raena hoped that they could be hunted down using Gavin's trackers, but feared that they would find the crates separated and moving away from one another. How many Outriders could there be?

Raena pulled out a brick of Messiah and cut a slab off with her knife. She wrapped it in more of the slave cloth and handed it to Mellix. Without a vaporizer or dosage information, it was mostly harmless. Besides, Mellix—not being human—couldn't get high off it himself.

She and Kavanaugh gathered as many of the Outrider pieces as they could and threw them into the crate of Messiah, burying each piece deep into the packets of the drug. When she felt confident they had collected up all the biggest bits, she pulled the thermeon from a pocket in her coat.

"Have you recorded everything you need?" she asked Mellix.

"I think so."

"Good. Go out to the street now." She nodded for Kavanaugh to go along and keep the journalist safe. After they left, she triggered the timer on the thermeon, pitched it into the crate, and sprinted for the door.

The resultant explosion brought the building down in the most satisfying way.

Raena was watching the building burn when Mellix swung the camera from the inferno toward her. "Why are you doing this?"

"Messiah was a trap set for humans by the Templar. That seems like reason enough." Raena turned away from him and started to walk.

"Hey, I would like your company," Mellix called after her.

She stopped and waited for him to catch up. "I will only speak off the record," Raena said, not looking at him. "By the way, it's not safe for you to walk around with that camera on the street. Too much of a temptation."

"Oh, right. Thanks." He disassembled the camera quickly, tucking its pieces into his tunic pockets.

Once they'd started to walk again, Mellix said, "Will Mykah be okay?"

She nodded toward Kavanaugh. "Both of us have survived worse. He'll be fine."

"He was my student," Mellix said, "one of my favorites. You can teach technique, but you can't teach passion. Mykah was one of the few who saw things wrong in the galaxy and wanted to have a hand in changing them. It didn't make him a good candidate for a standard news job, but he seems to have found his calling."

"He's been a good friend," Raena said. "It's been an honor and a pleasure to travel with him and his crew."

"Aren't you part of the *Veracity's* crew?"

She hadn't really thought about it, but she supposed it was true. "I've served on ships before, but the *Veracity* is the first place I've ever felt I've belonged. I feel more at home there than I have ever been anywhere else."

Mellix's next question took her by surprise. "Would you say you're fascinated by history, righting historical wrongs?"

"I would say that I'm finished digging through history." Raena paused, surprised by a sudden rush of emotion. It had been a long time since she'd felt free to look forward, instead of reacting to her past. "It's the future that interests me now."

ACKNOWLEDGMENTS

The first draft of this novel was written during Nanowrimo 2013. Of all my many attempts at finishing 50,000 words of fiction over the course of the annual National Novel Writing Month, this book (then called *No More Heroes*—now the title of Book Three in this series) was the first time I succeeded. Hurray for Nanowrimo and the hundreds of thousands of novelists it supports and inspires each year!

Thanks again to Martha Allard and Mason Jones, who held my hand and cheered me on as this book expanded from a rough Nanowrimo draft to the novel you hold in your hands. Their encouragement and careful eyes were a huge help. Any errors that remain are my own.

Thanks to Brian, Paul, and Kelly, fellow members of The Chowder Society, who were there with the *Star Wars* links when I needed my love for this genre to be re-invigorated.

Thanks also to Susan Holtzer and SG Browne, who read the first chapter cold when I was having a crisis. You said exactly what I needed to hear when I needed to hear it.

A special shout-out to Nick and the crew of San Francisco's Mercury Cafe, where I have spent many hours reading, writing, and editing. A good cafe is a blessing.

Finally, thanks to my champion, editor Jeremy Lassen, who believed I could write a trilogy and is helping me prove it. His questions and thoughtful reading helped flesh this book out to its current dimensions.

Thanks also to Jason Katzman and Cory Allyn, my knights at Skyhorse, for again being patient with my questions.

On to Book Three!

Photo courtesy of Ken Goudey

ABOUT THE AUTHOR

Loren Rhoads is the co-author (with Brian Thomas) of *As Above, So Below*. She's the author of a book of essays called *Wish You Were Here: Adventures in Cemetery Travel* and editor of *The Haunted Mansion Project: Year Two* and *Morbid Curiosity Cures the Blues*. Her science fiction short stories were collected into the chapbook *Ashes & Rust*. She remembers the Christmas there were men on the moon and looks forward to the New Year's Day there will be women on Mars.